# HERMANA

by

Becca McCulloch

*This book is dedicated to anyone who has ever reached for the lamp of divinity only to stumble over that pesky humanity. Keep trying—even a light that tumbles illuminates the darkness.*

*You are my inspiration.*

# Part 1: Las Guaranas

*For God has not given man the spirit of fear...Be not thou therefore ashamed of the testimony of our Lord.*
—2 Timothy 1:7-8

# Chapter 1

Beneath the plane, a patchwork quilt unfolds in green and yellow squares of land. The square edges tickle what I can see of winding blue rivers and gray-blue mountains. With this cross into the Great Plains, I am officially farther from home than I've ever been.

I am further from me than I've ever been, and I couldn't be more uncomfortable.

A woman sniggers to my right, lost in conversation with her seatmate. "I mean, I'm minding my business, nose in my book, and next thing I know, I'm surrounded by seven singing clones. It was unbelievable. I can't imagine how they didn't all die of shame, but they seemed completely unaware. I had to work not to laugh. But it did solve my bookmark problem." She slides the small pass-along card with a call line number into her book as her seatmate chuckles.

I hunker deep into my seat and spread my jacket over my knees to cover the navy skirt I'm wearing. Then I cross my arms to hide the omnipresent black tag, so the passengers won't notice I'm one of them—the seven Mormon missionaries who sang *Come, Come Ye Saints* in full harmony at the airport. I was in the bathroom for the big choral event, and I've found reasons to avoid pretty much every other missionary-type experience since we left Salt Lake City.

I go back to dealing with the lump in my throat that covers a fathomless ache. Each passing mile tugs Lannie Lewis from me and replaces her with a singing clone named Hermana.

I can't do this. I'm not this person.

The lump calls out for my mom. Everything calls out for my mom. Even the itch caused by the cheap wool of the seats begs for my mom.

Earlier today, I hugged my mom for the last time. She tucked Vagisil cream into my carry-on; the last words of wisdom from my mom were about yeast infections. Then I walked through security and boarded this plane. Barely a woman. Not really a missionary. I'm Lannie Lewis playing dress-up.

My gaze flits about in hopes that I'll find a parachute or unexpected ally. Instead, the only other sister on the flight, Hermana Olsen, comes into view. She grasps hands with an Elderly woman to her right. They each wipe tears from their eyes, and then both heads bow in prayer. Wow. She's brought a soul to God in the few hours since we became minted missionaries – the hours I've spent wondering how hard it would be to get home without anyone noticing.

My mind flips through images of my life like a forced near-death experience, searching for proof I belong on this plane. There must be something, somewhere that says this black name tag belongs on my chest. I've been Mormon my whole life, certainly I've defended the faith at least once. But I can't come up with a single experience where I stood like Captain Moroni with the Title of Liberty in defense of my family, my liberty or my faith. Most of the time, if someone says something negative about the church, I smile and change the subject. Not exactly spiritual brilliance. That's Lannie Lewis for you, a true spiritual coward.

Though, I did try. Once. My dad offered to pay for music school in California after I graduated high school. Dad lived in a tiny two-bedroom townhouse in North Hollywood with his live-in girlfriend, and he begged me to stay with them during my first year of college. I moved in to save money and maybe heal the rift caused by the divorce. My bedroom doubled as dog den and music production studio. Song notes and equipment covered every surface. No dresser or closet—my clothes stayed in my luggage under the bed. The bed and nightstand were all I had of my own. I placed a picture of Christ teaching the children at bedside with my scriptures and slid my violin beneath the bed.

My dad tapped on the door not an hour after I set the religious icons in place.

"Settling in?" my dad asked me, his too-big grin covering for how clumsy our attempts to be father and daughter had been.

"Yeah. Thanks. This is great." My forced smile joined his.

"We love having you here, Lannie, but…" He pointed at the nightstand and the four-by-six image. "Let's not offend Mikala, ok? It's her house, too."

I'm pretty sure Mikala wasn't the person dad protected that day. Regardless, the picture and scriptures hid under my bed for the thorny months I tried to coexist with my father.

For the most part, we ignored each other rather pleasantly, except for a few jokes about my mom. I needed a place to stay. Dad needed to convince Mikala he wasn't a deadbeat. Our disparate needs coincided to produce polite yet awkward silence.

My attention turns back to the patchwork quilt laid out below us. I'm not one for sewing, but I did make a quilt once as a Beehive. I cut one hundred and forty-four, twelve-inch squares from a random collection of old fabric pieces and abandoned clothing. Then my mom and I dug out my grandmother's old sewing machine and watched a YouTube video on how to operate it. The ancient machine buzzed over piece after piece to create awful, uneven squares. Then I stretched the quilt, filled it with fluffy batting, and tied each corner. It was probably the ugliest thing ever made, and it demanded months of work. I don't even remember how many, but long enough that my dad joked our living room had been transformed into a quilting museum. I developed a hard callous on my right middle finger that never healed— to this day, there it is, evidence of endless hours with a needle in hand.

I displayed the quilt, in all its mismatched beauty, at Young Women in Excellence that year. The women hovered, hunched in awe, and cooed their marvel at each uneven stitch and simplistic yarn tie that had become the hallmark of my pending womanhood. Something real and good and meaningful hid among the disorderly patchwork of that quilt. I bought a quilt display stand for my bedroom—that's how proud I was of the thing.

Then it came apart in the weeks before I graduated high school. The yarn untied, and my dog chewed off a corner to tug out pieces of batting. I laughed when the dog wore batting like a bad Santa beard. A quilt meant nothing, really.

I was eighteen and ready for the world beyond that quilt, a world of musical success and rapt audiences and talent unveiled. I believed myself to be the Mormon girl who would change the world, the one prophesied to come by Ezra Taft Benson in a talk before I was born—a Mormon who would participate in the world and leave it forever changed, part of a rising generation that would fill the earth—what else could I do but toss out the fabric of my childhood and quilt something new and frightening to be displayed before the entire world?

But the world is both larger and more unconquerable than I could have imagined. I've never done anything memorable, and I've learned that my own stitching—the human kind that binds too much fat and too little beauty into one form—doesn't interest Mormon boys. I'm as standard-issue and plain as a person can be. I envy the zeal of the missionaries who are on this adventure straight out of high school. I took two years to flunk out of music school, so I'm older and less wise than anyone else with a badge.

The other missionaries on the flight seemingly mock my early-onset cynicism with their energetic attempts to advance the gospel. Success and enthusiasm spill over earnest words shared with passengers. Their shoulders hunch over, engaged in deep conversation with an elbow partner while I slink ever farther into my chair and away from responsibility. At a loss, already, as to how to do this thing I swore I was ready to do.

No matter where I am, I don't seem to fit. Plain, old Misfit Lannie. The weird one with the book. Now, I'm the weird one with the Book of Mormon.

The patchwork land slips away under cloud cover, and I lose my last hold on home. The loss opens a wound in me like a hole in the ocean. Any feeling of home and comfort and rightness cascades into indeterminate freefall.

I'll never again be the person I was this morning. That's the purpose of this endeavor—this mission—to let God build something new from the scrap pile of my childhood. I feel God sorting through my soul, looking for sturdy pieces. His stitches will be even, his ties tight—if only my fabric doesn't fail him. The scissors raise, poised to make that first cut, and I try not to flinch.

# Chapter 2

After four weeks in the mission training center, we are entering the mission wilds of the Dominican Republic today. As a first step, we've been sent to the lush, vibrant foliage in the backyard of the mission president's mansion. We've met President Stathos and his wife before but seeing them in this context makes everything more real.

White metal chairs sit amidst green foliage in the ample garden. Mango trees and vibrant flowers as large as my whole head rustle under the force of a warm breeze that stirs the papaya and Plumeria into a fragrant and mouthwatering bouquet. That's the only pleasant part. The air cooks instead of cools. Moisture presses to my skin like a warm washcloth in the midst of a fever. The hot, wet air pins my nylon skirt to my thighs in an unfortunate sauna wrap that leaves sweat dripping in unfortunate places.

The mission president places large posters on easels. He's jovial—round and happy like a tropical Santa Claus—and makes jokes we don't understand. We blink at him and laugh on cue. My brother, Joe, advised me to stay on the president's good side. So, I'm nodding over here on his good side along with all the greenies.

The president grew up in Greece with multicultural parents and speaks four languages. Sometimes all at once. According to our trainers at the MTC, the president has a huge business of some kind and travels at least once a month to some not-here location to make sure everything churns out capital. He returns with grins and fine chocolate, which he doles out to the highest-performing missionaries in each zone.

The numbers he shows us are pretty. Pretty, pretty numbers. I've no frame of reference for how many baptisms a month is normal, so the goals seem A-Okay. I'm still so lost on this mission thing. I read manuals and memorize scriptures and yet have no idea what I'm supposed to do once I get out of bed tomorrow. Whatever it is, I'll do it on the president's good side by hoping my numbers match his numbers. That seems the clearest path to mission success.

The president has replaced the baptism goals chart when there's movement and noise behind us. We all turn to see Hermana Stathos leading a small parade of eight missionaries into the garden.

President Stathos claps his hand. We return to prompt attention. "We'll end here. The trainers have arrived. Let's put our most charitable foot forward, shall we?" The president laughs. Yeah. I don't get his jokes, but I laugh anyway.

When the president walks beyond our group, I crane around to spot my trainer. We're matched by home country for our first round. There are two American women. A pretty redhead waves at Hermana Olsen. A small, unremarkable woman with her hair in a tight braid approaches me. She has a sharp nose and flitting eyes—like the baby robins that would hop around outside my bedroom window each spring.

Her hand and chin jut forward for an introduction. "I'm Hermana Callister."

Even her voice reminds me of gentle attempts at birdsong. After we shake, she clasps her hands too tightly in front of her. I want to soothe them, place mine on top and coo at her until I can return her to her nest. Instead, I smile and nod in comfortable encouragement.

"We'll only speak Spanish after this," she says. "President says if we only speak Spanish, we'll feel more at home with the people. And we'll study the scriptures in Spanish every day. You need to practice."

My grandmother spoke Spanish, so the language flows through my brain, even if my tongue trips over the words at times, but I'm as blonde as a California pop song and Hermana Callister seems eager to teach. For her sake, I'll play the humble student. I nod and smile.

Hermana Callister beams at my acceptance of these simple orders, and then switches to Spanish. Or, she thinks she does. English words receive Spanish-style endings and mix with the occasional incorrectly conjugated verb. I stumble through awkward conversation until an Elder whistles to call us back to order.

Hermana Stathos sits perfectly straight in her flowered skirt and long-sleeved cream blouse. She's a slight thing that looks like she was meant to be somewhere much finer than wherever she is. President Stathos leans down to kiss her delicate cheek before leading the Elders away to his inner sanctum to discuss the manly things of the kingdom. I've no idea what to expect on the feminine side.

As Hermana Stathos announces the prayer, a giant, moth-like insect lands next to her on her chair. Its wings stretch like two pieces of recycled paper fastened to a metal binding. Its antennae rustle the fabric on Hermana Stathos' silky skirt. The woman gurgles with wide eyes, and then falls silent. She drops the prayer announcement without naming the speaker, and, instead, scoots herself and her skirt over three inches to accommodate the creature. Her eyes grow wider with each panicked sweep of our faces.

One of the Dominican trainers rushes in to scoop the bug away. The insect rests on the young woman's hands. Its wings click against her black badge. She releases the moth with the care I might take with a kitten or puppy.

Hermana Stathos' shoulders sink two inches once the creature is gone, but her spine remains perfectly straight. Then she talks about yeast infection. No joke. She forgets the prayer and jumps right into fungal overgrowth. If my mom were here, everything from the giant bug to confirmed fears about fungi would have her giggling throughout the whole meeting.

The bizarre health lecture continues while I fight off longing. I've never gone so long without laughing with my mom. Hermana Stathos covers an impressive array of topics. We discuss menstruation—most American women will stop their cycles due to stress, which leads to a collective sigh from both Olsen and I who yesterday confided in the other that we were late—and then an almost-humiliating discussion on weight management—a lost cause for me—that reminds us we'll all have to return home ready for dating and marriage.

The Dominican *hermanas* whisper behind me as Hermana Stathos transitions into foot care—all about shoes, all the time. The missionaries correctly assume I've a suitcase half-filled with tampons. They're eager to get to mine and discuss terms of potential trade with one another. I laugh, barely, at their machinations. It's enough to reveal I speak Spanish better than the average import, however. My shoulder is tapped almost immediately by one of the whisperers.

"For one box, I'll kill all the bugs if we're ever companions," says the woman who eighty-sixed the moth.

"I'll read your scriptures to you while you sleep an extra hour," another *hermana* claims.

A harsh hush worms its way forward. The taller of the two Dominican *hermanas*—their names are still unfamiliar enough that they get lost in my ear—leans in to whisper where only I can hear. "For two boxes, I'll let you have half my discussion numbers one week. No one will offer more. Trust me, you'll want backup numbers as you get used to the food and heat."

I reach behind me and shake her hand, whether she's serious or not. I'm not good at convincing people to do things, like get baptized, so I may need some non-spiritual help. The *hermanas* fall silent while Hermana Stathos lectures us about the dangers of street food vendors.

Then we smell the sweet freedom. President Stathos returns for a final pep talk before the doors of the mission home open. A host of white mission vans and cars wait to carry us into the lone and dreary world. The butterflies in my stomach churn through a long, long list of skills I've not yet mastered. Top of the list, super-spirituality. Joe told me to focus my energy in the MTC on repenting and drawing closer to God. Instead, I ate ice cream and read the entire missionary library. My brain and waistband are full, but I never did pray like Enos or speak to a burning bush.

Hermana Olsen gives me a double-thumbs up as she follows the shockingly pretty red-head towards a nearby bus stop. I follow my new crew. We're three greenies and three trainers all headed to the same house in Las Guaranas. Hermana Callister and I will be the only Americans.

Hermana Callister opens her scriptures in her lap as we start moving. The familiar words of scripture can't call my attention, though, when bright, new things pass by at every rotation of the wheels. Broad streets curve into roundabouts while concrete presidio-style buildings rise one on top of each other to either side of the road. The buildings climb up hillsides and spill laundry across strung lines. In the courtyards, people gather around pillbox speakers to dance and laugh and slap dominos on giant boards.

The women's snappy verbal cadences mix with the energy outside the car. There's something they have that I've never had, an energy that embraces life with passion. My life follows quiet, classic meters and rhythms, not the syncopated and rapid beats driving the energetic people on streets and in the car. I want what they have. I want it badly.

Hermana Hernandez jumps across me to point wildly at the Panda Express outside the window. An inland breeze catches her bright yellow dress at the border and flaps flowers before each of our faces. "My brother—he owns this! Finest restaurant in Santo Domingo."

The two Dominican trainers huff and shrug, almost in unison. They go home next transfer, so Hermana Hernandez calls them *las vampiras misioneras*—walking among us but dead inside. This mission is full of death metaphors. We're born, and we die the day we go home— or earlier, if Hermana Hernandez's jokes about these two are to be believed. *Las vampiras* are a funny pair, nearly-identical, with long, glossy, straightened black hair and red painted nails. Tidbits about the area get washed away in a sea of bickering over haircuts and fashion.

"Brazilian blowouts? Gel nails? How did we get stuck with you? You two are useless," Hermana Hernandez complains as she squeezes the hands of both women.

Hermana Vasquez—I've finally heard the names enough to remember—pushes Hermana Hernandez off her. "You'll be fine. Greenies were made for work. We need two more baptisms, so we'll be at sixteen each before we die. In six weeks—that's not even a baptism a month, so no problem. You won't even need us. We'll have plenty of time for the salon. And some weight loss. You heard Hermana Stathos. Gotta stay pretty. Or get pretty again."

I elbow Hermana Callister to ask if we have any baptisms scheduled. The tallies seem to grow in importance with each passing moment. She nods. "Two boys. You'll like them."

Only a day in and I've got two baptisms. I won't go home the loser missionary in the family. That honor stays with Joe who served in Italy. He got one-half baptisms, he claims, because the woman eventually converted—two years later. So, thank you, Hermana Callister, for saving me from a worse mocking than I have given him.

The white van eventually stops in front of a pink, concrete block house with tile roof. Up and down the street, similar homes shout welcome in a bright array of fanciful candy colors.

This is my new home.

The Dominican *hermanas* link arms to walk up to the steps. Hermana Callister grabs my arm to stop me from following.

"Serving the Lord starts now, Hermana Lewis," she says in a quiet, yet insistent way. Her bird-like eyes peer down the street, eager for gospel morsels.

The road changes from carnival-like to dusty. Heat blows in from all sides. And somewhere down that road, there are people I've never met. I'll have to talk to them about God, the thing closest to my heart. I'm supposed to spill my guts to a complete stranger. I struggle to open my guts to anyone. I speak in music, through my violin, not through tricky-sticky words.

No, I need a few more hours before I can face the strangling strangeness.

"I need to change and go to the bathroom." I smile brightly, hoping Hermana Callister is distracted once we get upstairs.

"A quick bathroom stop, but we have goals to accomplish."

Hermana Callister sits on a wooden step to wait for me as I climb the stairs to see our concrete box. That's what it is. A concrete box. Concrete floors. Concrete walls. Concrete ceiling. Spectacularly clean, but unadorned, concrete. There are three rooms. One large, open space with a kitchenette at one end. The tiny stove and refrigerator are smaller than the one in my family's RV.

Two rooms extend off the kitchen. The Dominicans occupy the one at the back. Hermana Callister and I sleep on what could be considered a porch. Slatted shutters substitute for windows in a long, empty space with two cots.

Not beds. Cots, like the kind in military movies.

I spin twice until I locate the tiny bathroom tucked in the corner of the kitchen.

Every few minutes, Hermana Callister shouts up to see if I'm ready. But I'm not. I don't know how to flush the toilet. The handle is broken, and the tank is empty. The urine mocks me, mocks my lack of readiness. *You thought you could serve a mission? You can't even flush a toilet.* Hermana Callister calls up again, so worthier souls will have to save the toilet. I'm glad there's at least a lid so I can hide my social sin.

Hermana Callister shouts again. There's evident frustration in her bird-like tone, as though she's trying to shoo other critters off her worms.

Hermana Hernandez jostles me as she lugs a large, brown suitcase toward her room. "Eh, she's a hard one, right? Don't worry, we'll set up your bed. So, go and make her happy, but then sneak over to our room for jokes and gossip." *Chistes* and *chismes*, Hermana Hernandez's two favorite things.

Hermana Callister calls out again, and I rush back into the oppressive heat and omnipresent dust of my new-found hometown. Hermana Callister rattles off a list of plans, beginning with a discussion and ending with two hours of street contacts—the dreaded activity, essentially a cold-call in person. I set my jaw and nod. I'm going to do this mission thing well, even if I am so bone-tired that I stumble over my words.

Despite my resolve, the day dissolves into every fear I've harbored. I get tongue-tied at the invitation. 'Can we come by to talk about Christ?' I've practiced the phrase in my head, morning and night, for weeks. Yet I gag on the syllables. Eventually, I sink on a bench and pretend not to cry by blaming dust and allergies for each sniffle.

Hermana Callister talks to a family waiting at the nearby bus stop. She jots more addresses and phone numbers on her yellow agenda. The mission is possible, but I'm failing.

The elderly woman who sits opposite me on the bench places a disfigured hand on my knee. She's impeccably dressed in a clean, shirtwaist dress with bright pearls in her ears. Yet her hands and shoeless feet turn in on themselves. Brown and yellow nails curl into the skin. She needs her nails clipped and painted to match her pretty dress, and someone should brush out the back of her hair.

She digs with two functional fingers through a small handbag until she finds a piece of white, blue and pink stick like an American candy cane. "Here, my dear, you deserve a break and a sweet."

The stick is sweet without a hint of flavoring. Straight sugar. Almost gag-worthy and yet equally divine. I suck greedily, hoping the sugar calms my nerves and shakes.

Juana chats as she sucks on her own piece of candy. "I've met lots of Mormons over the years. My boy used to be one of you. It's not an easy task to be a missionary. Is it?"

I gulp around an errant sob.

"Look at you," the woman says with a deep husk. "All sunburnt and exhausted. How long have you been here?"

"A few hours. I've come to share a message about Jesus Christ—" My voice shakes and a blink sends a tear down my cheek.

"Come now, tell Juana all your troubles." The woman squeezes my knee. "And I'll tell you mine. My feet are hurting. Had to abandon my shoes at the church. My boy's gone to get us a *motoconcho*. You ridden by one of those? I like squeezing the cute drivers. They'll forgive an old woman anything."

"My grandma used to say the same thing. I used to be the one that pulled the tangles from her hair. She said I had an angel's touch." The last sneaks out and I'm full of regret that I've mentioned her unkempt appearance. My internal filter glitches at the worst moments.

The woman's hand goes up to her hair, tries to pull through a knotted bit at the back. "Think you could help with this mess? My boy tries, he loves his mama, but maybe I could use a woman's touch. What do you say? I've got lots more candy."

"Yes. I say yes." I'm so relieved I cry again. The first name goes on my sheet. I did it. A contact. Service hours, not proselyting, but it's still legit. And I can help with her hair and nails. I write down the directions to her house, hoping they'll make more sense to Hermana Callister than they do to me.

Juana's son pulls up on a *motoconcho*—nothing more than a moped with an extra seat rigged onto the back. He lifts his mother and places her on the seat.

Juana wraps her arms around the driver and winks at me. "Don't forget, *hermanas*. Come to my house. Tell me everything about Joseph Smith."

Hermana Callister packs up the Book of Mormons sitting beside my bench. "Well done. See how fast the day goes when we work hard?"

Maybe. Not really. My thighs quiver with exhaustion and words get lost before they form on my tongue. John Gage's 639-year concert is progressing more rapidly than this day.

Hermana Hernandez waits on the steps for me. She waves and then grabs me for a hug after Hermana Callister slips inside the house. "We're like two pillows, no? All squishy fat and comfort. Did you make it through the day?"

A laugh works like electric paddles on a dying heart. My sense of humor surges. "I met an old lady you'd like. She rides *motoconchos* to hug the cute, young men."

"Definitely my kind of woman." Hermana Hernandez laughs. She keeps an arm around my waist as she steers me toward the bathroom. "Poor little, Americana. You need to rest. But first, a lesson in island bathrooms."

Hermana Hernandez uses an old margarine tub to scoop water from a 50-gallon bucket sitting in what should be our tub. "A demonstration on flushing," she announces with a grand flourish and dumps the bucket in the toilet. Like magic, the toilet flushes.

"No. Really? That's all there is to it?"

"One bucket and your sins are washed away, my friend."

One obstacle down. Dozens more to go. But I can use the toilet.

# Chapter 3

The next morning, my brain gulps the reality of a new day and then gags on the taste. Each muscle limp like overcooked pasta laid out across my bed sheets.

And I smell.

A night sleeping in my own sweat after a hard days' work has rotted me.

I may be dead. Except death wouldn't be this annoying.

Hermana Callister woke up thirty minutes earlier than our six-a.m. call time to perform military-style calisthenics. She huffs and hops, and I think uncharitable things in response.

At six, the alarm sounds. Hermana Callister jogs in place at the foot of my bed. She points at the Missionary Manual while she takes her pulse. "Chapter one. We start at the beginning."

The words grate on my bones over the entire hour of companion study. Then I struggle through an hour of individual scripture study that merges a dream-like Hermana mansion with brawny Nephites wielding swords atop a rock pile.

Three sharp bangs on our door startles me out of my dream state.

"Yo, *hermanas.* Open up!" A woman shouts for entry outside our door.

*La Vampira* Montez shuffles over to the door in fluffy bunny slippers. Her hair is wrapped in large, felt curlers like my grandmother used to wear. A toothbrush dangles from her mouth.

She opens the door, and the newcomer whacks her over the head with a flared and overused Book of Mormon. "You opened the door like that?"

Hermana Montez shrugs. She steps aside, and I get my first glimpse of *Mamita* Irene—our housekeeper—an old woman with more skin than substance. Her oversized AC/DC t-shirt hangs from her body, and she wears cheap, plastic, neon green flip flops on her feet. Her black and gray hair extends out at odd angles and represents every people to drop genetic code on the island. Tightly woven curls nestle near her scalp. Long, straight, and shiny locks pull into a blunt ponytail. Then there are wiry pieces that stick out like acupuncture needles.

She peers around the room with a hand over her eye to block the glare from early-morning sunlight. "The new girls? They came? I hear I've an American?"

*Mamita* Irene sighs and rubs her hands together. I expect her to come and scrub me down like Audrey Hepburn in *My Fair Lady*, but she flip-flaps away to the kitchen without a glance.

Fifteen minutes later, creamy oats and rich hot chocolate sizzle energy down to my toes. *Mamita* Irene wags a finger at me when I sigh in contentment. "Don't always expect such a breakfast. I'm too busy to treat you like babies. I got the Lord's work to do, too."

She points at the Rice Krispies box on the shelf. And a can of powdered milk.

Powdered milk makes me cringe.

My mom goes on food storage crazes every so often, so our cellar is lousy with the stuff. Before my dad left, we'd have annual creative food adventures to use up the foods saved for a never-realized apocalypse. We split into teams to create a week's menu. At Family Home Evening, we voted on the winner. Mom voted. Joe and I voted against each other, and Dad abstained. Mom chose the easiest menu to prepare. Still, we looked forward to the competition each year.

But after the divorce, the fun stopped. Mom hauls up canned food when it's about to expire. No fancy menus; we eat it straight. And straight powdered milk is the worst.

I can't eat powdered milk every day. Maybe I can go hungry for weight management. Or I can pretend it's a fast and maybe get some super-stellar spirituality.

Either would be a solid plan if I didn't hate being hungry.

I'll have to pass by a market later today to see if there's any hope for edible breakfasts.

The challenge of food yields to the battle for cleanliness. *Mamita* Irene walks me and my towel over to the bathroom.

"The water comes at ten and two. I'll fill the bucket in the morning for cleaning and safe water to drink—it'll be in the refrigerator. Then I fill it up for baths and toilet in the afternoon. This is all we have, so use a little, the littlest little you can to get clean. Three buckets. One to rinse. One to wash. One to rinse. Okay?"

Not okay. I don't even know where to stand for this. The barrel fills the whole bathtub. There isn't another drain. And worse, every so often, cockroaches scurry from beneath the barrel.

*Mamita* Irene hands me a small piece of grainy, brown soap. "And never, ever take off your *chancletas*." She points at the plastic water shoes on my feet. "Feet covered. All the time."

She tugs the door closed, fights it to latch, and then I'm alone. I stand naked, staring at a bucket of chlorinated water filled with invisible, dead parasites. The smell of bleach rises from the drips that fall from my washcloth to my body. The soap lathers nicely.

Red circles appear over my delicate skin along the path of the soap. The welts grow angry, puffing up in wide, red patches all over my arms and legs. The residue remains despite my single bucket rinse. Three buckets turn into five and yet still I burn.

A loud knock interrupts my tiny pain-filled gasps.

"Three buckets!" *Mamita* Irene scolds.

Tomorrow, I'll write my mom and have her send a gentler soap. And Benadryl. There must be something to make bathing possible on the island. But today, I can't get the reputation as the spoiled American girl who steals all the water. I toss the bucket back in the water, and then I pull clothes over the enraged skin.

*Mamita* Irene hurries in to collect the laundry while I pack my bag. She grabs Hermana Callister's bag of used clothing and tosses it down the stairs.

Then she turns to me. Her eyes roam my navy silk-lined skirt and white, frothy blouse with smart, black buttons up the front. "Tsk. Hermana. These clothes will never do. You'll be dead of heat in an hour."

I'm confused as I look at my clothes. We followed the guidelines in my mission packet.

*Mamita* Irene clucks and shakes her head. She digs through my luggage. Piece after expensive piece falls to the floor in a heap. My ugly skirt—a cotton button-up cream piece from Target, of all places, that my mom wanted me to bring for bike riding days—gets tossed towards me. "This one. But not a single shirt."

She moves over to a pile of clothes in the corner that I'm told contains the vampires' donations to the next generation of missionaries. *Mamita* Irene digs through the pile until she finds a light blue, threadbare cotton tee shirt.

"This. This will work. And pull that hair back. No pretty curls. No makeup. Just a girl with a badge."

She pins my mission tag in place after I switch outfits, and then pats my cheek. She speaks around a wide and almost-toothless grin. "Pack the fancy things away. I'll get you day-wear clothes at the market. Leave me twenty *pesos* on the table."

Hermana Callister shouts the time like a broken cuckoo clock. "10:25 am. If you need to use the bathroom, do so now. We won't be back until 1:45 and you don't want to use what passes as a toilet in most houses. Trust me."

Another day under the blazing sun. My name is gone. My clothes. My hair, my smell. Nothing is the same.

I'm *Hermana* now.

But stripping away my identity doesn't strip away my flaws. I'm stuck in my over-thinking place while Hermana Callister flies through appointments. There's a rhythm to this doctrine-question-commitment exchange, a melody sung by the Spirit. I feel it flow through negotiations, but try as I might, the song is beyond me, as lost on me as the advanced music that tanked my education.

Hermana Callister exacts perfection, as perfect as she is perfect, and yet my art is flawed. If she gives me a scripture, I interpret it wrong and she interjects. If she asks me for testimony, I speak too long and she interrupts. Over and over, I lose my phrasing and connect the notes poorly. She's kinder than any music professor I've had, but her pursed lips punctuate each fail.

By the time we ring Juana's door, thick tears bounce on my eyelashes. I've cried more in two days than I did in the weeks after I got the letter revoking my scholarship, maybe as much as I did the day my parents' divorce finalized. My brain sobs as much as my heart. Quiet tears of exhaustion plea the case for sleep, but we've hours still to go.

Juana's son lets us in with a shrug and guides us to where Juana sits in a large black armchair covered in plastic. A fine outline of sweat remains when she leans forward to greet us during a commercial break in her *telenovela*.

I don't wait on invitation or conversation; I grab a large orange bucket and go outside to fill it with water from the red spigot with pump handle at the garden gate. The water rushes out over my hands and feet, splashing as much outside the bucket as in. I wrestle the handle back to slow the flow and fill my bucket.

Five minutes later, my brain finds peace in the familiarity of *telenovelas* and wiry, gray hair that pricks my wet hands. I undo knots with my fingers and then pull hair through a wide comb while Juana chatters about the plot. Twins. Again. Juana suspects a hidden triplet will emerge. There's no end to multiples in the Mexican soap opera writing society. But the lead is handsome and the heroine youthfully sweet. Each passionate kiss causes Juana to clap her hands.

Hermana Callister washes the dishes in Juana's sink and then makes phone calls in the kitchen. She reappears at the closing credits.

Juana seems to anticipate her reason for hovering in the door. She reaches a hand toward the Bible that rests next to a red candle with the Virgin Mary's image that burns beneath a reproduction of the Sacred Heart of Christ. Rosary beads stretch over the top of the Bible.

"Would you read to me, dear? I've marked my place."

"Have you heard about Christ's visit to the Americas after his resurrection? I can give you a Book of Mormon to follow along." Hermana Callister grins and holds out the blue book.

Juana places her hands on her legs and grins back. "Oh, that sounds like such excitement. But I'm trying to read the whole Bible before I die. I'm not through the Last Supper yet and then I've got Paul-Paul-Paul and more Paul before I'm done. But I'll make you a deal. If you get me through the Lord's life, then maybe we'll read your story."

She leans back and winks at me, and then squeezes my hand where it rests on her shoulder. My hands quiver at the confrontation, calm as it was. "And you, girl, get on with things. I want pretty red nails to match my gorgeous hair. I've got my eyes on a widower at church and need to catch his attention."

Hermana Callister and Juana argue a bit over where Juana left off in her Bible studies. Somehow, I doubt the gray circles invading her pupils allow her to read much. Cataracts don't much like dim lights. The only source of electric light is a single bulb in the kitchen.

I move on to clip her toenails and scrub a lifetime of dirt from her caked and dried feet. The last coat of red polish applies as the timer rings on Hermana Callister's phone.

"There. We're done anyway. You're beautiful." My first real smile in two days lights up the space between us.

"No, dearie, that title belongs to you." Juana strokes my face and then pulls my dishwater blond ponytail. "But off you go. Make sure you come back soon. Can't leave the story of our Lord and Savior incomplete, can we?"

Hermana Callister leans in to kiss Juana's cheek. "We'll be back. I want to tell you that story of Christ in the Americas."

"I can't wait," Juana says and winks at me again. She runs her hand through her hair and smiles and that's all I need to return to the dust, heat, and confusion of missionary work.

Hermana Callister holds her hands over her eyes to peer at her cell phone in the fading light. "This phone doesn't hold charge worth beans. We've got one more appointment and contact goals to meet. I won't be able to call and reschedule, so we can't lose a minute."

A man leans on his parked moped across the street. He whistles across to us and then points with his lips towards the bike, a question in his eyes. I'm curious about these zipping public transport options. I've never ridden on a moped. But Hermana Callister already nixed the idea as an inappropriate use of mission funds and a lazy-woman's form of transport. I shake my head to refuse the driver and fall in step with my fearless leader.

Hermana Callister engages every single passerby. *Hi. Hello. Have you heard of Christ's visit to the Americas? Would you like to come to church? Can we visit with you to share a story of Christ? Would you like to be with your family forever?* The rehearsed words flow from her as she extends a hand and makes eye contact.

And I stare at my shoes, the mute and useless companion.

I've an intense need to bury my nose in a book to blot out the people and noise. Instead, I walk along, overwhelmed and exhausted, with hours yet to go.

About four thousand hellos later, we reach the house of the boys who plan to get baptized. Their mother lets us in by a gate and lights a candle inside a lantern. Two wooden chairs with stretched sugarcane husks for seats wait for us. The boys, who seem to be around age twelve, crouch to sit on upside-down tin cans placed on the dirt floor.

Hermana Callister launches a discussion of tithing. The boys whisper to each other. They laugh at a mangy gray cat sleeping in a spot of sun that raises its head every few minutes to hiss at nothing. They tune in to the gospel only long enough to agree quickly or give Hermana Callister a rote answer like *to be baptized*.

My patience hits the skids when a couple of girls gather at the fence, and it becomes obvious the boys can spare more attention for the opposite sex than baptism. At the next pause, I interject. "Wait— why do you want to be baptized?"

The boys laugh. A glance behind tells me the girls laugh in return. I snap three times—loud and harsh like my mom does when one of her kids steps out of line. "Hey. I asked you a question. Why do you want to be baptized?"

The older boy looks at me. "For what she said. Jesus did it. Right?"

"Yeah. But why do you want to follow Jesus?"

Now he looks at his brother. Confusion wrinkles brows. The younger one answers. "Because it's good. And we like church."

The older one follows his lead. "Yeah. Church is great. We like to play basketball there."

"You don't have to get baptized to play basketball at the church." The statement starts a revolution. The boys' eyebrows raise up and they squirm. Hermana Callister hushes me.

"We don't? But all the boys are baptized. On the team."

"You can go to young men's activities anytime. Baptism is something different. It's a commitment. You make a promise to keep going to church even if there's no basketball."

The younger one leans forward, worry draws his eyes into small slits. "They might not always have basketball?"

Hermana Callister squeezes my knee. Hard. Hard enough to hurt. "You're right." Hermana Callister says to one of the boys with great precision. "We get baptized to follow Jesus and that's good."

I talk over top of Hermana Callister. "But it's more than that. It's a lifelong commitment, a new way of being." I begin to run through all the covenants and commandments. With each word, the boys grow colder and make less eye contact and Hermana Callister's fingers threaten to puncture wounds in the side of my knee. "You can always play basketball, but you need to decide if baptism matters as much as playing sports with some nice guys. You can't be tepid. You can't go along. Going along only hurts people in the end."

It's true. I know this. I felt this the day my dad walked away, full of excuses that he'd never really known but done as he was instructed his entire life. You can't be tepid about faith; it has to burn a hole in your soul or it's never going to be good enough.

But the discussion is over. The older boy stands up and the younger follows. "We forgot we have something to do tonight. We'll talk at basketball, okay, Hermana?" The boys join the girls at the fence.

Hermana Callister yanks my arm. She drags me through the gate and then storms from the yard. At the road, she turns a fiery gaze on me. "What was that? Those boys are ready. They sought us out. We're not here to judge their decisions."

"They don't know anything. They weren't even listening."

"But they were ready. Ready enough."

"You'd argue with them if they said no, right? You'd want them to think about their decision, but you'd let them say yes without thinking it through? That's not right, Hermana."

Hermana Callister's lips form into a line. Then she rolls her eyes and wipes her hands down her skirt. "Let's go. We need to find more people. Our pool is too small, and we need to replace these guys. Just—follow my lead. I'll tell you exactly what to do and when to do it."

If I thought her energetic before, she's frenetic now. She pushes me out in front after every hello and then critiques my performance. I'm on an endless merry-go-round that leaves me nauseated. Hermana Callister doesn't stop spinning me until the street is empty except for one woman closing a shop.

"What time is it?" Hermana Callister says out loud.

"Almost 10:30," the woman responds.

Hermana Callister makes a strangled noise. We should have been inside an hour ago, but we can't tell time in a country with no clocks. Hermana Callister's watch needs a battery, and I left mine in my suitcase—something she lectures me about for almost twenty minutes on the pitch-black walk back home. How was I supposed to know my timepiece would be crucial to our eternal progression? I hate having time tied to my wrist.

The house is dark when we return. Hermana Callister runs to her room. She falls to her knees to plead forgiveness.

Great. Not even twenty-four hours into my first area and I've broken a major rule and ruined a baptism. My mom was right; my dad was right. The only thing they've agreed on in five years was that this mission was a knee-jerk reaction to quitting music school. And they were right. I'm a total waste, not called of God at all. I'll be that missionary—the one that gives their homecoming talk on tithing and doesn't mention a single mission success.

I'm so tired of crying and yet tears slip down my cheeks again. I don't want to be like this, but I hate the work and I hate this place and I want to go home. The depression I felt after my dad left tugs at the corners of my heart. I fight it back—or, at least, I try to.

Something scurries and scratches in the corner. The other *hermanas* argue in their beds about the noise. Hermana Callister calls out that she's praying and can't kill the rat.

A rat.

There's a rat in here.

Hermana Vasquez reminds everyone that someone has to kill it immediately per Hermana Stathos' lecture.

"You do it, vampire!" Hermana Hernandez shouts. "You want the blood." She makes a horrible sucking noise, and everyone laughs.

A child-like shadow passes by my bed, so small it can only be Hermana Diaz.

Whack! Squeal! Whack-whack! Silence.

"It's done, whiners. Now shut your faces and sleep. But if you snore, I'll order the rat-ghost to suck out your breath." She makes snoring sounds followed by a gurgled choking on a pretended final breath. The shadow passes my bed again and disappears into the next room.

I can still hear scuffling. "Is that another rat?" I hiss across the space.

"No. Tarantulas. Now hush. I'm praying."

I tuck my mosquito net tighter around my bed and curl into a miserable ball. Hermana Callister prays for almost an hour. I pray a minute as I lay on my back, but then I turn over and pretend I can sleep in the heavy heat of midnight with a rat corpse decomposing nearby.

# Chapter 4

The sound of bugs penetrates my sleep. Plopping. Scratching. Skittering about the floor. Restless dreams plagued me, filled with critters that swarmed my mosquito net and sucked out my breath. As the light comes, my mosquito netting rises and falls under the weight of insects that range in size from a fingernail to a whole hand.

My skin crawls.

Three days' mental and physical torture is enough. I can't do anything about the blisters on my feet or the daily heat stroke or my fear of parasites living in anything liquid or my utter uselessness as a missionary.

But the bugs?

The bugs can be stopped.

The morning alarm sounds my call to arms as an angel of cockroach death. Soon-to-be victims lurk out of sight, under every cabinet. Most of the devil's six-legged henchmen have dissipated into cracks to avoid the heat of the day. The bathroom and kitchen will still be inundated. Hard-soled *chancletas* make perfect murder weapons. I won't feel the bodies, and nothing will survive my stomp. As soon as I'm done with morning study, I'll reap undeniable vengeance on their shelled grotesqueness.

Hermana Hernandez and Hermana Diaz crawl under my net for companion study while *las vampiras* get their beauty sleep. A giant gray cockroach flutters in through the window to land on my shoe. Flapping little wings distract me; I miss my turn to read a passage in the Missionary Handbook, and Hermana Callister sighs. Another disappointment to add to her list. I try to shove aside excitement over bug massacre long enough to do the role plays.

At breakfast, a hard, brown body slips inside the box of Rice Krispies. My first victim. I grab the box to scare out the little bugger, but I'm distracted by Hermana Hernandez. She fishes something black out of her Rice Krispies. The small dots writhe on the table.

Bugs. In our cereal.

I slam the Rice Krispies box on top of the black dots. The cereal flings around the room as I whack again and again and again. Die filthy bugs. Die a vicious death.

When I look up, the other *hermanas* look at me in horrified amusement.

"You just fish them out. The cereal is fine," Hermana Hernandez says, her mouth full of previously bug-polluted grain.

"I hate them. I hate the bugs," I whisper. I sweep up the Rice Krispies and head to the bathroom while everyone else eats the cereal, including Hermana Callister.

*Mamita* Irene arrives while I'm in the bath. There are whispers and then the stove roars to life. The smell of chocolate and cream erase the sweat and sewage that permeates indoor spaces.

A confused cockroach emerges when I slosh water on the floor. I make a triumphant shout. *Mamita* Irene startles with her own squeak of surprise, and then watches me with her hand over her heart. I chase the cockroach out the door to where it bounces blindly off the table leg.

"Die, sucker," I say in English. My foot stomps down hard enough to rattle the chairs. There's a long squeal as the exoskeleton cracks.

*Mamita* Irene sighs at the sound. "Oh. That one suffered. Did you hear how long it screamed? I can't stomach the scream. It hurts my heart."

*Mamita* Irene sighs again, as though I have tortured her soul by killing a disgusting cockroach. Because it has feelings? No. That's a trick. They're dumb bugs. But, I harbor some doubt. What do I know about cockroaches? They're not common in white, affluent Utah.

Hermana Hernandez crunches a roach beside the refrigerator after she gets some water and it squeals, too, as its legs twitch upside-down. "Sorry, *Mamita*! I didn't see it!"

"Girls, if you must kill them, do it fast. Don't leave them in pain." Hermana Hernandez scrunches the insect again. It squeals, long and loud, and then falls silent.

Not one science teacher ever taught me that cockroaches are a higher order insect like ants. Ants organize. They mourn. I have a reasonable detente with ants. They stay away unless I leave food on the counter. But cockroaches? A cockroach does not detente. A cockroach overwhelms, inundates, and invades. If there weren't chocolate on the stove, I'd lose my appetite at the idea of having to live in peaceful cohabitation with cockroaches the size of my big toe.

"I brought your clothes, Hermana," *Mamita* Irene says and points to a large, black bag in our room. She follows me to the room, and then releases a long, horrified shriek.

"A dead rat? You've left a dead rat? Sitting there. The disease...Oh, you foolish, foolish girls." We each get a tap on the back of the head as the lecture continues.

I let the lecture fly in the air like the roaches I hate so much. The wardrobe's ugliness overwhelms me. Flowing gypsy skirts and strange patchwork jumpers combined with plain light-weight tees.

A lost vision of myself hovers out of reach. Dishwater blond hair with mahogany low-lights cut into a blunt bob. Black jeans and a frilly blouse with knee-high boots. A book in my hand and my violin at my feet. But the brown eyes that stare back at me through the dirty, bug-infested glass shutters don't belong to that girl. The sun-bleached strands are almost white, but my skin is turning brown. And my clothes are ugly.

I miss everything about home. Everything.

For vengeance on a life out of my own control, I kick at my luggage. Another brown-shelled body scurries for safety. I kill it without remorse and steel myself for the squeal.

It never comes.

*Mamita* Irene crosses in front of me, her lecturing on pause while she stirs the chocolate. Hermana Hernandez stands nearby and speaks to her in low tones.

I stare at the lifeless form at my feet. Then I crunch it again. I don't know why.

The scream comes this time along with a hush in the kitchen.

The world is weird here, but I'm pretty sure nothing can scream after it's died.

*Mamita* Irene rushes past me on her way from the kitchen with a black bag to dispose of the rat. I kick at a nearby cupboard. A cockroach emerges. I squash it and it doesn't scream.

Every time a cockroach has screamed, *Mamita* Irene has been in the kitchen.

When *Mamita* Irene crosses back to the kitchen, I lift my foot and squash it down to crunch the dead roach again. The squeal follows.

Theory confirmed.

My dead roach can squeal as long as *Mamita* Irene is in the kitchen. And every time I stare at a screaming roach, Hermana Hernandez covers her mouth. She's betrayed by her eyes. She can mute the sound, but nothing stops her eyes from laughing at me.

The women on this island love a good joke. And I'm today's joke. Screaming cockroaches to terrorize the American greenie.

Revenge and the need for a laugh combine to create a brave and grand plan. No one pranks me twice. *Mamita* Irene is about to learn there's no depth too low to sink in pursuit of a good laugh. I'm going to get her good.

In the dead of night, I walk the entire floor until I find the board that squeaks. It's right at the edge of the kitchen, perfectly placed so that *Mamita* Irene could work her greenie torture.

I lure cockroaches into *Mamita* Irene's prized iron urn with a bit of sugar water and flour. As soon as eight large, gray bugs crawl inside, I slide the heavy iron lid in place. The skittering and slipping make me gag but reassure me they haven't drown in the sticky muck I used as bait.

Then I grab a broom to shuffle resistant brown roaches into old margarine containers. The buckets slide behind chairs and boxes where I can easily tip them over by bumping the other side. Then I slip back into bed before the sun cracks open the night.

The next morning, I release my hoard on *Mamita* Irene. At first, she keeps up the ruse. She shoos the roaches away sweetly and reminds us to care for their families. She even suggests that we invite the roaches to pray with us after she sweeps ten or fifteen out the door.

I've requested stew for lunch so *Mamita* Irene will have to use the pot. The *hermanas* and I gather in the kitchen for one last prayer before we leave. I hover above the squeaking board, poised to enact revenge.

I volunteer for the prayer, and wax poetic until I hear *Mamita* Irene light the burner. The iron cauldron rattles. As soon as she removes the lid, she screams. Her hand slams down on the first beast to top the rim. The others come in a fast line. Then she whacks each with a spatula, a slaughter not seen since the Huns destroyed ancient Israel.

I squeal the board every time a cockroach dies. Hermana Diaz and Hermana Hernandez look puzzled at first, but then discover my trick and burst into laughter. Tears streak their cheeks. The *vampiras* shout *Mamita* Irene's lectures about caring for cockroaches as squashed bodies fall lifeless to the floor. I squeak the board a few more times to provoke more laughter.

*Mamita* Irene laughs as soon as the panic over the infestation subsides. I rush to her side for a hug and we laugh together.

As we quiet, she points at me, "Eh, Hermana, you'll do fine here. But you owe me a clean pot. One of the *vampiras*—" she grabs Hermana Hernandez's nickname for the island trainers "—can wait for you so that Hermana Callister makes her appointments. But you'll clean up your mess. Every bit of it."

I grab the bleach and the pot with a giant grin.

Hermana Callister picks Hermana Diaz, who remains doubled-over in crazed laughter even as Hermana Callister hauls her out the door, her expression as austere as ever. Hermana Callister doesn't make eye contact with me. But I shrug it off. Today, life is good and will be good. I'm covered in cockroach guts, but good. I feel it in my bones. There will be people to love, and the Spirit will flow without force, like it used to do.

The water rushing over my hands and pots whispers all my favorite happy scriptures. Maybe Jesus, the fount of living water, doesn't mind a good joke occasionally.

When I return to the kitchen, a tall, willowy and beautiful ward member named Mariana chats with *Mamita* Irene and Hermana Vasquez. I know her in passing—she wants to serve a mission, but her father won't let her, so she does splits several times per week with *las vampiras*—but she rarely interacts directly with Hermana Callister and me.

We shake hands, firm and strong. Mariana smiles at me, and nods towards the door. "We should go. Philippe doesn't like to wait."

Mariana threads an arm through mine. We walk three abreast down dusty streets as Hermana Vasquez retells my cockroach stunt. Laughter and easy greetings pass between them and the passersby. The two women's ease in the culture is so distinct from Hermana Callister's metered pace and forced friendliness. My foreignness fades over the course of our walk to the local secondary school.

The concrete block building with metal-framed glass windows rises along the outskirts of town. It towers above the wooden storefronts and brightly-painted stucco homes, part of a building initiative from the United States in the late 1960s. Inside, the age of the building shows. Paint peels from doorframes. Large gouges in the decades-old tile create trip points. Most of the classrooms lack doors. But there are still signs of care. The hallways smell of bleach. A woman scrubs a display case to a shine outside Philippe's office. Every classroom is filled with uniformed students.

Philippe ushers us inside with a large grin. He's handsome. His gray hair waves back from his forehead with Hollywood precision, befitting the principal of this imposing school and one of the most important people in Las Guaranas.

Unfortunately, he seems to be more curious about the church than interested in joining, per Mariana—his favorite student before she graduated. Philippe has spent three years on the investigator roll. He loves the visits and the intellectual challenge in theology, but his spiritual development remains on a stubborn square one.

He sits behind the large desk and rests his chin on templed fingers while Mariana and Hermana Vasquez occupy the only chairs. A Book of Mormon and Bible spread before him. He waits to be impressed.

With nowhere else to sit, I let books sing their siren song and summon me to lean into a large, stuffed bookshelf. Oh, how I long for a book in my hands, to be lost in characters and story, or even to wander the curious path of unexplored knowledge. The new, the unexpected, the curious—they call to me from the books.

And maybe it's that feeling of being with new and old friends that makes me interject when Philippe mentions *racismo*. Racism. A difficult subject for a church that once barred all non-white members from participating in church leadership.

I can't imagine how tough this issue must be in a room full of darker skin than my own, despite my complex racial identity. Thanks to light skin, no one would ever question my place in a fair-skinned world. But my grandma told me stories of resentment as white-faced boys led congregations while her Mexican father, a lifelong member, sat uselessly beside. My great-grandparents refused to baptize their children until my great-grandfather could wade into the water at his daughter's side. That great day came in 1978 when the priesthood was extended to all people everywhere.

So, I speak. Despite being the greenie and the whitest face in the room. I talk about how my own heart found peace with something my head wars against.

"I don't want to pretend I have any answers to this. I think it would be ridiculous for anyone white to pretend they understand how you feel. But I know how important the priesthood is. My dad left us when I was fourteen." My voice comes out wistful and soft, lost in memory and drunk on books. "We lost the Priesthood in our home. Every time I needed an ordinance, I had to beg a neighbor or a friend. I hated my dad for that, for taking the Priesthood away. But then a family moved in next door, refugees from Somalia. Brother Egwu did all the dad things from fixing broken doors to blessings. They never waited to be asked. If mom's car was in the driveway during a school day, Brother Egwu showed up with consecrated oil to see who was sick. He asked us, so humbly, if he could ordain my brother to the office of Elder. He took care of us. So, June 6, 1978, is my favorite date in history. It's the day that gave us Brother Egwu and the day each congregation could be led by its own people. From Mexico to South Africa, each ward owns its own soul now and I'm so grateful."

My fingers run along the book spines one more time before I move to rest against the desk near Philippe where his Bible lays open to the description of the Day of Pentecost. "I don't have an answer for the past, Philippe, but I'm grateful for the present day and for a prophet who asked an important question and then followed instructions, as Peter did."

Something beautiful pops from the barren ground in my gut. The first hint of the Spirit in too many months blooms dead center and spreads into a vast space. Then peace fills that hole, and surety radiates bright light to nourish the bloom.

The conversation in the room shifts. The women tell their stories of what it's like to watch their own people perform ordinances and lead congregations. They share scripture after scripture that illustrates God's love for all people. Philippe follows eagerly, marking passages with a bright red pen and scribbling ideas along the margins until the Spirit rests.

Philippe's eyes reflect my joy as he reaches across to grab Hermana Vasquez's hand before the closing prayer. "Today, *hermanas*, for the first time, I've reason to think seriously about becoming a member of your church. Thank you. The future is, at times, more important than the past, even for a student of history like this old relic."

Mariana and Hermana Vasquez walk silently behind me as we leave, a pall over us that's still pulsating with the occasional burst of light.

When we reach the street, Mariana turns towards me. "Would you come talk to my Papi? I think he'd like you, Hermana Lewis. He likes women who speak their minds. I think, maybe, he'd listen to you.

You're the kind of person he listens to. And you're cute. That never hurts." Her eyes sparkle with tears.

Mariana hugs me. As she lets go, there's a loud pop above our heads and a sizzle. Then the world plunges into darkness.

"*Se fue la luz*," Mariana whispers. The lights went out.

There's only one hydroelectric plant that serves this half of the island. When there isn't sufficient power for the capital, the lights go out in the outer regions. The problem is made worse by the people who splice into the main power lines and blow out the system. Las Guaranas is close to the capital, so blackouts are rare but still happen every few weeks.

Hermana Vasquez squeezes my hand as she kisses each of Mariana's cheeks. "Text me to let me know you got home safe. Take a *motoconcho*?"

She presses a five peso note into Mariana's hand. The streets aren't safe for women in this pitch blackness.

Three *motoconchos* summon at Mariana's shrill whistle into the seemingly empty street. My first ride. I follow Hermana Vasquez's lead by mounting sidesaddle behind the driver with my ankles crossed. I feel off-balance, but I don't tumble off as we start moving.

These mopeds sound like the bike gang I formed with my brother as kids. We'd attach a playing card to the brake cable so that it would flutter along the spokes as they spun. The mopeds buzz and weave as we did through our neighborhood. I'd be having fun, except the benign world sparked out with the lights.

In the shadows, men hover. Twice, we drive past a robbery in progress. Each time, Hermana Vasquez whistles and shouts for the drivers to hurry. There are screams of person and animal that punctuate an eerie, uncharacteristic silence.

Hermana Hernandez waits on the step with a single, lit candle. She clasps her hands and gives thanks to God when we approach. "Every minute felt like five. Did you not hear my calls?"

We couldn't hear anything over the roaring engines.

"Come in. It's our first Ceremony of Light. I've looked forward to this since I put in my papers." Hermana Hernandez ushers me inside with a hand around my waist.

A mission tradition has grown around the power outages. As soon as we walk in, the ceremony begins. Hermana Vasquez presents me with a long, white candle. "Because light is precious, both physical and spiritual. We're bringers of light, Hermana."

We light each other's' candles as we sing, *The Lord is my Light*. My voice rings loud and clear and echoes in the courtyard below.

When we stop, Hermana Diaz requests *Jesus, Savior, Pilot Me*. Then Hermana Montez asks for her favorite. Our neighbor pounds the wall and shouts a request for *El Espiritu de Dios*. We continue to sing in the gentle warmth of the Holy Ghost long past the return of the power.

Hermana Callister never joined us. Her form is indiscernible in the darkness except for the sound of soft breath. I don't think I'll ever understand her. Tomorrow, I face her world again, the world of harsh rules and constant criticism. My eyes close and I go back to Philippe's office in my mind. That's the world I want. That's the mission I can serve. But Hermana Callister groans in her sleep and I groan in my soul. The mission I want, and the one I have, feel separated by a thousand days of perfect obedience.

# Chapter 5

The weeks seem to fly by in an endless parade of exhausted parables. Morning street contacts have changed shape now.

"All you have to do is sing," she promises every morning. I'll do the hard part."

And that's where we are again on this fifteenth day of service. Hermana Callister pulls out a Book of Mormon. She nods at me to start a song. Like every morning.

*I am a Child of God* winds its way through the host of people at the town square. The streets hush. Slowly, a crowd forms. I sing all the verses with as much passion as I feel for the lyric. I'm not even that good, but on the streets of Las Guaranas, I'm Celine Dion accompanied by the London Philharmonic.

I wish I had my violin. They'd be headed to baptism if they could hear me play the violin instead of sing.

Hermana Callister moves among the people and makes ten appointments. The children follow us for two blocks before I indulge them with *I Feel My Savior's Love.* My grandmother sang to us in Spanish all our lives, so the words in the Primary songbook are more natural to me in this land than my own. As I sing, I feel her fingers brush across my forehead, giving me hope.

I haven't heard her sing or felt her touch me in several years. She has Alzheimer's and spends her day locked in inescapable memories. She has a heart of pure gold, even if her memory is made of pyrite. A sob threatens to disrupt my song.

Yesterday, I couldn't remember how to say cheese in English. I had to look up the word *queso* in my Spanish-English dictionary to remember how to ask for my favorite food in my native tongue. I can't remember my mom's voice. When I try to summon her, she speaks Spanish and wears flip flops.

I guess I sobbed in my sleep or something. Everyone is worried I might swim home. Over breakfast, Hermana Vasquez and Hermana

Montez told Hermana Callister to let me have a taste of normal. I didn't think Hermana Callister was listening until she starts to cast sideways glances at me. She chews her lip as we pass an office supply store that advertises computer time for rent.

"I asked President if it would be okay to check emails. Just this once. Since you've been..." She graciously drops the end of the sentence.

I speak before she can add anything. "It would be nice to hear from my mom."

We settle in behind two computers. Mine buzzes to life. Hermana Callister's remains silent. I almost sigh but then remind myself to take advantage of whatever flexibility she offers.

I dash off an email to Joe about *Mamita* Irene's prank before I open a single letter. I wish we'd talked more mission stuff before I left. We aren't chatty siblings except to complain about my dad. He'll like the cockroach story, though.

I hit send and then I look at the offerings in my inbox. My mom. The bishop. My one friend from school that still remembers me. And a couple from the Relief Society sisters who write everyone while they're out.

Nothing from my dad. No surprise there.

Joe's response comes as I read through mom's latest news, which is full of no news. Not that much interesting happens in Sandy, Utah. I write my mom a nice, newsy email full of happy stories and lies about how much I love the tropical weather.

A reply from Joe sits in my inbox. I click it, feeling deliciously guilty, as though I'm stealing a conversation between phone calls.

*Seriously? That's my first email from you? You touched some bugs? Actually, good for you. You gotta have a little fun. I wish I'd figured that out earlier on my own mission. So, have some fun. Don't go to that Lannie place where you freak yourself out and take everything too serious. Yeah, I wish I'd figured that out as early as you did.*

Something went wrong on Joe's mission, some story I've never heard. He came home a lost soul. Mom takes him to counseling, and he pretends to love life, but he spends most of his days playing video games after he works at a deli in town. He still loves Christ and the gospel, but his fire went out somewhere. I don't want my fire to go out, so I'll heed his warning. I'm going to keep trying to have a little fun.

My last email is definitely fun. Our stupid, amazing Bishop Hilyard films a three-minute video-gram that he sends out *en masse* to the eighteen missionaries from our ward. Today's video features the annual water fight on the church lawn. My mom laughs behind the camera as a group of youth drop two tubs full of water balloons over Bishop Hilyard. Both her laugh and his pretense at rage make me homesick again. I click off the computer and force my attention back to the mission.

Our next stop is Juana's house. The usual excitement flutters beneath my homesickness.

In less than an hour, we have a dozen contacts, and I'm sitting on an upside-down bucket clipping an old lady's cracked, yellow toenails. The cracks in her feet are deep and ooze something green despite my regular ministrations. She doesn't seem able to feel anything in her feet. She can't walk and doesn't react as I clip and disinfect. I've been stopping by every day to soak her infected feet in saltwater, pull off the dead skin and apply Neosporin. Mom would freak that I'm using up my whole supply on one old woman in my first area, but I know it's what Jesus wants. My Neosporin was intended for Juana.

She turns off the *telenovelas* now so that we can talk the whole visit. Today, she claims she was both a nun and a mobster's girlfriend. It's never the same story. At first, I thought she was senile, but then I caught her giggling at us. She's a con. An old, hilarious con. We don't even know if she's ever been a member. She changes her religion as often as her life story.

Hermana Callister is less patient with the stories. She wants outcomes. If Juana is a lost cause, then she wants contact names for her children.

"Juana, what's the name of your son? The one in the *campo*?"

"I've forgotten. He never visits." But her eyes sparkle. "Maybe his name was Freddy."

"No. Freddy is your son here in Las Guaranas. We sent him for sodas."

"We did? Are you sure? I thought Freddy was the one that lives in Miami. His wife is rich. They have two cars."

"I'm sure they do. But Freddy is definitely the one at the *colmado*."

"Hm. I'm too old to remember. I call them all Freddy."

"You called all your children Freddy? Same last name, too?" Hermana Callister's brow stays furrowed around her dark brown eyes.

"I didn't name them all Freddy, dear. I'm joking." Juana squeezes my knee.

Juana points her lips at a bottle of red nail polish. "Bring the magic. Takes twenty years off my feet. I'll be ready for striptease again."

We both laugh. Hermana Callister probes for more names.

"Alex. Alex Rodriguez," Juana says with an exasperated sigh. "*En serio.*"

No. Definitely not serious. "Does he play baseball?" I joke back.

"Would he like a Book of Mormon?" Hermana Callister asks.

I shake my head and this time I'm the one who takes pity. "No, Hermana Callister. Alex Rodriguez is a famous baseball player. She likes to joke."

Hermana Callister's face knits tightly. She's a confused lamb amidst the wolf pack.

I finish up the red polish. Juana's feet do look twenty years younger. "Okay, Juana. Tomorrow when I come to see you, we have to talk about Jesus Christ."

"Of course, of course. I love the Lord. We'll talk about him." But I know we won't. I hug her anyway and promise to be back. Her fence needs mending. We should bring the Elders by too, for service hours.

I text the men as I wait for Hermana Callister. She accosted the actual Freddy to ask him about his brother in Miami. Freddy wrinkles his nose in confusion. Eventually, he rattles off a name, but tells us the brother is a drug dealer and won't like religion. I'm not sure he's being any more serious than his jokester of a mother.

Hermana Callister huffs as we leave. "We're not going back there. They all lie to us. All the time. Every day, we lose a chance for a real interaction. We're not here to give pedicures."

"Yesterday, I washed her hair, too." I squirm. These visits are the best part of my days.

"She talks about nothing. I don't understand half what she says."

I bite on both my lips to stop from stating the real problem. Hermana Callister can't speak the language. She's been here for fourteen months, but can't order food, give directions for *motoconchos,* or follow non-gospel conversations. My heart aches as I watch her stumble through a phone call. I thought her reliance on memorized discussions was over-zealousness, but it's survival. Unfortunately, despite endless prayer, diligence and obedience—the gift of tongues has passed her by.

Hermana Callister walks on faster, still ranting about Juana. "If she won't listen to discussions and she doesn't know anyone that will, we can only spend two hours per week with her. Our service hours. Is that enough?"

I shrug. I love Juana. I'd be there every day. "How about we make it goal-dependent? If we meet our contact and discussion goals, we get to visit Juana?"

Hermana Callister scowls, but then she nods. She's a little desperate to get me to help more in street contacts. Maybe I will if I know there's a reward at the end.

My body feels heavier, though my clothes fit looser. Every step sinks into the ground and I must think to make my feet move. When I think about the pace of this labor, I'm surprised I'm still standing. Every day from 6:30 a.m. to 10:30 p.m. is a hard drive. Hermana Callister believes in the reverse law of the tithe on our mission: ten percent for ourselves and ninety percent for the Lord. Bathing counts as time for ourselves. Personal conversations, too. We get sixteen hours total down time every week. So, I'm exhausted. That's why I can't remember home or words or my own first name.

"Can we get a *motoconcho*?" I request with a yawn.

Hermana Callister shakes her head. "I spent all my money on ice cream."

The ninety-percent rule applies to money, too. Hermana Callister budgets eighteen pesos per week to spend on *motoconchos* and other frills. The average *concho* ride costs five *pesos*. So, it's nothing. We have to ride *motoconchos* to the ward building three miles away, so, by Sunday, we're essentially out of easy rides. I bite back a remark that money saved equals time wasted. Which one is more valuable to the Lord, Saint Callister?

Yeah. I'm testy today. Grumpy and a little impossible. Mom says I become a cat in a tree when I'm out of sorts. All hiss and no common sense.

A harsh hiss startles me from my angry tree. Mariana waves at us from across the street. "My dad is home! Can you come?"

Hermana Callister wanted to street contact down by the market. Her lips purse. Fausto isn't likely to be sober, according to Hermana Vasquez.

Mariana hopes for a miracle the way Noah did for rain. If Fausto refuses to sign the papers, Mariana can't serve a mission.

Hermana Callister's shoulders rise and fall in a giant sigh. She capitulates under the force of Mariana's eagerness. "Yes. We'll be right there."

Mariana leads us behind the series of wooden storefronts papered in pornographic magazines. The store owners mock our averted eyes, as though it's a shock that two Mormon girls don't want to see naked women in explicit poses.

Mariana's house is a two-room shanty hidden behind the stalls. We're welcomed readily by Mariana's mother, Ilsa. She's as tall as Mariana but not as fine. Her large bosom and wide shoulders swallow both of us in a single hug. "Oh, Hermanas, I pray you work a miracle with that old goat." Her lips point towards the back room where a large shape reclines in a lawn chair.

Fausto is drunk and half-asleep. Pungent rum mixes with sweat in the hot interior. Mariana wraps her arms around him. "Papi, it's the *hermanas*. You promised me thirty minutes."

Fausto opens one eye. I grin at him. Hermana Callister extends a hand.

"Sit," Fausto says and closes his eyes again.

Mariana shakes his shoulder. "No, papi. You promised. Thirty minutes."

He grumbles but sits up. "Okay. Tell me why I should give my daughter to your God."

Hermana Callister launches the first discussion. Fausto nods off before Joseph sees the column of light. Mariana and Ilsa huddle behind Fausto. Worry etches extra years on Ilsa's wrinkled face. The thirty minutes wind down with no progress.

And it's hot. Hotter than the usual hot. Boiling-skin hot.

Ilsa cooks a chicken over an open fire. The flames super-heat the tiny area. Sweat pours down my back. My eyes close at odd intervals. I was tired before we entered this sauna and now I'm wrecked.

"Come to church," Hermana Callister says, suddenly off script. "Just come to church and meet the men. They'll tell you why they give up their daughters."

Sunday is fast Sunday. Testimony meeting. He'll get to hear from members and not only missionaries.

"You can hear from the members as they…" I say. The right word slips my mind. Instead, I translate my sluggish thoughts literally. "*Desnuda. Testimonio desnuda.*"

I don't hear my mistake until I've made it. Not bear testimony. I've said bare testimony. Worse. I've said, *desnudas*. The euphemism for strippers.

Fausto roars to life with a laugh like the shout that brought down the walls of Jericho. "Naked testimonies? In the church?"

"So, will you come?" I ask.

My sense of humor overwhelms *gravitas* as the visual hits me. Strippers in church. I laugh at the idea of *Mamita* Irene jiggling her way to the front with nothing but the Book of Mormon and her faith. I guess bare testimony is better than if I'd literally translated bear. Oh, man. Now I'm seeing naked *Mamita* Irene giving testimony to a giant panda in the front row. That's fabulous. Testimony meeting would become my favorite week of the month.

"Very little I wouldn't do for *desnudas*." Fausto throws back another glass of rum with a twinkle in his eye. "Alright, alright. I'll come see your naked testimonies."

If it takes a stripper to get him to church, I can't imagine what might secure a baptism.

Mariana hugs us tightly as we leave. "It's a miracle. Thank you."

"He's not agreed to your mission yet."

"But he will. I know he will."

We wave at Fausto, Ilsa, and Mariana as we walk out. The fire had obscured night's approach. In the street, darkness nibbles away at the remaining light.

"We've got two more hours. Street contacts or member drop-ins?"

"Dinner. I'm starving."

Hermana Callister gives me that look, the *can't you wait?* look. A few minutes for food won't bring on the apocalypse. I ignore her and cross to the *colmado* to buy myself a banana and an ounce of goat cheese. Hermana Callister goes home in seven weeks. That's the maximum amount of time I must endure this companionship.

When I get outside, Hermana Callister stands with two men that rest against rusted *motoconchos*. They angle towards Hermana Callister with too-big smiles on their faces. One man's legs extend until his foot is a mere inch or two from hers. They laugh way too much. Hermana Callister can't tell jokes in English, no way she's told one in Spanish. Those dudes are flirting with her.

I doubt Hermana Callister has ever flirted on purpose. She's had the same boyfriend since the third grade. The skill set to catch a boy's attention changes once he's stopped eating glue.

"Hey, what's going on?" I ask, all smiles.

"Hello, Hermana," the man with light green eyes says, too low and breathy to be a proper greeting. His eyes travel the whole length of my body. The men here don't even pretend they're not contemplating nasty things. Makes me feel gross.

Hermana Callister bobs her head like a hungry parakeet with an eye on birdseed. "They want a discussion. Offered to give us a free ride to their house."

Yeah, I'm sure they're all about the free rides. Anywhere, anytime, any reason.

I grab Hermana Callister's arm and lean in to whisper. "Did you say *fecha* or *cita*?"

We've had this little problem before. *Fecha* is a date on a calendar. *Cita* is an act of courtship. She tends to confuse them.

The other guy removes her backpack. His hand covers her elbow to lift her into place on the scooter—*cita*. Definitely a date. Hermana Callister has arranged a double date for us.

The *motoconcho* roars away before I can interject.

I hop on the second *motoconcho* in one movement, my ankles clicking into place. I'm going to kill Hermana Callister, once I catch her.

"Well, let's go," I say and my date revs up the machine to carry me away side-saddle like the well-behaved missionary-lady I've been trained to be.

"Where you from?" The *motoconcho* driver asks as the machine whirs along the streets.

"America."

The driver laughs, as though I've been witty with my obvious and insufficient answer.

"I'm from La Romana," he says.

Great. I've no idea where that is. Conversation dead. He zips by the last streetlamp on the main road, the marker that delineates the end of our area. Up ahead, Hermana Callister shakes her head and points behind her.

"Hey! No. We can't go any further than this. We have—geography—area—we can't go beyond the lamps."

"No worries. It'll be fun. We like party-girls." He says the last word in English.

Party-girls. You've got to be kidding me. Oh, Hermana Callister is so, so, so dead.

"Take us back," I say low in his ear. My no-kidding voice.

"*Rubia*, don't worry. We live close. It's a big party. Then we'll take you home."

*Rubia, Blondie.* One of many code-words for spoiled American princess. I'm not an American princess. But I am one-fourth Mexican. He's about to learn what that means. My anger boils over when he reaches back to touch my leg.

I throw my weight around to rock the *motoconcho*. "I'm a missionary. I'm not going to be anyone's party-girl."

"That's what they all say at first."

Ridiculous. This is ridiculous.

I have to get off this bike.

I rock the *motoconcho* again. Harder. The back wheel skids.

"Hey! What're you doing? Stop that. We'll fall."

"That's the point."

I rock us again. Twice each way. My captor lets up on the speed enough that I can place my foot on the ground. The increased friction yanks the bike. Pain explodes as my ankle rolls under itself. Worth it, though, when the speed backs off again. I push both heels into the ground as we turn left. The back tire skids twice and the driver saves us with a hard push back upright.

"Stop! You'll kill us. You're crazy."

"You're gonna let me off this thing." I rock harder. Back and forth with all my might. "Signal your friend to pull over and let me off this stupid bike."

We nearly collapse when I shift all my weight to the right. The driver swears at me with words I no longer recognize. "Crazy American women! I'm going to speed up to signal my friend. Just don't kill us."

"If you try anything, I'll throw us both. Don't think I won't."

"The crazy ones. I always find the crazy ones."

He pulls up alongside his friend to whistle and shake his head. In a moment, the *motoconchos* have slowed enough that I jump off. The man tosses my bag at me, and then spits on my shoe. I kick dirt on him. My charity faileth when I'm about to be kidnapped.

The men roar off into the night.

I grab Hermana Callister's shoulders and shake them, harder than I should but not as hard as I'd like. "*Cita* means date! As in two couples on a romantic outing. If you hear *cita*, you say no! Who knows what might have happened to us out there. Sheesh, Hermana Callister, how do you not know this?! You've got to be smarter or you'll get us hurt."

I push up into her face, not pausing enough to let her derail my rant. "So, here's how this works. The person who speaks the language is the person in charge. I don't care about seniority or spirituality or consecration or anything. I speak the language, so I make the decisions."

To make my point, I put two fingers in my mouth and whistle, loud. The sound startles a cat crouched over a rat carcass. The starved beast squeals and runs across the street. A cab puffs and spits and then sputters to a stop in front of us. I rattle off perfect directions back to the house, and then hold open the door while Hermana Callister slips inside.

Her sniffles don't dissuade me from showing off my conversation skills as we chat about his family up north and beloved dog. He was baptized once, a long time ago, but he likes rum more than church. The entire story makes me laugh. Our handshake obscures Hermana Callister pushing a Book of Mormon at him.

At the house, my bag skids across the floor when I toss it. Hermana Callister collapses to her knees by her bed and that makes me even angrier. I walk into Hermana Hernandez's room to tell the kidnapping story in whispers while I lay across her bed and eat peanut brittle she got from home last p-day.

*Las vampiras* speak up from the darkness of their sarcophagi as I finish the sad tale. "Hermana Lewis found her *esposo de isla.*"

Island husband. A Dominican Happy Meal. Buy a mission, take home a husband. I don't know how often it actually happens, but the Dominican *hermanas* complain about it all the time. American women who take the good ones.

"Don't worry. We'll let you take that one home. No complaints from any of us."

We all start to laugh. *Las vampiras* bring me a wedding bouquet made of old schedule sheets and hum the wedding march. No one mentions that we should hush our laughs out of respect for Hermana Callister's prayers. When we calm enough for our own prayers, Hermana Diaz prays that we'll all be happy in the holy sacrament of the marriage and we start laughing again mid-prayer.

Somewhere in the giggling, I fall asleep for several hours next to Hermana Hernandez. In the dead of night, I summon the courage to brave the bug-scape and return to my own netting. Hermana Callister is still on her knees.

# Chapter 6

A few very quiet days later—it's a little shocking how long you can go without speaking to a person that can never be out of your sight—the Elders' white Ford truck skids to a halt in front of us on the road out to Juana's house. They came today to mend the fence.

The large, funny one—Elder Alexander, I think—leans out the side window. He points at me. "Hey, President Stathos wants to see you. Tomorrow, 9:30 a.m. You gotta take the bus cuz we haven't met numbers yet. Can't afford a day off to run you two in."

The car backs up and the Elders are gone again.

This must be about Hermana Callister. She probably mentioned my mission rebellion in her weekly letter. The president has heard that I injured an angel and now I'll catch hell for it.

I deserve a good bashing. I may speak the language, but I'm a hopeless mess as a missionary. Other than laughing with Juana and a long academic discussion with Phillipe about the four versions of the Joseph Smith story, we've done not one valuable thing since I nearly toppled those *motoconchos*. The longer I'm in charge, the more the numbers will plummet until only big fat zeroes populate the goal board. I'll drag home with proof my dad was right, and that I'm not the right kind of person for a mission. I'm no more righteous than the mosquitoes that buzz about our beds, hopeful for a sip of nourishing blood as I hope to obtain celestial glory by sponging off the righteous.

Time flows sticky, pungent, and slow like old molasses. The sunlight globs onto the earth and refuses to let the night come. Then night clings to every corner. When the day does arrive, the trip to the President's mansion mires in unnecessary delays and unexpected stops because Hermana Callister insists we take the cheaper public bus rather than the air-conditioned tourist ones. I don't deny her. I can't add more sins to those piled around me already. The yellow VW bus bursts with people. A free-roaming chicken clucks its way up and down the aisle.

We hold onto a pole at the front and let the creature pluck at our shoes.

The smell of fifty people and an ill-behaved chicken doesn't leave us on the half-mile hike to the house. I smelled much better the last time I arrived at this door.

The maid wipes her hands on her white apron and ushers us inside. The Americanized home shocks me now, though I barely noticed it my first visit. Carpet instead of cement. Painted plaster. Chintz couches. The dish towels and washrags match. *Mamita* Irene would die over the pots and pans. She protects her single, iron, do-everything pot, like the royal guard watches over crown jewels. Here, there's a restaurant-worthy collection of such pans hanging from the ceiling. And everything is quiet. No shouting from the streets, no loud music.

Fresh *bolo* bread cools on the clean stone counters. The woman offers me one, but my stomach churns in protest.

Hermana Stathos opens the door at the other end of the house. The president lifts his head and motions me towards his large, mahogany desk. Hermana Callister should say something encouraging—surely, that's part of the Gospel, too, right?—but she chomps her bread and asks for hot cocoa even though it's mid-day.

The rug runner that lines the path to the president's office looks like a plank, and my imagination forms a pirate's ship around me. My thoughts take on an unfortunate argh, and a grin threatens. I've always had the weirdest reactions to being in trouble.

How am I supposed to behave? Do I lead with apology or wait for accusation? I try to tuck my injured ankle under the chair. My smile is probably not solemn enough.

I've never been to the Bishop's office for anything other than praise and interviews. One big sin would have been a good idea. Then I'd know what to expect, how this would go down. But no. I'm the vanilla-est of vanilla Mormons. Not interesting enough to be righteous or sinful. I've floated through my life with nothing but a series of appropriate yes and no responses to temple recommend questions.

Hermana Stathos slides the door shut behind me.

The president rises to shake my hand. Then he perches on his desk with one butt cheek on the desk and most of his weight on a single leg. Argh, my brain repeats.

I'm going to laugh. Do. Not. Laugh. I cannot laugh. I take both lips between my teeth and bite hard. Mission death happens when you laugh at the president. It's not written anywhere but it must be true.

The president steeples his fingers and draws them to his mouth. "I've heard some things about you, Hermana Lewis."

My emotions flip in a moment. Tears replace the hidden laughs.

"And so—I think we need to discuss some changes to your assignment." This I didn't see coming. An embarrassing conversation, a little shame. Not a transfer. Never a transfer.

The president comes off his perch. He walks behind his desk and withdraws a black case. Fat on one end and skinny on the other with a single scratch that happened when I slipped on some ice my junior year of high school.

He has my soul in his hands.

My violin.

My name is engraved along the front.

It's mine. How does he have my violin?

"I asked your mother if we could borrow this, picked it up in Miami myself. You've been in orchestra since you were eight, yes? Youth orchestra? Then a music scholarship but you gave that up to pursue—"

"I don't quite know yet."

Oh, I want my violin. Is he going to make me earn it? The last thing I did before heading to the airport was to play my senior recital in the hotel room. I've longed to play again on bad days, even stood in the bathroom and pretended to bow the strings.

"And I'm told that's burying your talent in the earth. The people here need beauty. Music has power, Hermana. Incredible power."

I'm not sure what he's saying. I hope what he's saying involves him handing me that case. And I'm right. As soon as I nod, the black case moves across his desk. The thick black handle melds into the groove of my palm. When the black case is in my lap, my fingers scramble to unlock the latch.

My hand runs along the smooth wood. The pads of my fingers stroke the strings. The president nods at me, looks at the violin. Play? He wants me to play? Hermana Stathos nods, too.

"Okay, but I'm pretty rusty."

My chin finds its favorite spot. Love for this chunk of wood delayed my mission almost two years. Claremont College. I moved in with my traitorous dad and the awful new girlfriend, so I could accept a partial scholarship and play in an orchestra with some of the most talented people in the country. I don't regret it. I love my pretty thing too much.

In my mind's eye, the conductor stands before me to signal the tuning. I pull the bow for a single e-flat. The perfectly clear note shakes hands with the silence. The concert can begin.

I play Nearer, *My God to Thee*, the Horner version from a movie soundtrack, but still a hymn. The first chord calls forth the second and then the third and then the whole song whines and sings. My eyes close. In my mind, I join the Titanic. My fingers warble on the strings at the right moments as the lifeboats load and so many are left behind. The music shivers inside, and my brain goes still. The violin and my muscles move in divine purpose. I hold the last note an extra measure, so the sound fades instead of stops.

Then I open my eyes.

Hermana Stathos wipes away tears.

The president holds his scriptures in his hand. "We'll take them the light of Christ, Hermana. In song and through the Word of God."

I feel like me, the real me. And I finally know how I'll serve my God.

Hermana Callister follows me out of the house. We don't speak. My mind is too full of music and her mouth is too full of fresh bread.

The concerts start almost immediately. Every Sunday. The new best day of the week. Our area is only forty-five minutes from the president's mansion and on a main highway, so I usually get a ride to the concert with the Mission President or one of the training *hermanas*. Hermana Callister stays behind with the housemates. Heaven on the Lord's day.

Ten days later, the second concert falls on Mother's Day. I'm eager to share my excitement with my family on one of my first phone call home. I sit on a small stool in a local *colmado* for the Mother's Day call. My rear end wedges into a shelf with the fruit and *Telenovelas!* Magazines. Hermana Callister waits across the street where she can see but not hear. I did the same for her.

"So, I'm playing in these concerts," I blurt out when Joe answers the phone.

The bad connection makes Joe's voice sound like he speaks through water. "What concerts? My mission never had concerts." Intermittent chomps and bleeps tell me that he's eating something and playing a video game. I close my eyes to block out the brightly colored houses and giant mango trees, and transport back to our basement where I lounge on the couch while Joe wishes I'd go away.

"Of course, you didn't have concerts. You don't have any talents. But I do. So, anyway, the president and I travel all over—"

"Wait. Just you and the president?"

"And his wife. Obvs."

Joe gurgles whenever he thinks. The rough, wet sound amplifies over the connection. When the sound stops, he says, "Hey, just be careful, ok? They may be missionaries, but they're not perfect."

"Huh?"

"Just—it's not good to be the president's favorite. That's all. So, watch yourself, ok?"

Joe can be paranoid. He's missing the point. Totally. "No one thinks I'm his favorite. I never make numbers, and I'm a waste at baptism. Seriously. I'm the only missionary here with a big fat zero on the baptisms chart."

"Yeah. That's kinda worse. Just watch your back, okay? Jealousy happens."

"Yeah. Sure. Of course." The sounds of video game violence resume.

Joe is twenty-three, but he's been on pause since his return home from his mission three years ago. He's not exactly qualified to give life advice.

Mom's voice cuts in. "Okay. I'm done giving Grandma her pills. She couldn't wait another ten minutes, I suppose. I guess it's better that she remembers them. But now you get to repeat yourself." Mom carries the burden of my dad's family without a hint of resentment. Ex doesn't mean unloved, Mom says. Grandma will live with us until she dies.

Mom rambles on. "How is the food? Are you eating? Is the food safe?

"Yes, mom, everything's fine, and so far, no yeast infections, either." Joe fake-gags and then his shouts turn muffled. Mom probably smacked him. Or sat on his head.

"So, what do you like? Oh, tell me everything, Lannie." I love my mom. I really, really love my mom.

After five more minutes, Joe breaks in, having wrested free from Mom. "I hate to do this, but—" His phone alarm beeps in the background. Our time is up.

Mom's exhale rattles across the line. Her voice is tight when she speaks again. "Bye honey. We love you. We're so proud of you."

I'm too choked up to say goodbye. Maybe I'm glad I can't hear their voices for seven more months.

I'm feeling lost when the president and his wife arrive to pick me up for that night's concert. They insist I arrive on time, unwrinkled, and in full makeup. Tonight's concert is in *Guayubin*. Hermana Callister and the rest of my district will come on a bus rented by the branch. The breaks from Hermana Callister make the days bearable. I count down every day until her transfer home. Only 56 more days to go.

*Las vampiras* snigger as I collect my bag to go. They pretend not to be looking at me when I glance over. No—they're *not* looking at me.

Joe's paranoia is infectious. The only thing anyone thinks about me is that I know how to play the violin.

I rush down the stairs and throw open the door to see my beloved instrument. The violin lives at the mansion with the president and his wife. I'd never risk it being stolen or manhandled by Elders at transfer. My fingers stroke the bumps and small grooves on the rough plastic case as we drive; every sign of imperfection is as precious to me as the perfect instrument inside. Sadness after the phone call lingers and fills my head with Wagner. Wagner plays as soundtrack whenever I'm sad.

Wagner ended my music career. My major professor selected the work, *Träume*, for junior level juries. At Claremont, junior juries were pass or fail. If I passed, I continued in the program. I practiced so hard my fingers bled, as a good virtuoso should, but I never mastered the long, lyrical passages that bleed with emotion.

My teacher ordered me to immerse myself in the pains of life. I watched hours of sad movies about the Holocaust—a fitting apology for so many hours spent on a song written by a notorious anti-Semite—and I tried to pour those tears into the melody, darkening the deep tones and barely touching the high ones. But at juries, my instructors found my performance hollow, uninteresting, and complained I lacked the correct vibrato to tease out any nuance from the notes. In fifteen minutes, I lost my position in the music department.

Goodbye scholarship. Goodbye California. Goodbye future.

I play *Träume* over and over again. It's become the echo in my heart. Drama and pain and passion and beauty—so many moments covered by one impossible-to-master song. I hear more than notes in the melody. Sometimes, God comes to me through the music, but I rarely know what He says.

President Stathos interrupts my sorrow to ask me if I've been to Mexico. He's recently returned but had a very difficult time due to some changes in airline policies. I have nothing to contribute. President Stathos continues on, not bothered by my silence.

The ocean peeks out of trees as we turn west. The stake building in Nagua stands stark white against the blue ocean and brown sand. All the usual foliage surrounds the building, except the green leaves and beautiful flowers all bow towards the blue God that holds the island in His arms. Gorgeous. Heavenly. If the temple is the Lord's house, this must be His vacation cottage.

The president strides confidently towards the open-air chapel. He places his scripture bag on a real, cloth-covered bench like we have in the States before heading to the pulpit to practice the speeches that narrate my music. Hermana Stathos sits on the stand next to president. At the end of his speech, she claps silently for him. They're a weird pair.

The ocean crashes behind me. *Träume* swells in my head. I slip into the courtyard to find a private spot for rehearsal.

A slight wind rustles branches on the far side of the courtyard. The leaves clap together, harsh and staccato, like a director's call to attention. The wind quiets and there's a hush in the ocean as I strike the first chord. The beginning is almost inaudible, lost in the usual cacophony of street sounds. The initial run up the scale leads to gentle high notes, the painful heart twist in this melody. Then it's back down the register for a dramatic passage. A crashing wave matches the next run up. Over and over again, I match the swell of violin to the ocean's movement in a strange duet with the moon. It's all wrong, artistically and technically—definitely wouldn't pass juries—but the dramatic cat-and-mouse as I chase the effects of gravity set up an emotional climax. The turbulent ocean orchestrates around my last three chords. I hold the finale until a large wave mimics cymbals that end the movement.

When I open my eyes, a woman stands in front of me. She's dressed in simple gray dress and white Keds. Her gray hair pulls back into a tight bun. A callous-covered hand reaches out to grab mine. She tucks her face into her shoulder to sniffle.

"Wagner," she says, her precise pronunciation a surprise. Tears slip down her cheeks.

"Yes." I wrap my other hand around hers and squeeze.

Her mouth works over unformed words. Noise disrupts our moment. The woman's eyes jump to the chapel where the crowds have arrived with all the hisses and shouts common to island greetings. A male voice calls *mama* from within the chapel. The woman leans forward and kisses my cheek.

"I have tapes of Wagner. From the library," she whispers to me. "We'll listen together when you come to my town. I know you'll come. I'll pray you come. I'll pray every day."

The male voice calls *mama* again. The woman squeezes my hand one last time and then shouts back that she'll be right there.

She's going. Already gone, really. For a moment, I'm lost in my silence. Puzzled. Unsure. Maybe even delusional. The connection to the ocean and then the random woman appeared from nowhere. It's surreal and yet more real than anything. And so buzzy. Light and buzzy as though God Himself stands a few feet away.

A flailing arm grabs my attention. Hermana Stathos gestures at me from the chapel, her eyes full of panic. I'm obviously late for my curtain call.

The gray-haired woman stands at the back as I perform. Her hands clasp in front of her heart with head bowed and tears streaming. Her mouth mutters along with the music, lost in prayer and something more.

The woman is gone when I open my eyes after the closing prayer. Instead, Hermana Callister stands in front of me. "President says you should ride the bus back."

The concert is over. My soul slips back into a black case carried away by the president. And I'm back in my loveless marriage with Hermana Callister.

# Chapter 7

On Wednesday, two piglets fighting over a teat bring Hermana Callister and I closer to unity than we've been in almost a month. We laugh together as one baby pig bites the other's nose and gains the win. She whistles a little as we cross behind the giant hogs that sleep in the Bishop's back yard, her hands shoved into the pockets of her favorite red gingham, oversized shirt dress. Hermana Callister's green backpack bounces along. There's a masculinity in her walk and person that reminds me she's military or plans to be. The little bird who loves discipline and calisthenics will report to basic training in a matter of weeks.

But there's more to the story of her good news than excitement for home. A small, silver CTR ring appeared in the mail yesterday. She wears it on her right hand and she wears this shirt dress almost every other day. They're linked somehow—the ring and this dress and her joy—but I don't know for sure.

I won't know for sure.

Guilt stings somewhere too close to heart center. I didn't do well by this bird. I push and I'm too rough. I want to coax her back into our nest, but the idea of forced, painful, immature Spanish conversation plagues me.

Plus, pride. I've got plenty of pride.

We duck under a broken fence post to get back on the main road. Mariana waits for us on her moped. A pink helmet dangles from her hand. She called us a half hour ago. We're to try once more with her dad. We haven't seen Fausto since the strippers incident. He's been on a banana plantation in the *campo* since the day after we spoke.

We both mount the back of the moped in a move that must violate a law of physics. Yet somehow, three women can, in fact, occupy a single moped seat on this island.

Mariana chatters away as we speed along. "The stake president is in town this week, and I want to have my mission interview, but I need my dad's signature. Then my dad showed up unexpectedly today. We weren't expecting him at all. It's a sign from God. Today is the day."

Ilsa's large frame fills the cramped space of the storefront. She leans out over the ledge to kiss our cheeks. "Aye, *hermanas,* you're on a fool's errand. He's drunker than the governor at a rum factory. Planning to drink every peso he earned, I think."

She shouts the last towards Fausto as he passes by the back door, shirtless with pants hanging perilously low on his hips.

He shoos us away with his hands. "Get out! I've no use for Jesus today. Out!"

Fausto stumbles backwards into a chair as he mumbles something about invasion of his sacred castle.

"Have a seat, Fausto," Hermana Callister says with unexpected sarcasm. She crosses to the living room and plops her bag on the floor. Then she sits atop of it with both hands on her knees. Their eyes level on each other. Fausto belches, long and loud.

Hermana Callister leans into what must be the scent of sin. Her joy came coupled with daring. She smiles at Fausto.

"Mariana wants to serve a mission. You'll sign the papers today."

Hermana Callister speaks in a voice not her own, not a loud voice or a harsh voice, but a pointed one, as the scripture in third Nephi says. The room acquires an otherworldly hush that pushes mute on the noise from the storefront and the street.

"Do you hear me, Fausto? God wants Mariana to serve a mission. You're not going to stop her." The soft words poke at my heart with the sword of truth. And they're correct. Every, blessed word is perfect in grammar and pronunciation. A much-sought miracle.

Fausto sputters as Mariana places the papers. He waves a sausage-like finger in Hermana Callister's face. "No. No *Mormona* is going to rule my house. Mariana stays home and works the shop. She knows her place."

Hermana Callister straightens her spine and moves forward an inch. Fausto slouches in retreat. "Her place is with God. As a missionary. If you pray, you'll know that's true."

"No!" Fausto knocks over a lamp with a wide, emphatic gesture that slices air and rocks a table. He growls at Hermana Callister. She presses harder into her knees. She's more than willing to take him by force, if that's the fight we need.

But we don't need it. We can't need it. Maybe Hermana Callister doesn't know that life gets less certain once alcohol is involved. I do. There were enough drunken parties at my dad's house that I know you want drunks laughing, not looming.

"Hey, Fausto, come on," I interrupt with a joke in my tone. "I got you strippers, what else does it take?"

Fausto's attention shifts to me. A slow grin spreads across his face at the joke. Then he starts to laugh. "*Desnudas*. Were they good? Scared those American boys?"

"Yeah. There they were, but you weren't anywhere. I was mad at you. You promised me you'd come."

Mariana follows my lead. She sits on the arm of his chair and wraps her arms around her father. He's relaxed into the joke and puffs on a large cigar with eyes half-closed. Mariana kisses his cheek and he pats her knee. "Papa, please. I want to be a missionary, but then I'll be back."

Fausto's eyes twinkle when he looks at his lovely daughter. "If I let you go, you'll marry a *Mormón* and he'll carry you to the States. Then you'll never see your papa."

Mariana grins at him. Her own eyes twinkle a response. "A pasty *Mormón*? Papa, our children would be pink. I don't want a pink baby."

"We need brown babies. Like you and your mama. Beautiful brown babies." His eyes close and he leans back, content in the idea of future grandbabies.

Mariana rests against his shoulder. She picks up the paper and rests it next to her father's hand on his knee. "I'll bring them by every Sunday after church."

Fausto glances at the paper, softening. But then he looks at Hermana Callister and rallies. "No. I've said no." His stubby finger knocks the paper to the ground and then points at Mariana. "And you'll obey your papa. Honor your papa."

Mariana throws her hands in the sky and stands. She paces as she rants. There are many, many words about feeling imprisoned and maybe running away to the capital. She's not the type to be content at home. She already takes classes on the sly at the local business college. The only way she'd work at her dad's business would be if she owned the thing. And then it wouldn't be a small-time shop for very long.

Hermana Callister shushes Mariana. She's retrieved the paper. Her brow furrows, but she squares off with Fausto again. Each time she's settled into this battle, a funny, quiet glow has sparkled in the air around her. I can feel the energy, the slight flutter in my heart. This is Hermana Callister's fight, as much as Mariana and I want to make it a group effort.

"God wants her, Fausto." Hermana Callister's voice is quiet but firm. And correct. The gift of tongues is as real as anything. Whether it's her or the Spirit, every word is perfectly made.

Fausto moves forward until he and Hermana Callister are eye to eye. "And Ilsa wants a new dress. No one gets what they want today. Not even God."

Hermana Callister's eyes narrow. "But if Ilsa gets her dress, then God gets what he wants, too, right?"

Fausto laughs, thinking he has her beaten. But every weird piece of Hermana Callister's person and mission life have pointed like the Liahona toward this showdown. The ridiculous reverse law of the tithe means there's no dress on the island that Hermana Callister can't buy. She has several thousand pesos in the bank, which would be nothing in the States but is a quantifiable fortune on the island.

"Ilsa!" Fausto shouts for his wife. Ilsa wears the only clothes I've ever seen her in—a grease-spotted denim skirt and stretched-out navy cotton tee.

Fausto waves a hand at us like he's a great king granting petitions. "What dress do you want? Tell the *hermanas.*"

Ilsa wrinkles her nose in confusion, but then she shrugs. "Any dress. This one is rags. I want a nice dress. A pretty one. One like Hermana Callister's would be nice." Ilsa wipes her grease-soiled hands on the front of the denim. More black spots join the others.

"You heard her." Fausto looks back at Hermana Callister. "She wants your dress."

"A dress like hers, Fausto," I interject. "We'll find one like Hermana Callister's dress."

I've spoken to the wind. No one even blinks at me. The terms of this agreement are set, ridiculous as they are. Ilsa is twice Hermana Callister's size, a large-boned woman with extra-large chest. It'd take a miracle on par with loaves and fishes to make Hermana Callister's size-six shirtdress fit.

Hermana Callister's head bows in prayer and tears glisten her eyelashes, but, when she raises her head, her face is resolute. "Okay. Ilsa can have my dress if you sign the paper."

"Dress first," Fausto says. He pushes Hermana Callister, dares her to fail in her quest.

Hermana Callister walks back to the room with Mariana. Ilsa follows them. I swear I hear the executioner's drums.

Fausto cackles and then points at me. "Now, you tell me more jokes."

If Fausto is king, then I'm the court jester. Something about that makes me feel dirty.

When Hermana Callister emerges, she's draped in a simple red dress of Mariana's. The tall woman has done her best to exchange like for like, but Hermana Callister could make two dresses from this one and still drown in fabric. Ilsa has the opposite problem. The shirt dress strains at the chest and hits her above the knees.

"Looks good." Fausto cackles again.

He points at the bottle of rum on the counter. Ilsa pours him a drink and then sits on his lap. Mariana brings over the papers, and he signs them. Mariana squeals and hugs everyone two or three times. She and her mother talk over each other as they initiate a plan in the works for almost a year. Everyone except Hermana Callister seems thrilled at the turn of events.

Hermana Callister tugs on my arm. Her fingers quiver against my skin. "Can we go?"

"Yeah. Of course." Our task is done. Ilsa offers us a lemonade that I politely refuse.

We don't make it far outside the house before sobs overtake Hermana Callister. She sits on a bench while she shakes and gulps air in a pointless attempt to calm down.

My hand covers her knee beneath the cheap silk. She bites her fist, and then turns the CTR ring in dozens of circles as she tries to speak. "I... I... wore... that dress... when my boyfriend... asked me.. ." She twists the ring on her right hand again and sobs anew.

And that's when I get what happened, what Hermana Callister gave away. The ring and the dress—they were the tokens of a beyond-the-mission happily-ever-after.

A flash of anger washes out with a wave of awe. Hermana Callister will walk into heaven ahead of me for good reason. Maybe she's rigid—she definitely lacks a sense of humor—but Hermana Callister puts nothing between her and the Lord. Absolutely nothing.

My hand covers her shaking ones. "Let's go home, okay? I think the Lord will understand one early night."

She leans on me and cries the whole walk back to the house. At the top of the stairs, Hermana Callister heads straight to her room. Hermana Hernandez teases her about wearing her fancy gowns out tracting. I shake my head at Hermana Hernandez and follow my trainer.

Hermana Callister kneels. I grab the Missionary Handbook and sit on her bed through the entire length of a near-endless prayer. The air tingles and glimmers even as she sobs through prayer. God is pleased.

When she finally opens her eyes, I slide the book in front of her. "I was thinking maybe we should start over. At chapter one? I think I need some more practice."

Hermana Callister's eyebrows knit together. "We were on chapter four."

My hand rests on hers, gentle and protective. "You're right. Chapter four is perfect."

Hermana Callister climbs next to me on the bed. "We should do all the role plays, don't you think? Even the ones about tithing. We never teach anyone with money, but we might if we go to the capital."

"Of course. Every single role play. I have a lot to learn. From you."

She switches back to Spanglish—the miracle lasted only as long as the encounter with Fausto—and I repeat Doctrine & Covenants 4:6 over and over in my head. Charity. Patience. Faith. Godliness. Maybe she can't speak Spanish, but Hermana Callister is still the perfect missionary and it may not be the worst thing to spend another transfer with her.

Hermana Callister's miracle is the first of several over the next few weeks. My humility, and our collective effort, breaks my baptism curse like the walls of Jericho. The proof stands ten feet away. Philippe—the schoolmaster, the ultimate ungettable—has finally taken the plunge for us. He beams despite his waterlogged Hollywood waves dripping water onto his suit.

The courtyard hugs us in tight amid the deep green foliage and bright pink azaleas. Ward members mingle with Philippe's family members while soft Christian merengue music plays. Hermana Callister matches his grin and hands out small stones inscribed with scripture as baptism gifts to each attendee. She finally found a reason to spend the sacred funds of the church. Philippe laughs, Hermana Callister grins, and I'm so happy I could burst.

The Elders came to town to complete the ordinance and eat our food. They're alien beings, loud and full of weird hand gestures. Joe went through this phase after his mission. I avoided him until he stopped insisting on clapping and snapping his way through every hello.

"Hermanas," Elder Cortez drags out each vowel and holds his fist out for a bump. Hermana Callister pretends at distraction, so I fist up.

Elder Johnson waves with chili burgers and cookies in both hands. He speaks around a wad of dry almond cookies. "So, a little change-up on transfers. We'll be over tomorrow for Lewis. Sorry for the late notice. We didn't get the call last night and assumed that meant no transfers. Then the zone leaders had to chase us down. Like, literally. We had to jump out of the way of those numbskulls this morning because Elder Cortez, the genius, forgot to plug our phones in last night. Sent you a message. Did you get it?"

Hermana Callister's attention is now fully fixed on the conversation. "No. I don't have a message. My phone's been acting weird. The office is supposed to get us a replacement."

I'm too shocked to say a word. Me? I'm going? It makes no sense. I'm a greenie on my first transfer with a companion that transfers home in six weeks. There's no way I leave the area.

Hermana Hernandez drops the bag of almond cookies. She places her hands on her hips and speaks in broken English. "What? Taking my Hermana Lewis away? No way. This is—how do you say it?—a bad joke. You're a bad joke, Elder Cortez."

Elder Johnson takes another cookie from the tray. "Hey, it wasn't us. President shook everything up this morning. Changed the whole transfer. Nobody's all that thrilled. But President had a dream, so Hermana Lewis goes. We'll be there at six tomorrow morning."

"A dream? The President changed the whole transfer over a dream?" Hermana Callister wrings her hands and her mouth does the baby bird thing.

"Geez, it's just a transfer. Sixteen of them make a mission, fewer for *hermanas*, I guess." I squint at his rude assessment and facial expression. A tear rolls down my nose, though, and ruins the stink-eye effect.

Elder Johnson turns away to shout Philippe's name and extends a fist. Philippe is so happy that he puts aside his usual *gravitas* for a bump and giant laugh.

There are too many people I love. Mariana chats with *las vampiras.* Juana sits in the corner next to Freddy. *Mamita* Irene jokes with Ilsa near the food table. This moment is my last with these people I've loved, and it all feels cruel. Transfers feel cruel.

Elder Johnson and Elder Cortez say something as I float away. I need Juana, her stinky feet, and her terrible jokes. Her shirt smells of dirt and sweat and cheap perfume when I sit beside her to lay my head on her shoulder.

Her fingers stroke my hair as my grandmother's did on the day my dad moved out. Loss has never been my thing. Joe and I packed up my dad and issued the personal invitation for him to live elsewhere after his affair was discovered and my mom melted down. Yet I still collapsed on my grandmother when Dad pulled out of the driveway. Maybe I believed his staying would mean he'd not taken a twenty-year-old musician along with him on every business trip for a year. That hope was as irrational as my wish to stay in Las Guaranas forever. My dad's affair happened. My transfer will, too.

"Oh, pet. What's brought you to this? If you must know, I'll tell you the name of my son in Miami—"

My sobs mixed with laughter create terrible hiccoughs and now telling her why I'm behaving childishly is impossible.

"Transferred! She's been transferred!" Hermana Hernandez shakes her fist at the sky. There's a collective gasp that would make me laugh if I could stop crying or hiccoughing.

"What?" *Las vampiras* wander into my eye line. "No. A greenie gone after one transfer when her companion goes home next month? That never happens."

"The president had a dream." The words bounce out on broken air. It explains nothing, and, yet, it explains everything.

Juana hugs me close. Then Hermana Hernandez, Mariana, *las vampiras,* and Hermana Diaz pile on. Hermana Callister's tiny hand rubs my shoulder.

Juana makes a gurgling noise. There's very little air at the bottom of this love-fest.

"Guys, I think we're going to kill Juana."

"There are worse ways to go, little one," Juana whispers against my hair.

Hermana Hernandez shouts to everyone as the group disbands. "Add another name to this party. Anybody got a birthday? Anniversary? Let's celebrate everything."

She walks to the old-school tape deck churning out tinny music. The tape deck pops open and soon the air fills with Shakira.

The party stops being subdued and appropriate, but Philippe doesn't seem to mind. He dances with *Mamita* Irene. Hermana Hernandez teaches me the salsa. Elder Johnson eats two more *chimis* while Elder Cortez chats up *las vampiras*. Hermana Callister taps her toe and almost smiles while everyone has the best sober party in the country.

The next morning, I sit on a disorganized heap of luggage outside Las Guaranas house. Everything that once was odd is normal now. I know how to bathe in three buckets and shuffle my feet to scatter cockroaches. I'm no longer scared of tarantulas, and this morning I strained weevils from Rice Krispies covered in powdered milk. Like a boss.

Hermana Callister sits beside me. She broke a rule last night. She stayed up until midnight to help me pack. I fear for her next companion. The repentance for that bit of rebellion could be intense.

A white truck appears at the end of the street. "That's the Elders," Hermana Callister says. I stare at it bleakly. My last tear fell around dawn, but I snuffle around a plugged nose anyway.

"*Los Limones* is great. Hermana Schulz, too. She's been everyone's favorite companion. I never served with her, but that's what they say." Hermana Callister sniffles.

"Then I'll have had two great companions." I drop my arm around Hermana Callister. "You're pretty amazing. Best mission mama ever."

She chuckles into my shoulder. "You didn't say that two weeks ago."

"Sorry about that. I like ice cream and *motoconchos*. I'll try to repent."

"No. You won't." She sniffles again.

The truck arrives, and a lanky American Elder hops out. He's handsome in a traditional sense, but his eyes are bloodshot. His name tag reads Elder Blank. Under less serious circumstances, I'd laugh at a name like that, but Elder Blank doesn't look like he'd appreciate a pun, good or otherwise.

"Schulz is inside. If everyone can get the sniveling done fast, we'd like to get back up to *Los Limones* before it gets hot. A/C in the truck's been broke since last transfer."

He retrieves a soft-covered luggage set from the back of the truck. Pink flowers and pretty tags. My set is utilitarian brown, a gift from my mother when I went to music school. Her best advice to me is scribbled on the edge of the largest case: Be good and drink plenty of water. We're not poetic people, but that advice has never failed me.

The truck door opens again. A red-haired woman as beautiful as her luggage alights. She sparkles, even her tears glisten as they hover. Behind her, a tall, weathered woman emerges. If they both didn't have name tags, I'd assume the beautiful Hermana Litchford traveled with a bodyguard. Hermana Schulz isn't much taller than me and certainly isn't fat, but Hermana Litchford absorbs so much beauty from the air that even the cockatiels in the trees look dowdy and uninteresting.

A perfectly white and manicured hand extends towards me. The crimson-haired goddess speaks. "You played beautifully at the fireside. *Los Limones* is lucky to have you next. Our *mamita* is overjoyed you're coming." Her voice is lyrical, quiet but not mumbled.

Litchford's hand squeezes mine gently, perfect ivory not cooked by the sun, unlike my tanned and rough one. She's a slice from the loveliest cake ever baked.

Hermanas Litchford and Schulz hug once more. They both cry heavy tears and their goodbyes seem to go on an uncomfortably long time. Rumor is that Hermana Schulz wrote a request to the president to serve the next transfer with Hermana Litchford, who transfers home next month. I'll bet she'd be as beautiful in mission-death as she is in mission-life.

Hermana Litchford disengages from Hermana Schulz only when Elder Blank beats twice on the side of the truck.

Hermana Schulz looks at me, pained. Her eyes go from me to Hermana Litchford. I'm a disappointment, a heavy loss. But she points at the truck. "Well, let's get you to *Los Limones.* Ydria hasn't stopped cooking since we told her you were coming. Hope you don't mind a little weight gain."

"Best cook on the island," she promises with a squeeze to my shoulder.

Elder Blank bangs on the side of the truck, louder this time. "Let's roll, *hermanas.* I'm missing my mountain."

Hermana Schulz hoists herself into the van. She wipes her nose on the back of her hand and then her hand on her skirt. "Lewis, meet Blank and Monsen. I'm Schulz, not Hermana Schulz. I'll stop blubbering soon and we will show these two idiots how missionary work gets done. We have a friendly wager each month and these dopes think they're going to win 'cause I cried."

"You really think you can get your girl feelings in control that fast, Schulz? Isn't your period due soon, too? That'd be a real shame if two girl problems collided. You'd be out of commission a whole month."

Schulz cuffs Blank on the head. "Even grieving and bleeding, I'll wipe you two from the leader-board. You can't concentrate longer than a boob jiggle."

The estrogen bath from Las Guaranas house gets a sharp shot of testosterone. We make one right turn and Las Guaranas house disappears. Then another right turn and the town is gone. Deep foliage appears on either side of an unkempt highway. There are no marks on the road; instead, the lanes in either direction form or dissolve based on a crazy form of car-chicken in the middle lane. Thirty minutes of mostly-sexist jokes later, we turn off the paved road to jerk and bounce our way up a winding mountain road.

# Part 2: Los Limones

*For thus spake the prophet:*
*The Lord God surely shall visit all the house of Israel at that day, some with his*
*voice, because of their righteousness, unto their great joy and salvation, and others*
*with the thunderings and the lightnings of his power, by tempest, by fire, and by*
*smoke, and vapor of darkness, and by the opening of the earth, and by mountains*
*which shall be carried up.*
—1 Nephi 19:11

# Chapter 8

Gentle after-rain sun warms the wide green canopy and sets brilliantly colored birds to sing from their perches in intricately-shaped, moss-covered trees. The sun rolls in and out of view through the large, tropical leaves flapping overhead. We have paused in conversation and movement; the moment is too beautiful to disrupt with sound.

Giant melons and juicy fruits sway in the breeze and occasionally plop to the ground in the ravine below us. Papaya, kiwi, mango, lime, and coconut—the air blends fruits as smoothly as the smoothie shop where my college friends and I chatted about Mozart and our lamentable lack of dates. The scrumptious air is warm, but a cool mountain breeze rustles my skirt and lifts the heat from my skin.

*Los Limones.*

Beautiful, charming, peaceful *Los Limones.* A song and a prayer brought me to this magical place. The woman in the courtyard whose tears blessed my performance prayed that I would come to her. Then President Stathos had a dream that I should go to *Los Limones.* I doubt he knew what he did, but his dream carried me to the house where Ydria works. My first mission miracle, and I'm the prayer's greatest benefactor. God himself kisses every leaf and lightens my every step. I'm in love with *Los Limones.*

I've had six weeks of full felicity in this village with my housekeeper, Ydria, and my companion, Hermana Schulz. Today, we look forward to at least six more weeks of perfection. Together. The world's best trio in the world's best area. To celebrate, Hermana Schulz and I have chosen to *siesta* in our favorite spot above the earth.

A small stone wall serves as a seat while I eat a green citrus fruit whose name I don't know. The fruit is fresh from the tree, plucked moments ago by the nimble Schulz.

Schulz has climbed out along a low-lying limb. Her legs dangle over the steep drop of the mountain. The back of her long skirt loops through her legs and tucks into the waistband. She cracks open one of the giant melons and hums to herself. I read my scriptures. I can't seem to shift my diurnal rhythms. I lie awake until midnight. Then six a.m. rolls in like a giant wheel parked on my chest. Schulz lets me sleep if I read scriptures at siesta.

Schulz breaks the silence with a laugh and sets a nearby bird to flight. I cringe around a grin. We've been joking about the same story all day.

"That goat has it in for you." Schulz plops a piece of green melon in her mouth.

"I hate the way that goat hates me. He watches me with those black beady eyes. Butts the gate every time I pass."

"Co-o-me herma-a-a-na, le-e-t me e-e-eat your ski-i-i-rt." Schulz's bleating is eerie good.

I laugh, take aim, and nail Schulz on the shoulder with a piece of melon skin. "Oh, hush. Didn't you want a nap?"

"Right. I need one. Some of us were up at dawn." She teases me. In good fun. It's who we are together. Always at a laugh.

Schulz lays back and sleeps until we both see the sun shift. We don't wear watches. I love that about Schulz. We keep time like the Dominicans. Waning sun means time to work.

Schulz stretches and begins the tightrope-style walk back to the ledge. "Where are we off to? Your week in charge."

With a sigh, I remove the folded yellow schedule from the front pocket of my backpack. I glance quickly over the goal report on the right side. Discussions. Contacts. Baptisms. Each column sadly empty while the service column is four hours over goal. These yellow sheets might as well be marked Lannie Sucks at Missionary Work.

Yet I keep trying. "It's only Wednesday and we aren't anywhere near our contact goals. So, street contacts. I have to do them. Make me do them."

"Maybe I could get the goat to goad you on."

"That goat is Satan's own. No way he moves the labor forward."

"The labor always goes forward, Lewis. It's you that lags behind."

"Not anymore. Starting today, I'm awesome at contacts. Gonna open up my mouth and find the three people left in *Los Limones* who haven't been baptized at least once."

Schulz laughs as she jumps down from the branch. There are over six hundred members listed on our church records, but fewer than fifteen people attend church each Sunday. I've not yet made a street contact who doesn't eventually dig out a photo of themselves dressed in white and flanked by two LDS missionaries. Our reactivation list is insane, but we don't have a single investigator on the list.

"There are always more kids, Lewis. You gotta ride this bandwagon."

"I hate baptizing children without active parents. What do they even understand?"

"You know what President says. It's not about what they understand..."

"...it's about opening the gate. I know. We open the gate. So, let's go meet some kids."

"Maybe we'll get lucky. The way Dominicans move about, there's gotta be someone still dry in this town. Let's find 'em and get 'em wet."

We hike up the steep hill, barely catching our breath. The houses sit on stilts that look ready to stand up and walk away like Baba Yaga's hut in Slavic Folklore. Dominican men and women perch in the door and hiss at us as we climb over thick tree roots. Schulz nods in greeting at everyone, even the silent ones who chew sugar cane without teeth and spit the pulp at our feet.

Atop the mountain, the winding road carves haphazardly into the mountain edge. The street erodes in large chunks at its edges, making the last part of the climb treacherous. I'm grateful for my replacement wardrobe. Flowing skirts and cotton shirts guard our modesty on these crazy climbs between town and river.

Schulz steps too near the edge. A piece of asphalt gives way under foot. She grabs my arm and I yank to give her traction, but the move pushes me out into the street where a *motoconcho* whizzes by close enough that my two-layer gypsy skirt flies up in the cross breeze. Two old men across the street cat-call at my exposure and gesture at me to join them.

It's a contact. Not sure I believe the Lord speaks through flashing, but I like old men and old men like me. They make me laugh. This group has a wide, curbed board set up with dominoes. As I wait for Schulz, the men resume slamming the pieces and shouting support or trash talk. One old man bangs his domino and rattles the table. He shouts *tranqua!* and is joined by others. The game is over.

"Not a contact, Lewis. I already banned goofing around at dominoes."

"Oh, come on. You know they'll let you teach a discussion while we play. Fifteen minutes and we get two contacts and a discussion. Plus, I'll have fun and not hate the next two hours as much."

Schulz shrugs, though disappointment etches on her face. "You're in charge. Let's go hustle some drunks into hearing the first discussion."

We dart across the street at a pause in traffic to join the men. I'm immediately offered a seat at the board. My reputation proceeds me. Schulz sits on an upside-down bucket and dazzles them with her dramatic retelling of Joseph Smith's first vision while I win three games in a row.

"Your Joseph Smith teach you how to cheat?" The old man yells for the shop owner to bring us a Coke.

"I don't have to cheat. God is my partner." The younger of the two hisses and erupts into laughter. The older man grins at me. Then he wiggles his two teeth with his tongue. I cringe and laugh while he sets up the board again.

Schulz looks towards the darkening horizon, her indulgence of my playtime over. "We better get going if we're gonna make those goals today, Hermana."

The cold Coca-Cola pressed to my lips hides a sigh. Dutifully, I bid farewell to my fellow dominoes-enthusiasts. They clink bottles with mine.

As we played, Tito told me his youngest daughter was killed by the last dictator, and he's questioned God's existence since. I'd like to finish that conversation with something more sacred than dominoes in my hands. "We'll see you tomorrow, Tito. Your house. Dinner time, right? Finish our talk on God?"

Tito's response is interrupted by the arrival of a girl on a bicycle. Her thick black hair winds into tightly twisted pigtails held by bright pink baubles. She chomps gum between words.

"Nabihah wants las *Mormonas* to sing her to sleep."

There's no need for more info. Our friend, Nabihah has been at death's door since I met her my first day in the area. This is our third summons to her side. We always go. Eventually, her request will be the actual event.

Schulz hands the girl a peso to thank her for the message. We jog back across the road. Schulz leaps over the edge. I climb down an area with minimal give and run down the mountain. Schulz easily wins, but I give a decent chase. Maybe it's indecent to have a race toward a dying woman's hut, but I think Schulz and I have grieved Nabihah so much over the last six weeks that it's almost a relief to think the time has come.

Nabihah's hut sits on the edge of the river. Smoke slithers out the windows and doors to engulf the small crowd gathered for what might be her final hours. As we approach, body heat and fire rob the evening of its cool crispness. People shift, and we follow pockets of incense-laden air towards Nabihah's sick bed.

When she sees us, Nabihah reaches out a withered arm. Large red and purple nodules run like leopard spots across her arm and back. The cancer moved to the outside, she says. She has no breasts—doctors removed them at diagnosis—so she sits bare-chested in the light of more than a dozen devotional candles and whatever burns in the blue-and-red, crackling fire that spits pungent odors. *The* resident witch doctor, the *sancista*, tosses a handful of powder from the leather bag slung over her shoulder

Like most here, Nabihah endorses a strange medley of religions. She is technically Mormon and loves the missionaries, but the candles and *sancista* are part of *Los Misterios*, a combination of traditional Vodou and Catholicism. And in *Los Limones*, everyone is a Catholic when they die; the cathedral has the only safe cemetery. The Priest boasts that everyone in *Los Limones* is born and dies a Catholic, no matter what happened in the middle.

The Elders give us a respectful half-wave as we move into place next to Nabihah. Blank leans on Schulz's shoulders with his elbows. Stoic Monsen stands uncomfortably in the back. I sit next to Nabihah, in my usual spot, to stroke her hair and sing when she asks.

"The old witch gives me the creeps. I can tolerate the Priest, but why does she have to be here?" Elder Blank whispers in English with eyes on the *sancista*

I hush him harshly, even though the *sancista* freaks me out, too. Rags hang over her bony, sagging frame, looking like wash hung out to dry rather than clothing. Chicken feet stick into unkempt corn rows and a black mortar and pestle hangs from her belt. I don't dare look at the collection of things that roll around on a giant tin plate.

My mom served her mission in Honduras and spoke of the ancient religions there with respect, but, growing up in Utah, my head got filled up with stories linking traditional religions to satanic cults and ritualized abuse. Those stories overshadow my interactions with the *sancista* and make even the mundane seem sinister. When she moans and shouts prayers in a language I don't understand, I shiver involuntarily. The women and men nearby cross themselves and murmur, seemingly as disturbed as I am, but no one interrupts the woman's ministrations.

There's another kerfuffle at the door. A large, white man in long, black robe pushes through. The Priest. All the religious players now sit in the room.

Nabihah places her bony hand on my knee. Her mouth moves, but the crowd and sparking fire drown out her words. I place my ear near her lips to hear the command: *cante*.

"She wants us to sing."

Schulz produces a hymn book opened to *Lead, Kindly Light*. She gives us a note and we tune to it, an odd coincidence that we all sing well and in separate parts.

After we sing, the Priest prepares last rites and the *sancista* pounds something in with a pestle to form a fine powder she mixes with water to rub across Nabihah's shoulders. The Priest anoints Nabihah's brow below the oil spot from the Elders' Priesthood blessing. She's sure not to offend God or the devil now, as the Dominicans say. This is death in *Los Limones* where everyone is everything, religiously speaking. Nabihah is more overt than the average person who sneaks one religion out the back as the next knocks the door.

The heavy silence pushes out the *sancista*'s chants and intermittent sobs from family. I bow over Nabihah's hands as they clench mine. She moans as I pray. Nabihah speaks in half-formed mutterings. Her eyes look beyond me, locked in hallucination or maybe something more significant. The light and comfort pull us closer together, as though God wraps us in my old quilt and kisses our foreheads.

Nabihah's eyes to find mine. She's more lucid than I've seen in a half dozen visits. I say what I always say when death comes to visit in this village. "It's okay, Nabihah. There is something waiting for you. It's okay to let go."

Her eyes close again and her breath starts to slow. A low rattle begins in the back of her throat. At the sound, the Priest calls for her children. They press in around me to say tearful and heartfelt goodbyes as Nabihah holds my hand tightly. The rattle intensifies and then turns to a relieved gurgle that signals the end. The feeling of peace around us intensifies, a buzz and light that accompanies death. I stroke her black hair one last time as her hissing exhale releases what remained of her life. Nabihah's chest relaxes after that final breath, but her hand does not.

The family begins the other-worldly wailing that marks the commencement of Dominican mourning rituals. The sound echoes the bitter winter winds that rush out of the canyons in the mountains back home to freeze the earth—the howling breath of death itself.

No one notices I'm stuck until everyone moves outside and leaves me alone with the *sancista*. Her eyes are pale green like algae covering a still-water lake. She walks over and releases the fingers grasping mine one by one.

Her words hiss through missing front teeth. "You did well today. Everything right. You have the gift. You'd make a good *sancista*." The word *sancista* seems uttered by a snake. A shudder rattles my bones. Old biases against witches and magic are hard to shake.

"I only play for God," I whisper and force a smile.

"We all play for God. Light draws from the same source. You're a healer. It's in your eyes. There's goodness in your eyes."

The *sancista's* hardened hands clench mine while my attention stays on Nabihah's vacant face. I'd rather stare at nothing than the searching eyes that want to read me. Odd how empty the body feels once the spirit has flown.

The *sancista* turns my hand over in hers to run a leathery finger over the lines in my hand. She clucks her tongue. "*Anaisa* is with you, child. The spirit of love and joy. She says love is on the horizon, her greatest gift." The *sancista* lifts laughing eyes to greet mine as her thick fingernail taps my palm. "But be careful. *Anaisa* is nothing but trouble if you reject her gifts. You Mormons never have enough beer and cigarettes to keep her happy."

My eyes open wide enough to water as I turn towards the *sancista*. Her green eyes sparkle. Teasing me. My fist closes to end the discussion. "Thanks. I think I'll be fine. Let me know if you want to talk about God sometime."

The *sancista* cackles. "I talk to my gods all the time, dear."

She laughs again. It's not a cackle. Just a laugh. The eerie light and strange experiences and ingrained prejudice played tricks on me. She's an old lady practicing an ancient religion, nothing more.

The Elders stand outside beside Schulz, who's developed a close friendship with one of Nabihah's daughters. Schulz's arm wraps

Graciela while all four of them listen to the Priest pontificate to the remaining family. There are uneasy looks and murmurs as I exit the hut.

"Unbelievable," Blank says and spits on the ground, an action rude in any culture, but worse here, where a woman has died. "He's blaming us? There's a crazy priestess inside washing the body, but Nabihah's death is the Mormons' fault? That guy is a piece of work."

Schulz hugs Nabihah's oldest daughter, Graciela. "Do you still want us at the funeral? The Priest…"

"Yes. Come. Mama would want you there. Ignore the Priest. He thinks giving last rites means he gets the last word, too."

Blank gestures at us to get in the truck as the wailing resumes. We don't lose the sound until the Elders turn onto the main road well above Nabihah's hut.

The Elders drop us at the door of our yellow cinder block house as the sun slides over the mountain. Light flickers through the wooden slats that cover our windows, interrupted by shadows as our *mamita* and her daughter move inside the house.

Blank taps the side of the truck once we get out. "Hey, we tried to call you a half dozen times today. Think you can charge that cell phone for a change? Not that I mind paying for bike messengers, but the church provides cell phones for a reason."

Schulz rolls her eyes and points at the candle-lit windows. "We've got a small electricity problem up here, in case you haven't noticed. When was the last time we had light, Lewis?"

"Last week. I think. The day we made brownies."

"That was, like, ten days ago. So, yeah, I'll charge the phone every ten days or so when we've got power."

"What about solar charges? Neither of you has one?"

"Nope. Lewis had an awesome one, but she dropped it in a creek. Mine was crap."

Blank bangs the door again, this time in frustration. "Okay. Then let me take 'em. I'll charge 'em tonight and find you tomorrow. You know where you're gonna be?"

Schulz gestures at me. Cell phone chatter and death have her in a perilous mood.

I step forward, yellow schedule in hand. "Yeah. We'll be at Ydria's daughter's house until noon. Then we could stop by your place and get them."

Blank nods. We hand him our phones. They're useless up here, even when we have power. The reception is lousy.

An irritated bleating erupts next door. There's a bang and then the gate shakes. Two eyes reflect flickering candlelight. It's the goat. That evil goat. That goat hates me.

But the gate locks in place, so I can be brave. With hands on hips, I face that stupid beast. "I'm not going anywhere, so give this up. It's you against me, and I'm going to win." The goat rams the fence twice more.

The mission truck roars off with Blank and Monsen laughing at my recent zoological encounter. My animal hijinks have become favorite punch-lines.

We push through the door to greet Ydria and Liliana. Ydria tosses a pan across the kitchen to land in the sink. Her hands fly in the air and she mutters. Clangs and bangs accompany the rousing swells of *Ride of the Valkyries*. Only celebrity chefs cook with more passion and curse words than our *mamita*.

Liliana does homework at our table. They live down the hill from us, but Ydria is always at our house so Liliana comes straight up the hill after school. Ydria's three children were raised as much in this house as their own.

Schulz tugs Liliana's tight braids as I walk toward the banshee in the kitchen.

"Valkyries today, Ydria? Must be a serious cooking dilemma." I drape my arm over Ydria as she curses at our dinner.

"I burned the *concon*! Like a girl. I'm not a girl. It's this pan." She bangs the offending bit of iron three times. "I need a new pan. This pan is..."

Ydria swallows the word she wanted to use. *Concon,* a popcorn-like layer of browned rice at the bottom of the pan, is her specialty.

"So we buy a new pan. How much do you need?"

Ydria chews her lip. "Oh, I don't need anything fancy. Five. Maybe ten pesos."

For a moment, she's the woman at the concert again, quiet and intense. She won't tell me why she wanted me to come. I think she assumed I travel with the violin. She's kind enough not to be disappointed at my violin-free state.

I love this woman like my own mom. Despite her tears at the concert, she's feisty and unrestrained and deeply intelligent. She reads deep, dense, literature and yells at the library—which houses perhaps a half dozen books—for not stocking the current Pulitzer Prize winning novels. She cooks and cleans to a soundtrack of classical music. Wagner when she's angry. Bach when she's pensive. And Brahms when she's happy. We don't hear enough Brahms.

I dig a twenty *peso* note from my bag and drop it on the counter. "There. Buy the nicest pot. No more burnt *concon.*"

Any joy over the pending pot fades quickly. Ydria moves aside a brown bag and then exhales in frustration. "And I forgot the papaya!"

Ydria's intense, but rarely this intense. I squeeze her shoulder as she chops a tomato. "I'll skip over to the *colmado* and grab a papaya while you finish up, okay? What's up with you today? You got a reason for this series of cooking emergencies?"

"No. No, not no. Yes. I'm—" Ydria sighs. She puts down the knife. "Henri is coming home. There's a big protest at school, so they've closed for a few weeks, but I rent his room out during the school year. So I don't know what I'm going to do. He doesn't want to stay with his sister or sleep on the couch."

Dominican men are spoiled. My brother would never dare to refuse to sleep wherever my mom told him to park.

"Henri's coming home?" Schulz's interest piques at Henri's name. She's a fangirl for Ydria's children. Henri is the mythical, handsome student while Hetty is a she-beast that lives in town. Schulz obsesses over both. Ydria loves her madly for it.

I tease Schulz as I turn to leave for the market. "I guess if there's nowhere at your house, Ydria, then Henri can always sleep on our porch, right, Schulz? It'll be easier for you to drool over him if he's nearby."

Ydria swats me on the rear end with a towel while Schulz scowls at me. "Oh, you girls. Always joking. Now hurry back with my papaya. It's dark and dinner is ready."

The house door swings behind me on its hinge as I breathe the crisp night air. A few minutes alone will be the perfect end to this crazy day. Schulz will perch on the window ledge where she can watch me walk to the *colmado* as soon as she finishes asking every detail about Henri's pending visit.

The first hit comes as soon as I clear the gate. A hard whack to my right buttock. I jump forward and would turn to face my attacker, but another crack hits my hip and I stumble over my own feet. The devil's horns snare the arm of my blouse. The beast has finished knocking over the fence and invaded our yard.

"Get back. Get away from me." The words are useless. The goat rams again. Less force this time, but he keeps the pressure constant to push me out the front gate.

Then he bleats so low it's almost a growl. He backs up five steps and lowers his horns with perfect aim at my stomach as he paws at the earth.

The beast intends to gut me. Burst of moisture emerge with every huff. He's revving his engine, preparing for the kill.

I turn and run.

Like a lunatic. Arms flailing. Screeching nonsense. Tripping every third step.

I run down that mountain faster than I've ever run. My beige skirt waves behind me with a ravenous, enraged goat's jaw firmly clenched around the cotton. The goat hits me time and time again. I leap with each hit to stay upright. If I fall, I'm dead.

Behind me, Schulz screams in a dead chase, trying to keep from violating the mission rule that we must always stay in each other's eye-line .

Ydria shouts, too. "Help her! Someone help her."

All around me, candles fill doorways. No one offers help, though. As they witness my plight, laughter becomes the soundtrack of my escape.

"Stop laughing and help her," Ydria yells.

Two men take notice of me as I near the crossroads that leads to the town square. They drop bags and dash up the hill toward me and the goat. One grabs Satan while the other grabs and steadies me. My feet have multiplied. I'm a wet noodle trying to tap dance.

"You okay? If I let go, you think you can stand?" The guy holding me is only a few inches taller than I am. He wears a gold cross around his neck.

My nod is a lie. As soon as he lets go, I slide onto a nearby stoop. My rear end chills at the unexpected touch of concrete. Great. As if it weren't humiliating enough to be chased through town by a goat, I've flashed everyone, too.

Ydria arrives, her hair disheveled and the dish cloth still in her hand. Schulz is a step behind, wearing her *chancletas* and holding a piece of bread she'd pilfered from the kitchen. Liliana calmly brings up the rear until she sees the men with me. Then the young girl squeals and launches herself three feet to land in the arms of the man holding the goat.

"You've arrived," Ydria puffs.

In confusion, I look at the men for the first time. I couldn't see them well in the blackness. They're young, my age or younger. Both are dressed in *chinos* and button-up shirts. The moonlight shifts and now I can see that the taller one has Ydria's unusual green eyes.

"Just got off the bus. We were headed up the hill to find you," Henri says with a nod.

Schulz shakes both men's hands. "Well, we found you. You can always count on Lewis to make a dramatic entrance. She's got this extra foot she's always tripping over."

"And apparently, a real gift with animals. This one seems to really love her." My rescuer grins at both of us.

"Nothing but a bitter spurned lover now, though." Schulz laughs at her own joke.

Goat escapades. Nabihah's death. The *sancista*'s sinister warning. They all hit me at once, a bubble of emotion I can't control. Crazed half-breathless laughter overtakes me. "She warned me... the *sancista*... *Anaisa*... I displeased *Anaisa* and now the goat... And I don't have any beer or cigarettes."

They all stare at me as I shake my head and wave a hand in front of my face to dry the tears chasing my giggles. My spurned lover—a gift from *Anaisa*, apparently—hoofs the dirt and bleats, eager to charge at me again. And all I can do is look at him while a million emotions spill out through laughter and tears.

# Chapter 9

That night, a dream catches me as soon as my exhausted head hits the pillow. My quilt from Young Women's has been stretched across the living room of my home in Utah. I lay the batting over top, but our stupid sheepdog—Lacy, but we called her Lazy—tugs on the opposite corner. The batting tears off in giant chunks. I chase Lazy and push the cotton back together, but when I look up, the dog has the next corner in her mouth. On and on, in endless repeat, I chase the dog around the quilt. Lazy lets out a loud bark when I grab at her tail. The imagined sound startles me awake.

Bitter darkness and penetrating silence surround me when my eyes open. A shift in the weather has frozen the night. My single blanket isn't adequate warmth.

I slip on my *chancletas* to search for my sweatshirt in the back room where Ydria does laundry. No creeping crawlers scurry away from my lit candle, all hidden somewhere to wait out the cold. Maybe I'll get a snack while I wait for my limbs to warm. I was too exhausted to eat much of anything once we got back to the house.

While I rummage the house for food and clothes, the dream stays with me, as though I'm an ancient Pharaoh being warned of famine. The dog runs round and round. The dizzying and disorienting action chases sleep away with every revolution. There's no point lying back down.

An unopened letter from my dad sits on my desk, the first communication I've had from him. I should face that now, without eyes on me.

My fingers caress the envelope. The sight of his handwriting renews my shivers. There's a sick finality in the paper cut I obtain by sliding my finger under the fold. I suck the small line of blood and begin to read my dad's first communication with me since I moved out last spring.

*Hey, Lannie,*

*I hope you're having fun. Having you out there's got me thinking back, a lot, to my time in Mexico. The friendships. Language. Culture. Those pieces meant something, I guess, even if the rest was a waste of two good years.*

Sobs erupt before the first tear falls. He can't be supportive. Not even for a single paragraph. My dad is a self-proclaimed expert of everything. Once upon a time, I thought him the greatest man I'd ever known, but now the only thing my dad excels at is avoiding child support payments and making me and my mom cry.

The remainder of the letter swims past me until the last paragraph's memorable line.

*Well, I've got one last bit of big news. Mikala and I are having a baby.*

Disappointment and anger hit harder than the goat. Unsupportive. Immoral. Sinful. A waste. He's the waste. Not my mission. My dad is the waste.

The corner of the letter dips into the candle. The words flame away where I drop them on the concrete floor. With a puff and stomp, the flames extinguish. Each bit of ash twists and turns on itself until it becomes dust—the final resting place of what I felt for my father. I pad back down the hall and slip under the threadbare blanket where I beg for sleep—for blackness—until, finally, God is merciful.

But the dream returns. The dog tugs the batting. I chase the dog. My parents argue in the background, a detail I didn't notice the first time. Near them, a candle burns on a corner table. The goddess, *Anaisa*, laughs in unholy reverence from a bed of beer and cigarettes.

The next morning dawns quick and cranky. Ydria rattles my bed twice before I stop growling at her and sit up. The room is a tilt-a-whirl manned by a psychotic clown, spinning and careening and risking my life every second. Ydria holds me in sitting position when I moan and threaten to collapse.

"Here. Drink. You'll feel better."

Oatmeal. Usually my favorite, but today the milk churns into butter in my stomach—a lump of grease that nauseates rather than nourishes. "Take it. I can't go out. I'm sick."

Ydria's hands touch my face. She exhales on a long, frustrated sigh. "No fever. Stayed up too late again, did you? Are you responsible for that scorch mark on my floor, too? Only thing drama gets you is a headache. Get up. Walk around. You'll be fine. "

"Yeah. I get it, Ydria. I'm up. Work of the Lord moving forward."

"Pfft. Work of the Lord dragging itself to the bathroom, at best. And don't use too much water. Your laundry is piled to the sky. I can't wait until the next time water comes, so we'll be short by tomorrow."

The mirror doesn't give me any hope. The bags under my eyes could swallow the Grand Canyon. I shake off the grumpies after a splash of water to my face. Not the people of *Los Limones's* fault I couldn't sleep. There's work to be done. A whole bucket splashes over my face in attempt to wash off bad dreams and worse realities.

Ydria pounds the door. "Two buckets. No more."

Right. Low on water. Again. Only the armpits get attention today.

Schulz brushes her teeth in the kitchen sink. She tosses me a bottle of Tylenol. "We start the day with Hetty."

Hetty. I'd forgotten. Ydria's daughter scares me worse than the *sancista*. She's a bitter beast of a woman, angry at the world for all her own choices, and she lives with a terror of a man. She's a million months pregnant. Ydria wants her to ditch the jerk before the baby comes. Hetty likes Schulz, so maybe she'll listen to her, but I get to sit on the stoop and look stupid for an hour because Hetty won't even let me in the door.

"Maybe we could get splits. You could go with Ydria—"

"I don't have time for social calls!" Ydria shouts at me as if it's not her own daughter we're discussing. She's in a mood and I'm in a temper. The house pulsates danger. When things go wrong between Ydria and me, the whole town hears the explosion. I capitulate before Ydria's hackles rise any further.

"I wish we had our phones so I could make calls while I sit on the naughty spot. Why does she hate me anyway?"

Schulz huffs and a fine, white spittle sprays the new pot Ydria bought on her way up the mountain. Ydria explodes in reminders about not brushing where she cooks. If this is Ydria when Henri's in town, then I'll thank him to leave.

An hour later, I'm drawing lines of music in dirt while I wait on Schulz. An empty Coca-Cola bottle clinks and rattles as I kick it between my feet.

*Los Limones* proper consists of a wagon wheel of streets that turn around the park and cathedral. No more than eight paved spokes make up the town and the streets are rarely full. The Elders work inside the wheel, we work outside. Technically, Hetty lives in the Elders' area, but Hetty's viper venom and relation to Ydria, make her a special exception to geographic limits. This one house inside the wagon wheel belongs to the *hermanas*.

Laughter sounds inside the house, and then the door behind me opens. Gray chinos hang at eye level rather than Schulz's pink and green *running shoes*. My pounding head forces me to ignore the newcomer. The sun will worsen my headache if I look up in greeting.

The *chinos* sit beside me. Henri considers me with eyes so like his mother, green and rimmed with thick lashes that caress his cheekbones when he blinks. Tightly-wound, silvery-brown curls fall near his ears, unkempt and rebellious—a touch of long-haired bad boy in an otherwise proper frame. He's uncommonly handsome in this land of beautiful people, enough so that I'm embarrassed to look at him for very long. I turn back to the dogs and passersby and my game of Coke bottle soccer.

"The goat let you out of the house today," he says with no attempt at a grin.

"My tarantula and cockroach roughed it up this morning. He won't bother me again."

For a moment, I think the joke failed. Awkward silence consumes any humor. I risk a glance at him. His pouty mouth has quirked up on one side. He doesn't laugh, but his eyes shine a bit brighter. I have to look away again. Or, I should. But I don't really want to. Instead, I smile.

Too quickly, his mouth resolves back into a line. He drops his head and stares at the dirt. "And you're funny, too."

His voice is low, almost imperceptible on the busy street, except the street is quieter than usual, muted despite the *motoconchos* whizzing by and the market playing merengue. Two men drop bottles in to bins, but the sound seems far, far away when I'm staring at Henri.

I smile deeper, as I do when I'm teasing Ydria. "A good sense of humor opens doors."

A smirk deepens his lop-sided grin. "Not my sister's. She's harder to please than Judas."

Henri blushes when I laugh. The heat rushes off him as we hold eye contact. The heat and my poorly-washed armpits take up way too much mental space.

"I really need a shower." What? Where did that come from? Henri wrinkles his nose twice. Now I'm blushing, too, and too talkative. "I mean, I usually bathe—always bathe—but we're low on water and your mom wanted to do laundry..." Does that sound worse? Like I'm blaming Ydria for my disgusting body odor? Oh, shut up, weird Lannie. Just shut up.

"You're out of water?" Henri repeats.

I shrug, nod, and then lift my hands and shrug. The full encyclopedia of gestures plays itself out to try and erase my second embarrassing moment in twenty-four hours. Not that it matters what Henri thinks of me. I'm a missionary, not a woman.

A whistle disrupts the self-destructive tendencies that have tanked my non-mission romantic life. A small woman in a skin-tight skirt and red lace and satin bra waves at Henri. He stands up and walks across the street, which should be a bigger relief than it is.

Two dogs cavort nearby with barks and growls. They scratch at fleas hidden between patches of mange in between violent lunges at one another. As I stare at them, the heat and my own stench reawaken my headache and remind me of everything wrong in my world.

I hate today, even though I'm trying not to let it show. I'm not even thinking about my dad and his stupid baby and I still hate today. Except now I'm thinking about my dad and his stupid baby and how uncharitable I'm being in hating a fetus simply because half his chromosomes come from a complete embarrassment in the dad department.

The baby is lucky, though. He will never know Ben Lewis, the church-going family man born to a white LDS father and his Mexican convert bride. Ben Lewis wreaks havoc on a childhood. Trying to understand Ben Lewis. Remembering Ben Lewis. Mourning Ben Lewis. But the lucky baby won't have to do any of that. He'll only know Benito Lantana, the trendy Latin music producer in Los Angeles who shares nothing in common with Ben Lewis, except some pesky children and an ex-wife.

My father didn't even keep our name—the name my mother took at marriage and the one he gave his children. Benito Lantana uses his mother's maiden name to get in touch with the Latino roots that matter so much to Mikala. Because Mikala matters. Not my mom. Not Joe. Not me. Only Mikala and the baby.

The woman talking to Henri reminds me of Mikala. They're both loud—I can hear this woman from across the street—and neither can manage to put on a full outfit. And both have made a man abandon me. I have psychological damage over how many times I've been ignored while men chase after young, beautiful, scantily-clad women.

Not that Henri is like my dad. But everything is about my dad today.

The dogs edge closer. I kick the Coke bottle hard in their direction to scare them off. The noise attracts Henri's attention. He whistles and gestures me over. I point over my shoulder at the window and shrug. I'm stuck on the stoop as long as Schulz is inside that house.

Henri drops an arm around the woman and they walk back across the street. They're almost on top of me before I rustle up the energy to stand.

"Hermana Lewis, meet Celia. She's Hetty's best friend. Only friend."

Celia leans into Henri, her breasts riding his arm. "Eh, you. Hetty isn't that bad. You're no fun, that's the problem. What happened? You used to be fun."

Henri looks over at me and blushes again. "I got religion. You should, too."

He crosses his arms, but Celia doesn't take the hint. Now she has one arm for each breast.

"Learn religion with *las monjas Mormonas*?" The Mormon nuns. A phrase we hear often. "They give me shivers. I'll have to drink extra rum to warm myself."

"Well, it's always good to have plenty to repent of when we stop by," I quip.

Henri looks down the road to hide another half-quirked smile.

Celia cackles. "I've got plenty to repent of. Right, Henri?"

Celia pulls Henri's face back to look at her. She's brazen. I'm a little jealous of her confidence. I wonder if Mikala went after my dad with as much gusto.

The door behind me opens. Hetty exchanges Celia for Schulz with a giant squeal.

"Guess we all know where we rank with Hetty, don't we?" Schulz says.

Henri looks through the slats at his twin sister and her best friend. "Any luck with Hetty? None of us want the baby raised in this. It's only quiet here if that jerk's gone." Like Ydria, Henri refuses to say Hetty's boyfriend's name. I don't even know what his name is. He's never been introduced.

Schulz shakes her head. Henri chews a lip for a moment before looking at me. "Maybe one day she'll let Lewis in. See if she has any luck."

Every hackle Schulz has raises whenever anyone sings my praises too loudly. I think it's part resentment over President's dream ending the Schulz-Litchford dynasty. The other part has to do with the concerts, since she doesn't get to come. She gets to ride a bus down a mountain to pick up one of the traveling *hermanas* while I go sightseeing every other Sunday. The President's golden girl—that's what she calls me when she's mad at me. So Henri's intimation that I've got magical talents unleashes unseen barbs. One pierces my throat and stops my voice with a jealousy-infused poison.

Salvation comes in a big white truck. The Elders honk and pull up alongside. "Hey, Henri. You busy? Got time for member visits?"

Henri slaps hands with Blank and hops in the back. "See you later, *hermanas*. Be nice to my mom."

Blank dangles our phones out the window. "Say pretty please, *hermanas*."

"Say shut your mouth, Elder Blank." Schulz swipes the phones as Elder Blank drives off.

She stalks up the hill. I follow lamely. When I catch up, she turns on me. "Geez, Lewis. You're like catnip. Do you have to flirt with every guy we meet?"

This is one of her favorite golden girl barbs. I'm a flirt. I suck the attention from the air.

"I don't flirt with anyone. I'm as interesting to men as athlete's foot."

"Then Dominican men must love a good itch. Just—not Henri, okay? He's an actual decent guy. And Ydria loves you. So tone it down around Henri."

"Sure. Fine. Whatever it is, I'll stop doing it." My headache blasts back into full throttle. A pounding, grinding, whining pain squeals its way towards migraine central. I can't take a fight right now. "Hey. How about we do those street contacts we didn't get done yesterday?"

"Yeah. Let's do it." Schulz strides over to the market to get a Coke. Her body language says it all. I'm doing street contacts; Schulz will ride sidecar.

The day drags by. Countless faces, numberless conversations. Street contacts have never gotten one stitch easier. My natural introversion turns each hello into a vampire bite that drains me. Schulz saunters along, sucking juice from a mango. I lost track of how much she's had to eat or drink. Whatever my sins have been, they earned her a day of rest and relaxation.

Each step back up the hill costs double the energy and sends painful sparks up and down my legs. I could sleep right here, on the dirt, if Schulz would stop moving beyond me.

Schulz stops, and I wonder if my wish came true. I'm regretting it, if so.

"Who's at our house?" she asks.

The waning sun forms haloes around my visual field, but I can make out a boxy car. "I don't know. Ydria won the lottery, I guess. Bought a car."

"Gah, but you've been in a temper today." Pot meet kettle. She's been a beast, too.

My little white migraine pills dance a jig in my mind's eye until Schulz's gasp disrupts their rhythm. She rubs her hands across the front of her skirt, and then messes with her hair.

Henri and his friend from last night lug our large water bucket into the house. It's my turn to stop dead. I don't move again until Schulz has reached the gate. For all her accusations that I flirt to convert, she's doing a fine job employing feminine charms with Henri. He smiles at her, no reservation.

I push past them both without a word, pausing only to introduce myself to Henri's friend, Tavo. I want inside. I need my migraine medication and some people-free space.

Henri calls out to me as I open the first door. "You've got water now. We brought it up from the river."

Kind. He's being kind. But it feels every level of weird and I don't want to engage Schulz's wrath again, so I acknowledge with a nod and quick word of thanks.

Ydria leans on her broom as I enter. She watches me. Everyone seems to be watching me and I don't need watching.

# Chapter 10

Eight days later, the only thing that's changed is that God's eyes are on me, too. Narrowed glances that mirror Ydria and Schulz. As I climb the concrete stairs outside the large yellow cathedral, every eye seems to find its way to my face or back and every whisper seems to carry my name.

Giant bells peel out welcome to Nabihah's funeral. We walk in and take our usual places toward the back. I wish I felt like being in church. Any church. Since my dad's letter, I've struggled to feel the Spirit, and I'm so frustrated with myself. I can't generate a single charitable thought or feeling for my father or the baby.

I wrote my dad back, hoping that would dispel this gloom. I composed fourteen words that stung my soul. "Great. Thanks for telling me. Love, Lannie. P.S. Mission is great. Glad I came." I sent a photo of Schulz and me at our last baptism. He'll either claim me or hide me. No more facilitating his fantasies of me being Ben Lewis's self-made sequel.

I'm better than this falling-apart thing that I do whenever my dad hurts me. I hate that he can tumble me. I want to forget him, forget everything, and go back to where I was before I opened that envelope and his out-of-wedlock baby. With his live-in girlfriend. While I'm on my mission. Completely ridiculous. Disgusting, really.

As I sit, I feel eyes on me again. Christ hangs on the cross above the altar, carved in mango wood and painted in renaissance style with heavy, sad tears. His presence presses upon the congregants but smothers me as I face His judgment.

I'm failing Him, failing everyone. Again. I came out here to move beyond this thing with my dad; instead, it strangles me. I'm sorry. I really am, but I have no solutions. I've prayed so many prayers over my dad that every possible word combination is a rote recitation. Isn't the Atonement supposed to fix this? Make it magically disappear so that I'm never choked by my dad's betrayal again? But no. A few words and the muddy waters of Ben Lewis overcome the Spirit and make me useless to my Lord, the only man that matters.

The wooden eyes peer harder at me until I can't stare back anymore.

Ydria walks in with Henri, so I slouch another two inches. Schulz probably thinks I'm flirting with Henri by wearing my black dress shoes rather than my running shoes.

Which is dumb. I haven't said a word to Henri in a week. I haven't really said a word to anyone outside of discussions, including Schulz.

The liturgy starts with the usual kneeling and standing for prayers. I focus and sing my hopes for Nabihah's salvation. Then I open the magazine for the recitations. I like the recitations. The words of Christ and the prophets on my tongue may alleviate a little of my sour mood.

"I love the Lord, for he heard my voice." The lectern begins Psalm 116 for the call and response.

"I kept my faith, even when I said, 'I am greatly afflicted'"; I said in my consternation, "Everyone is a liar." The reading hits me at my core. I don't remember this stanza, and I can't speak the response along with everyone else.

Everyone is a liar.

My father is a liar. I'm not sure if he lied to us as children or if he lies now, but he's a liar. The people who disappear from church the week after their baptisms. Schulz, who chastises me for flirting while she sits and laughs with Henri during the service.

And me.

I'm a liar. I'm the worst liar for being here when I feel like this.

I gulp around a dry lump. Ydria presses a white cloth in my hand that becomes a flag of surrender. I can't do this. None of this. The liturgy. The mission. My life. I run out the door to find a bit of stairs behind a pillar and indulge in hysterical, snot-filled weeping that I've held in since the night I read my dad's letter. After a good long cry, the bells ring to signal the end of the liturgy and, maybe, everything else.

There are a few footfalls that move past me, but then a pair grows closer.

Gray chinos stop beside me. The scent of Ydria's handmade oatmeal soap competes with cheap cologne, a scent combo I wish I didn't recognize or care about.

"My mom's worried about you." Henri sits, and then he hands me another white handkerchief.

"Why? I'm doing so great." A laugh-sob turns into a snort that gets buried in the cloth.

"Want to talk?"

To Henri? No. But if I don't talk to someone, I'm going to quit my mission and open a bead store on a beach somewhere. "I got a letter from home that's... It's dumb. I'm being stupid about it."

Another sob sullies the new handkerchief. I'm a rather uncomfortable blend of feminine grossness at present. I wipe my eyes and swallow so I can make some rational sense. "My dad left us a while ago. He has a new family and he's having a baby with his girlfriend. They're not even married. He's the guy who gave my brother and me the chastity lecture, and now he's having a baby with a girl that's only three years older than I am."

"I didn't know American Mormons had fathers like that. Like mine."

Henri kicks at dirt and fiddles with his sleeve. Henri's father has three known families, one in each area where he does business. Ydria is the legal wife. Divorces don't come easy in this Catholic nation, so as much as she'd like to say otherwise, Luis is still a part of their lives. Ydria's closed-mouthed on the subject, so I know a lot less than I wish I did about how he interweaves in the pattern of her life.

Henri's gaze fixes far away from me, down the street toward his house. "Do you know that Liliana isn't my mom's daughter?"

"What? No. I mean, she looks different from you and Hetty, but I didn't—"

"Our birth was bad. Mom could never have more children. But when I was eight, my dad came home with a baby, and said it was ours. The mom had died in childbirth. Her family didn't want the burden. So mom adopted Liliana, never said a word about it." Henri's voice grows quieter each sentence. His body stiffens at the last.

I understand all the things he doesn't say that hide behind the facts, and I know there's no good response to make it better. A good dad fixes your broken things. A bad one breaks apart the whole world.

The doors of the cathedral open on priestly chants. The coffin moves past us. Henri rubs the back of his neck while lines of mourners make no notice of us. They press small bouquets to their chests in preparation for the burial.

"I need to pray." I say the words, and then I feel them. I do. I need to pray. It's a commandment as much as a statement.

Henri follows me back to the front of the chapel to stand beneath the wooden cross. Maybe it's a trick of the light, but Jesus doesn't seem to be crying anymore.

"Hey," I say to the carving, out loud and with less embarrassment than I should feel with Henri right beside me. "My dad is having a baby with his girlfriend. I don't know what to do with that, so I'm hoping you'll help me out so I can help you out again."

There's a burst of hope, a soft smile from heaven. I grab a small, purple flower from the bucket that stood beside the casket. I owe Nabihah her moment.

Henri comes forward as I move back. He crosses himself, and then grins at me. "Everyone is everything in *Los Limones,* right?" I bite my lips to stop an undignified grin, but I know my eyes shine too brightly because his do, too, as he looks at me.

Then he looks up at the sculpture as I did. Any mirth falls under a curtain of heavy burdens. "My dad left my mom with nothing but pain. If I don't make it, then nothing ever gets better for any of us, so please don't forget us. We put all our trust in you a lot of years ago." He grabs a pink star-shaped flower I don't recognize.

We make our way out the doors, down the wooden steps and past the black iron fence to the poorly-kept cemetery. Gravediggers eat mangoes with their legs dangling over the dead. Henri walks ten feet behind me, close enough to be seen but not near enough to be seen as being with me.

Schulz holds Nabhihah's daughter at the gravesite. One by one flowers and dirt fall into the grave. The wailing intensifies. I kiss mycluster of posies as the others have done and then the flower falls. My rose hits the casket. I add my personal epithet. I'm done letting my dad hurt me.

Henri catches my eye as he, too, kisses his flower and drops it. His eyes close for a moment. When he opens his eyes, he taps his chest twice in a gesture the Elders sometimes use that seems to mean brotherly love or camaraderie, but I don't know for sure. I take a risk and repeat the gesture. The sparkle in Henri's eyes intensifies, despite overall solemnity, until we bow our heads for the grave dedication.

The final amen signals an awkward shuffling. There's a constant, tight circle around the grave, but the bodies in the circle switch up as though they're playing musical chairs to the wailing and chants. Henri and Ydria make a quick escape. My shuffle to the back serves no purpose. Schulz remains glued to Graciela. We stay until the last wail loses breath, and then walk Graciela back to her house.

Halfway down the muddy mountain path, a eucalyptus tree guards a small path up to a blue hut. Four dirty yet happy children play with cloth dolls and chase each other about. They shout greetings to their mama. The two oldest take our backpacks and tags to play at Mormon missionary while we help Graciela settle back into her routine.

Graciela grabs the boiling pot off the spit. Unlike Ydria's beloved cookware, this black iron pot is hammered and rough with sharp edges where plates of iron meet in poorly-welded seams. "I need coffee. Do you want a juice? I need to start the beans. Jose Luis will be home soon and hungry."

Schulz breathes into the red-orange embers in a small fire pit to re-ignite the morning fire. She's adept at so many skills in this place. The children gather round in awe of her.

The youngest speaks from behind the thumb stuck in her mouth. "*Papi* is here. Napping. With his Auntie."

Schulz glares at the house. Auntie usually means a second wife or lover.

Graciela erupts into movement, the iron pot swinging at her side. "That *bruja*! In my own bed! On today of all days!" The pot jolts around by her side in a stormy march.

Schulz and I move towards each other with flight in our eyes. The shouts start before we retrieve our bags. Indecision overwrites our previous clear thinking.

Jose Luis stumbles from the house, his language full of words I don't know, and his belt undone. Then a woman flies out on a scream.

Celia.

Blood pours from Celia's nose and a deep cut below her eye. She clutches her red bra to her bare chest. Graciela stands behind her and twists a hand into the younger woman's hair. Each twist brings another shriek.

Too much of my own story is written on Celia's too-available skin and Graciela's fevered face. My mother wore the same pained look on the day she confronted my dad about Mikala.

Dad came home from a business trip to Los Angeles in his usual state of nervous disappointment. He jabbered to mom about the acts he'd tried to sign and his failed attempts to book performances while Joe and I wrestled luggage up the back stairs. Joe disappeared after dad's briefcase had tumbled backward down the stairs and burst open.

Later, Joe came to my room with a long, yellow lease form for an apartment in Los Feliz rented to Ben Lewis and Mikala Alvarez. Dad had been telling us there was no money from the new business. Mom worked two jobs to cover our expenses while dad chased his mid-life crisis career change. Times were tough in the Lewis house. Every LA trip drained already-empty reservoirs. No money for anything but necessities. Yet mom persevered. Whatever dad needed, that's what we'd do, because we were an eternal family.

But her sacrifices supported my father's lies, not our eternity. There was money. Mikala had both at her new apartment in Los Feliz.

The iron pot thuds against Celia's arms. She screams as she falls. Graciela kicks her and pushes her down each time she tries to rise. Physical and emotional damage will never repay the full cost of stealing a woman's security and her children's stability, but they give the rage a place to go. My mom has never had this moment. An evil part of me cheers for each tortured cry and blackening area of skin.

Maybe I would've watched the whole beating without remorse if Graciela hadn't raised the iron pot above the cowering woman's head. The pending fatal blow broadcasts a new image. Pharisees and Sadducees surround us with stones at the ready. My Savior writes in the dirt. Then He raises his eyes to look straight at me.

Let he who is without sin... His words write themselves on my heart. I'm far from sinless. I can't cast this stone.

Schulz springs forward with a shout, but somehow I win the foot race. I place myself between Celia and Graciela. My arms cover my head as Graciela delivers that fateful blow. The crude iron pot thuds against my arm and knocks me over the top of Celia. The world pulsates with a raging pain that clears after a minute but leaves me shaking and gasping for air.

Schulz hauls Graciela backward and wraps her in a giant hug. Her sobs hurt me as much as her violence. At the edge of my sight, Jose Luis lights a cigarette and disappears into the foliage. Too easy. His escape from this is too easy. He deserves a slice of this rage. Graciela. My mom. Celia. Mikala. Me. We're all victims, to some extent, of a man who can't keep his pants on.

Celia coughs up blood. Red patches turn blue all around her rib cage. The next cough comes up clear, though, and she stands easily, so she should survive. Celia tries to cover her large breasts with her hands as she limps toward the path.

The Savior's eyes are still on me. He seems to nod towards the bruised and broken woman. And I can't ignore her pain, either. I must be the Samaritan. I chase after her on the path to help guide her arms back into the small bit of dignity afforded by a red, lace bra.

"Do you want a doctor?" I ask. Celia shakes her head. "Can you walk? It'll be better if she can't see you." Another head shake, much smaller than the last and intended only for me. Her arm slips around my waist.

I betray Graciela, as I betrayed my mom when I went to LA after high school. My mom is amazing, but Mikala broke her in a dozen ways, and watching me move into that apartment and live dad's life— even if only to keep the peace—nearly smashed my mom to pieces. That moment lives in Graciela's eyes, too, as I walk Celia down the path. But Celia needs me, needs someone to bind up her wounds and care about her pain. Maybe Mikala did, too. I never showed Mikala much pity: Celia can be my penance.

We limp together down the path. Both our legs quiver as we pour sweat. My injured arm hangs useless. The pain intensifies on occasion, then quiets into a rhythmic throb.

At the bottom of the path, Celia lowers herself to a stone outcropping near the creek to splash water over her feet and face. Dirt and blood form rivulets along her dusky skin like waves from an ancient sea carved into rock. She refuses help even as she flinches with each movement.

"Do you live in town? We can get you a *motoconcho*."

"*Conchos* don't go where I live." She must be river people, hidden in the ghettos with the farm migrants and the cast-offs from the regular community.

"Don't worry. We'll get you home."

Celia's dry laugh ends in a cough. "You know what I am? What I do? *Monjas* don't have nothing with a girl like me."

"Good thing we're not nuns, then, isn't it? I don't care what you do. Jesus says help people in need. You're in need."

Celia's shoulders waggle and she spits out a wad of blood. "Jesus don't want me."

"He does. You're God's daughter. Just like me."

Purple, swollen skin squeezes her eyelid closed. A single tear forms a path through the lashes. "My back hurts. Will you clean it?"

Blistering red stripes fester amid old scars. A few eucalyptus leaves serve as band aids, but no matter what I try, blood shows up somewhere. My shirt and skirt have deepening red patches. There's so much blood that I feel a little faint. But her skin doesn't look broken.

Schulz descends when only low horizontal light cuts through the heavy rainforest growth. Exhaustion followed the shakes. My legs quiver when I try to stand. Schulz lifts me up by an arm. I point at Celia who looks as wrecked as I feel.

"She can't get herself home. She's still bleeding somewhere. And who knows what this water carries. If she's not infected with something now, it'll hit soon."

"Graciela will have a fit. We can't play both sides of this."

"A walk home. Nothing more. She's hurt. Plus, if we abandon her, you've got no chance with Hetty. They're best friends."

Schulz concedes, and we carry Celia between us, down the mountain and around the bend. The river peoples' gathering of tin glows in reflected candlelight. Celia points us towards the first hut in the rear.

The door squeaks on its hinges. Schulz lights a candle beside the door. The tin amplifies the outside lights into a single sliver that points to a tiny crib with an infant inside.

"You've…That's a baby. You have a baby? Alone in here?" The baby blinks large, black eyes at us in silence like a Roswell alien adjusting to life on earth.

"Yeah. I've got a baby." Celia opens a drawer from a bureau. She pulls out alcohol and takes two sips for every drop she dabs on wounds.

"How old is she?" My hands reach for a child but fill with bones. No chubby baby softness anywhere. When I lift her small arms, she bleats like a lamb. Starvation sings its sad song, complete with buzzing flies. "When did she eat last, Celia? She needs milk."

"With what money? Jose Luis was going to give me money but his *bruja* of a woman ruined that, didn't she? No money. No food."

"You don't breastfeed?"

"I need my breasts for other things. And what of it? American women don't breastfeed."

Celia's hand tightens around the bottleneck, and she chugs. "I don't want to watch her die. I thought she'd be gone already." She gulps more and lies down on the floor.

"What about Hetty? Or Ydria?" I can't imagine them letting a baby suffer like this.

The baby bleats again. "Make it stop," Celia mumbles.

She rouses to my hard shake of her hurt shoulder. "How much is formula?"

"Twenty pesos." The same amount as Ydria's fancy new pot. Babies go through a can every few days. Milk will cost at least three hundred a month. We pay half that in rent.

But we can't let a baby starve. I'll figure out a long-term plan tomorrow. Schulz shoves thirty-six pesos in my hand. I have another twenty-two. Outside, we find a man with an older motorcycle. "Does that run? We need to go to a store. We'll pay you."

He revs the bike to life and we both climb on back. It's a rough and dangerous journey up the mountain. The wheels squeal and skid. The *colmado* owner argues hard, but we turn our fifty-eight pesos into three cans of formula and a tip for the driver.

Back at the hut, I cradle the baby. Celia snores on the floor. The last of the rum disappeared at some point. The tin hut is so hot, like living in a tanning bed. The heat hurts—I'm pouring sweat—and I'm overwhelmed by this situation. I vary from tears to giggles with little impetus. Everything is sad and funny all the time.

"We can't leave the baby here," I whisper to Schulz after she gives me the bottle. My right arm cooperates enough to hold the baby while my left tips the bottle. She has tiny little faux rubies in her pierced ears. There's barely enough flesh to support the small studs.

"We can't take her. I'm lax on rules, Lewis, but this is my line. We can't raise a baby."

My right arm screams with pain. I shift and notice fresh drops of blood on the bed.

Schulz notes it, too. "Where's that blood coming from? Is it you? Are you hurt?"

The forearm seems fine. The pot came down on the back of my arm. The strangest sensation settles over me when I raise my arm and push up my sleeve to try and see the injury, like an unseen pot of dry ice melts over the back of my neck, making me both freezing cold and burning hot.

Schulz makes a strange, strangled noise. A funny flap of skin hangs from my elbow. When I relax, it falls in its natural place, but when I lift my arm, the skin hangs like a butt-flap from old flannel underwear. Blood oozes and drips from a dull, white almost plastic-looking plate. My bone. I'm staring at my own bone. The whole thing makes me laugh. I hold my stomach and laugh as the butt-flap leaves my elbow buck naked in the breeze.

"Lewis, this isn't funny. You don't feel that? You're in shock. Lewis, all that blood is yours. Lewis, can you hear me?" The world is a bit hazy. White and fuzzy at the edges. Things sound funny, too. Distant, but also too loud.

Schulz puts the baby back in the crib and bolts out the door. The bang of tin resonates deep in my head. I'm starting to feel tired. Maybe I should lie down for a minute until my head feels better.

The *sancista* slaps me, arrived from nowhere in the space of a breath. Schulz chews her fingernails behind the old woman. "No. You don't sleep. Not yet."

The old woman grabs my arm and begins to wrap it with a foul-smelling white cloth. On the second revolution, I scream and pass out only to be slapped again. This time, the darkness doesn't let me go.

# Chapter 11

Crisp sheets rustle when I move. My heart beats and skin tingles when cold air blows over me from a vent in the ceiling. I'm alive. I had some doubts about that last time my eyes fluttered open on this all-white room.

President Stathos sits beside a window with scriptures in his lap. He looks at me over his wire-framed glasses. "Well, you gave us a scare."

Outside the window, giant palm trees flap over matching sky and sea. A bandage as white and sterile as the room winds my arm. Above me, a bag drips liquid into my veins.

I've life, sustenance, and safety, but no companion. "Where's Schulz?" My voice is gritty and dry, my throat thick.

"Hermana Schulz is back in *Los Limones* with Hermana Litchford. The work goes forward even when one of our own tries to play hero." President Stathos presses his chin into templed fingers.

"It happened so fast," I murmur.

Hermana Stathos lifts my head towards a cup with straw. Fresh, clean water matches the all-white, sterile hospital room. "I'm sure it did, sweetie."

Lines appear around Hermana Stathos' mouth as she non-verbally orders the president not to chastise me again. The lines morph into cracks when he defies her.

"You're going to need time to heal. I've cancelled the upcoming concerts." His words carry enough finality that I doubt I'll see my violin before I go home.

"We should let her rest." Hermana Stathos closes the discussion.

The President snaps his Quad closed. He rises with a sideways glance of frustration at Hermana Stathos. "Your family expects an email by tomorrow. Hermana Ángel has a mission iPad. She'll be with you until you're released from the hospital."

Hermana Ángel enters when the door opens. She was Hermana Callister's favorite companion, known for her strict view on obedience and austere approach to emotion. There's no question why she's here with me instead of the lovely and compassionate Hermana Litchford.

The iPad drops on my lap. Hermana Ángel sits without word, her eyes on her scriptures, but I somehow feel she judges every word I write. I don't write many. The whole thing wouldn't play well with my mom. For now, it's an accident. When I'm done, I lie back and try to put the pieces together without thinking about a starving infant or my dad's infidelity while I'm locked in a cell with an unfeeling warden.

The Lord in his mercy limits my sentence to three days' interment. Baby-pink skin regrows over the bone with no signs of infection. The flap gets sewn shut once that first layer forms. All I'll have is a grotesque scar from medieval-style emergency stitches. *It's a miracle*, the doctor declares at least three times. Checkups will bring me back to the hospital every two weeks, and I have to keep the arm covered, but I'm free to go. For now. Hermana Ángel insists *Los Limones* won't be home long; I'll be moved to safer areas in the Capital. I mourn *Los Limones* as much as I worry about Celia. Both in silence. Both severe.

The Elders bring down Hermanas Litchford and Schulz. Schulz and Hermana Litchford worry over me for the two minutes it takes to exchange companionships. Then Schulz and Blank relax into their usual banter along the winding road. I try three times to ask about Celia and the baby, but, each time, Schulz changes the subject. My heart breaks for all the worst-case scenarios I've crafted during my week in the hospital.

Ydria buries her head in my neck on arrival. Her fingers claw into my back for a fierce mama-bear hug. "*Mi estupida*. I promised God if he sent you I'd protect you for your own mama, but then you go and be so stupid." Her grip tightens before she releases me to yank the discharge papers from my hand. She turns up a Bach concerto and begins to make long lists of care instructions. Very long lists.

"I'll have no peace, will I?" I say to Schulz, who munches on *concon* at the table.

"Nope. She's been laying down safety rules from the moment you left. Wait 'til you see our map. She's crossed out the houses of every known drunk and brawler in town and made off-limits every dirt path."

"So we have—what?—three safe places to proselyte?"

"One of which is Hetty's house. First stop of the day." Schulz pushes back from the table. She tosses my bag at me. There's a large bloodstain on the left side.

"The doctor distinctly said I'm not to sit on a dirt street for an hour."

"Liar. Stop complaining and boot up." Schulz points at a new pair of hiking boots on my bed. She's herself, but not herself. Probably irritated I broke up her and Litchford again. "By order of her majesty, Queen Ydria. Don't hurt her feelings by refusing. She's done nothing but cry and pray for a week."

The shoes tug and sweat all the way to Hetty's. They hurt more than my arm. Yet it's so good to see my streets again. All the usual faces in their usual spaces restart my happy thoughts.

Schulz pauses outside Hetty's door. "Ready for your surprise? It's a good one."

My nose crinkles at the bridge. I'm not one for surprises. The door swings wide. Hetty stands framed in the doorway with a newborn in her arms. Her eyes stare at the baby with tenderness but look up at me with fire. If my surprise is that she gained telekinesis when she spawned, then I'm dead. But instead, she shrugs and points with her lips towards the sofa.

I've been granted access. My ugly, yet sensible boots, step inside Hetty's inner sanctum.

A loud squeal startles me and then I'm overwhelmed by a still-mostly-naked Celia. She kisses me a half dozen times. Her octopus arms grab at every malleable inch, including my rear end. Her effusive everything gets me giggling even as I try to stop tendrils from feeling me up. "Celia! That's enough. I'm alive. You're alive. We're lucky."

"Oh, stupid! That's not why I'm kissing you. Look!"

My gaze follows hers to where Henri stands behind the door. A baby pats his mouth and he kisses her fingers. His eyes sweep past mine with a quirky side grin. The floor falls out at the same time I learn to fly, but then his eyes land on Celia and gravity finds me. My attention goes back to the baby. Celia's baby. The same small fake rubies in tiny ears that I saw that first day. I can't believe it. She's still thin, too thin, but there's light in her eyes and death no longer claws at her frame.

Henri presses the little girl into my arms. My kisses echo Celia's and everyone laughs when the baby pushes back my face with soft puffs of protest. She's alive. I've prayed for nothing else since I woke up.

Schulz reaches over me to pass a finger along the somewhat-fuller cheek. "We wanted to surprise you. Celia has promised to ask for help when she needs it."

"Eh, lay off me. I like to provide for myself."

"That's only okay until your baby needs help, Cels." Henri's voice is quiet as he half-whispers to Celia, who relaxes once she's wiggled under his arm. They seem cozy, cozier even than they were that first day.

But none of that matters, not a thing matters but this beautiful ball of shy smiles and recently-bathed baby smell. She relents and lets me kiss her baby fist again. Our eyes lock and I think the two of us have known each other for a dozen generations in another space and time. She thanks me, somehow, with those wide and brightened eyes.

"I don't even know your name," I say in awe.

"Issa. But I should rename her Lewis. It's nice, no?" Celia reaches out to let her baby wrap a hand around her mama's finger.

"No. You wouldn't dare. Lewis is too ugly for this angel. How does she look this good? There were only two cans of formula."

Hetty rolls her whole head with her eyes. "I've two breasts. There are two babies. Does math make your head hurt?"

Schulz hisses at Hetty before she gives me a real explanation. "The *sancista* took the baby to Ydria. You know Ydria can't resist a baby.

Then Hetty had her baby the day the formula gave out. The midwife helped Issa learn to breastfeed. But if we hadn't gone... everyone says..." Schulz swallows, and her eyes turn red.

"You saved my baby." Celia throws her arms around me and Issa. We both accept our kisses. Again.

Celia pushes away this time. "Now we'll have cake. And dance. Unless you and Schulz both have cement in your hips." She grabs my hips and forces them to sway. "Ah, not Lewis, she's made to move." She makes a high-pitched trill of triumph.

All my plans for stricter obedience sink into the pressed dirt floor. Hermana Ángel's mind-numbing lectures inspired no change. I'm a lost cause. Schulz is no help. She was complicit in this party and already has cake stuffed in her mouth while she indulges in a dance lesson. Only Henri stands with me against the back wall while I cradle Issa.

"Are you really okay?" Henri stares ahead to where Celia licks sugary frosting from her fingers while marching in a wild merengue.

"I'm a miracle, they say." I lift my injured arm to show off the bandage.

Henri settles into the wall, dropping another inch and leaning toward me. "My mom is going to watch your every move, you know that, right?"

I try not to smile at him, dropping my eyes to my feet. But then I can't resist a joke and lift my eyes to his. "I've got the boots to prove it."

He pauses, his eyes on mine. Then he grins at me. "Well, I left you something at the house, something that helped me tune her out when she rode me a little too hard as a kid."

"What is it?" I look to him, but he looks at his shoes and then heads to Celia's side. Celia immediately changes to a dance far dirtier than salsa. She cackles when Henri blushes.

Hetty shoves cake under my nose. "Cake. For what you did."

As soon as my hands close around the plate, she's gone, too. Her body sways to the rhythm with her baby as partner.

No hope, there's no hope for me. My hips sway on my last bite. I've only two weeks left in my home until transfers, and I'm not wasting a minute. Celia turns the dial up another notch.

Our private dance party continues until Schulz forces a stop. Ydria has demanded I return for siesta. My arm throbs its own unfortunate alarm.

Celia walks with us to the door. She sobers a bit. A little. She's not capable of much sobriety. "I know what others say. And what I am. So you didn't have to help." Tears form, but she bats them away with her wrists. "You're alright, *monjas*. Come teach me about Joseph Smith sometime." Celia turns and rushes back to where Henri cradles Issa.

"You've got to be kidding me," Schulz whispers under her breath to a closed door.

"Right? The Lord works in mysterious ways, Hermana Schulz."

"Ugh, lose the *hermana*. I've worried for days about what I'll have to undo in your personality after so many days with Hermana Ángel. I'll get started on your retraining as soon as we get you home and resting. That arm was the most disgusting thing I've ever seen."

"Don't sugar coat it for my sake. Just say it straight. I can take it."

"Good. Then hear this: don't ever scare me like that again." Schulz whistles for *motoconchos*.

Henri's gift shows itself when I sit down to take off the horrible boots. A Spanish copy of Treasure Island has been slipped under my cot cushion. Inside, he's written, *Adventure for an adventurer. Stay safe.*

The book undoes any possibility of sleep. As soon as I hear Schulz and Ydria start up a conversation, I slide the book out to lose myself in the story of Jim and Long John Silver.

When stolen moments get me to the end of Treasure Island, an Isabelle Allende novel appears under my mattress. But I'm only a few chapters into that one when the day I've dreaded arrives. Transfers fall on the day of my first appointment with the doctor one more indication that

I'm leaving *Los Limones*. My hair lifts off the back of my neck as a kind wind lays cool kisses against over-sunned skin. The sun's touch isn't cruel anymore. Autumn has come, and everything is gentler under his care. But sadly, the touch reminds me that my season in *Los Limones* has ended.

The Elders knock our door five days after my birthday. They've been to a meeting in the Capital called last minute by the President. They'll have the news.

A giant, broken, and bent cardboard box sags between them as they cross the threshold.

"Special delivery for Lewis. You owe us first dibs on any snacks inside," Blank says.

Ydria points with her lips towards the back corner. A recently-dead chicken fills her hands and our sink with blood.

The Elders drop the package before collapsing on the chairs at our table. Schulz scoops in for the gossip. She sits backward on one of our crappy sugar-cane chairs, facing the Elders. Her sideways baseball cap leans over her right ear. She's our ace mission reporter hot on a lead. Her eyes beg for information. She licks her lips and leans the chair towards Elder Blank, but Blank smirks and pretends not to notice.

A pack of Poker cards lie on the table. Elder Blank picks them up, shuffles them, and raises his eyebrows at Schulz. Schulz rattles her chair and groans in impatience.

"Hold on, Schulz," Elder Blank says. "I've got to do my priesthood duties. What are you doing with tools of Satan, *hermanas?*"

I lean against the end of the table. Schulz will have a stroke if she doesn't get gossip soon. I snap my fingers and gesture for the cards in Blank's hands. "They're Ydria's. She loves tools of Satan. But I'm the one doing evil. I'm telling her fortune and predicting only good things, right Yds?"

Blank withdraws a Queen of Hearts and winks at Monsen who solidifies into an embarrassed, pink porcelain statue. Poor Monsen. He never seems to know what to do when Blank gets to teasing us. Schulz rocks her chair in perfect imitation of demon possession, and the urge to send her into fits sparks my humor as it enlivens my compassion.

I grab at the pack of cards, snatching them from Blank. I play the game, too, prolonging Schulz's torture "I couldn't say no to Ydria. I was the best fortune-teller in the eighth grade. I predicted Harper and Lilly's breakup almost two days before it happened and without knowing they were bickering outside the girls' bathroom because Lilly wouldn't eat with him in the cafeteria. Everyone thought they were true love, but I knew better. The cards don't lie, friends. Not when I play them."

"No one better at pointless card games than you, Lewis." Elder Blank picks up the scented candle we burn to chase off the chicken gut smell. "And are you burning incense, too? The President may need to know about this."

Schulz throws her hat at him. The cap clips his ear. Then she grabs a Book of Mormon and takes aim.

I wrestle the book away from her. "Not the word of God, Schulz."

"Tell me!" Shulz bangs a hand on the table. The pig next door squeals and snorts in response. Ydria shouts at all of us to calm down and remember the solemnity of our callings.

"Fine. Ruin the fun. The real missionaries stay another transfer, which means you're out, Schulz, so get packing. And don't get comfortable, Lewis. You only get a ten day stay of execution. Just long enough to teach the area to a new companion. Then you're in a threesome in the Capitol so the President can keep an eye on his reckless golden girl. The mission's in a mess, President's spitting mad. First, Lewis plays vigilante. Now a mysterious something shuffles the mission deck—see what I did there?—and we all get a refresher on mission rules at next month's zone conference. Whole thing must be bad. Hermana Ángel has been called back to active duty. Which means—drum roll, please, Elder Monsen—Litchford requests Schulz's not-so-honorable presence for the last six weeks of her mission. She says no one else could kill her but you. I hear President gave in because she wanted to extend her mission again, but he wants her to go home and find a big, strapping man to be her next calling."

Schulz has sat back on the chair, too quiet and calm. I expected her to be running about throwing imaginary flowers in the air. She'll be back with Litchford. Instead, she stares coolly at Blank, like she's trying to figure out if this is a trick. "Blank, you're a sexist pig. I've wanted to say that since we met. Now that you're no longer my district leader, I speak in truth."

"Thanks, Schulz. My momma raised me right."

Blank pulls on the baseball cap. Schulz pulls it down over his face. They struggle for control of the hat for several minutes. Then Blank tosses it aside and opens his bag to grab out a large book. "Given your status as a she-woman, man-hating feminist, I grant you the superlative most likely to stop shaving her legs, if she hasn't already in my mission yearbook. Make the signature legendary, Schulz."

"Oh, gag. You disgust me, Blank. I'm not signing that book."

"Doesn't matter. Your picture will go on that title. If you don't sign, you'll look like a bad sport. You don't want to look like a bad sport, do you, Hermana?"

Schulz grabs a bright pink pen to write: You're a sexist pig. Never change (cuz you won't). Love, Schulz.

Blank pushes the book towards me. "Lewis, I give you most likely to be pinned in a teenager's locker one day. You know why, right? Remember that day? The shirt? Who could forget the shirt, right?"

Monsen colors at the reminder. We all remember. A cat pooped on me one day because all animals hate me here. The investigator loaned me a sweater two sizes too small for my considerable bust. We ran into the Elders in the park. Neither could make eye contact but admirably avoided making contact with anything else, either.

Blank flips the page. "See? Your photo's already there."

Everything fades from focus. How did they...? I remember the pose. Schulz laughed about the Elders and dared me to turn and blow them a kiss. It was a joke. A big, stupid joke. I didn't see the camera. If I had, I wouldn't have popped a 50s-style pinup pose.

"Get that out, Blank. She'd been pooped on by a cat. If anyone sees that, they'll think she posed on purpose and wears those clothes tracting."

"No way. Best hidden camera shot ever. Soon as I'm home, this one goes on the interwebs my friends."

The chair scratches against the floor and falls when I stand up. Behind me, Schulz whispers, "I thought I'd miss you, Blank. I was wrong."

A hiss stops me at the kitchen. Ydria points me back to the table with firm resolve. She's wise in quiet ways. Storming off confirms every sexist thought in Blank's head. I can save face by using the bathroom, but the only dignified course requires me to follow Schulz's lead and joke my way through insult.

When I've returned, Ydria crosses in front of us to feed the chicken remains to the pigs. She digs into the new box. I'd forgotten about it in all the drama. The box comes apart with ear-piercing pops and shrieks as the tape separates.

Two pieces of paper sit on top of a pile of my favorite things from home. The first bit is a note: *Thought you might need a touch of home for your birthday. We're so proud of you. Love, Us.*

The second piece of paper is a photo. My mom sent me a new family photo. She and Joe smile next to Cardboard Lannie. The life-size cardboard cutout shows me in full missionary uniform at the MTC. I don't look like that young woman anymore, all clean and not-leathery. Cardboard Lannie, Joe and mom smile and wave. I wish I could wave back.

Beneath the papers, there are pulverized cookies, candles, new shoes, a boxed cake—which makes Ydria huff in resentment at the intimation she can't make a decent American-style cake—birthday candles, and all the party gear I could hope to have. Ydria, Schulz and the Elders pull out the party gear and get to work on my belated fiesta. The Elders chow down my chocolate. Schulz goes to the market for an egg to bake the cake.

But the bottom of the box contains my real gift: a handmade blue sign. The letters are roughly done. They say, you can either laugh or cry and crying gives me a headache. Yellow paint dried in drips beneath each letter, yet this sign is the best present I've ever received.

The blue sign hung for years over our back door. Mom painted it the day the divorce papers arrived in the mail. She grabbed an old slab of wood and sanded for hours. Then she used finger paints for the quote from Marjorie Hinckley. We laughed at her, perhaps unkindly, but the first real laughter since we threw my dad out. A simple nail hammered above the door without any measure of precision held the sign for years. Most of the time, it hung crooked. We would throw shoes at it until it righted, or whenever we needed a reason to laugh. The sign became our family motto.

The sign makes Schulz laugh as much as it always has me. We translate the quote for Ydria, and she laughs. Then we all fall into an unplanned hug. Schultz sniffles. Ydria repeats the quote and we all laugh again. *Crying only gives you a headache.*

The postmark on the box is two months old. The passage is weeks late but managed to arrive at the perfect time.

# Chapter 12

I float through Shulz's transfer like the in-focus character in a *nouveau* French film. Figures move past me, obscured in a fog. Loss slows time and shifts experience inward. Other scenes in this film replay in my head. My grandfather's funeral. The day my dad left. Juries. Saying goodbye to mom in Salt Lake City.

Schulz and I stand beside each other as the training *hermanas'* car approaches. We've not spoken all morning. Stoic Schulz preferred the view to conversation. A few jokes passed between her and Blank, but nothing for me.

"You'll be a great training *hermana*, Schulz."

"Thanks, Lewis. Try to stay alive."

That's the end of Schulz and me. She climbs in the car with Hermana Litchford, who still looks like she should be cavorting on a beach in a Pac 'Sun ad, and Hermana Stathos, who spares me a small wave and inquiry after my arm.

My new companion will come by bus. She's been part of a threesome, so her poor comps get to waste a day on this transfer. No one knows when the bus will arrive. We sit and sweat while ancient buses stuffed with Dominicans and livestock rattle and sputter by at uncommonly high speed. The dirt whips into dust devils and makes the heat hotter. My Coca-Cola tastes gritty.

"I volunteer to get us all fresh sodas," I murmur to the Elders. Everything already feels different without Schulz. Without her, we're the sad pictures from the 1920s American dust bowl. Faces filled with deep lines and dirt. Nothing exciting at all.

When I get back, Hermana Olsen sits on her luggage opposite the Elders. This is the first I've seen her since we left the MTC. She's changed, too, roughened at the edges. I hold out the 7-Up and Coca-Cola bottles for her to choose. She rejects both. The Elders take their Dr. Peppers. My insides feel like dried-out paint trays, so an extra soda is fine by me.

The Elders toss the luggage in the back of the truck. Conversation spurts and sputters like the buses. Elder Blank is unrecognizable when on his best behavior. Monsen is nice but runs out of welcome to the area chatter in five minutes. Olsen answers in rhythmic monosyllables. She shifts about on the seat and inhales sharply each time the truck tires slip near the cliff edge. Like the people on those hot buses, we, too, lapse into silence.

Tavo's car sits in front of our house. Tavo waves mid-text with his back resting against our giant water bin. We must have run out of water again. We only see Tavo when Henri needs a favor. He's the son of the local magistrate. I'm not sure what that means except he lives in a house with an electronic gate, has a car, and never puts down his iPhone.

The Elders hop out before the truck stops. Tavo is the ultimate ungettable. Blank wants a yes on any gospel commitment from Tavo to stand as the crowning glory of his mission. Henri says Tavo is as Catholic as we are Mormon, so I doubt Blank will succeed. Henri emerges from the house with his arm around Ydria.

Olsen's hand pauses on the half-open door. She slides back in and pulls the door closed. "There are men in our house." A statement of fact with no emotion but color bleeds through her pale neck and ears.

"Don't worry. You'll get used to Henri and Tavo. They don't pop in often."

"But they go inside our house?"

Irritation sizzles and stings at heated patches near my neck. Henri claps hands with Elder Monsen when he emerges from the house. Tavo laughs. Ydria buries her head in Henri's shoulder to hide her own amusement. These are my people, officially included in my no-judgment bubble. "Yeah. Guys come to bring us water. Welcome to *Los Limones*. Best area of the mission, but we function a little differently than the rest."

Olsen presses her lips together with gaze glued on the jovial company outside. The Elders lean against our gate in perfect ease. "And the Elders are okay with it?"

*Yes, they've approved our bathroom schedule, too,* I want to say. Reassurance feels more Christian. "Ydria has cared for missionaries for fourteen years. Her children grew up in this house as much as their own. They know their place, and no one respects our calling more. So, please, don't embarrass her. I'll talk to her about Henri and Tavo if it really matters to you. But let's get out of the car. Everyone wants to meet you."

Her eyes widen, but then squeeze shut. "I'm sorry. I'm out of sorts. The day started all wrong, and I wasn't prepared for this transfer. I don't feel prepared to be here."

For the first time since Schulz's transfer was announced, the world focuses in on someone else. Olsen's nails end at angry red, bare ridges. Her feet rub together at the tops of the toes; a dime-sized yellow spot tells of frequent worrying. She doesn't feel like the same woman that sang in the airport and responded first to every question in the MTC. I wonder what's happened to her over the past four months.

A flood of compassion leaves residue of shame. I've been so worried about the end of my happy kingdom that I failed to see her world ended at some point. I cover her hand with mine. "It's okay. You'll love *Los Limones*. Everyone does."

"I'm afraid of pigs. Everyone says there are a lot of pigs up here."

I reach across and push open the door. "More than people. But they aim for me, so you've got at least two weeks to learn how to avoid them."

Olsen almost smiles. "Now I see why you became senior companion so soon. Everyone remarked on it, but they're wrong. You're more than the president's favorite."

"I'm not the president's favorite." Or at least, I'm not anymore. I hadn't really processed the reality of being a senior companion. Olsen and I were each mission-born on the same day. I'm a year older, chronologically. To me, that's all there was to the choice between us.

We slide out of the truck and move to Ydria's side for introductions. The men pay us little attention. They're in full guy mode, bragging and joking. The Elders chafe, huff and street talk as though they've met Henri and Tavo on a basketball court in the projects. Well, a sanitized projects where *oh no he didn't* is the dirtiest phrase uttered.

"Look, brothers, no mountain beats me. I can climb that thing blindfolded in a thunderstorm," Blank says.

I can't resist teasing all the men in that tight circle. "I'd love to watch anything beat Blank. Can I put money on this match? Maybe come along? I hope it's bloody."

Ydria taps my head with her chin. "These locos want to hike to Point of Heaven. And no, you may not go with them."

"Isn't Point of Heaven the place President Andres talked about on Sunday? Where you can see the whole island?" My interest is definitely piqued.

Olsen surprises us all with a happy inhale and full sentences. "Oh, that sounds gorgeous. I've heard *Los Limones* has amazing waterfalls."

Ydria's mouth is firm. She waggles a finger at me and Olsen. "The Elders can take you to the waterfalls another day. Point of Heaven is not for *hermanas*. You have to slide through mud to get down." Ydria glares at me. "So it's especially not for *hermanas* in bandages."

The feminist quills along the back of my neck raise and fire. "I'll bet I'm as good a climber as any Elder. My dad loves to white water raft. I've hiked mountains that make Point of Heaven look like a mound of sand at the beach, and I did so with a thirty-pound backpack and carrying a raft. I can hike, gentlemen, and I want to hike Point of Heaven."

"Oh, shut it, Lewis. You've probably not hiked more than a mall. But maybe your shoe bags weighed thirty pounds," Blank says. Monsen and Tavo laugh. Then Blank finally introduces Olsen to everyone.

After Ydria shakes Olsen's hand, I thread my arm through Ydria's and lay my head on her shoulder, another issue more pressing than Blank's blatant sexism. "*Reina de reglas,*" I whisper. *Queen of rules*, a phrase used among *mamitas* to warn each other about very strict missionaries.

Concern steals Ydria's smile. She turns her head towards mine to whisper back. "Oh, no. Henri was inside."

A quick squeeze of her arm is the only comfort I can offer. I've no idea if my explanation served beyond getting Olsen out of the car.

The Elders drop our luggage inside the door and then take off with Henri and Tavo. In the bedroom, Olsen asks Ydria for cooking lessons. My hands fly in the air, and I walk out. Let the Elders take cooking classes. Let the *hermanas* hike. It's a free world isn't it? Shouldn't it be?

But injustice is the rule of the day. Last night's *concon* is missing. I may have to hunt Schulz down in the Capital and hurt her if she ate my piece.

Instead of delicious *concon*, I withdraw a piece of cabbage to try and tempt Max from the crack in our table where he scurried a few minutes. He hisses at me when I approach, disturbed by the changes. "Oh, come on out, you old grouch," I tease as I slide the cabbage towards him.

Max has the task of keeping our cockroach and spider population under control. Ydria keeps him well-fed so he'll stay at his post. I hum soft bars and wait until small green limbs reach up to sample the safety. I've almost succeeded at convincing Max to emerge when a loud whistle startles both of us. Henri shakes the bars with a shout and then laughs when Max the gecko sticks his head up to hiss again before burrowing back into the crack.

I roll my eyes at Henri, who dangles a large, brown *colmado* bag through the bars.

"You can't prefer that thing to me, too," Henri pretends to pout.

I plop a plastic cup over Max's hiding place to shield him from Henri's teasing. "It'd break Ydria's heart if Max disappeared."

"Everyone loves that stupid gecko. I'm jealous.

The lilt in his tone is a little too flirtatious. I don't make eye contact as I cross to the gate to retrieve the bag. We don't have much reason to talk beyond the niceties. The gender boundaries with which we live mean that Henri belongs to the Elders.

"Did Ydria forget something?" I ask, all facts and no stories. That's the safest way to be.

Henri drops the teasing tone. He's serious again, too. "No. The new *hermana* wants *habichuelas con dulce* so mom sent me for sugar."

"Well, whatever Olsen wants is the order of the day." I lean into the gate in feigned good humor, but I keep my eyes fixed down the road. "That bag is awfully big for a pound of sugar."

"It may also have a little something by Julia Alvarez."

My eyes snap to Henri's before I think better of myself. "I'll see that finds a safe place," I say with an automatic grin.

Henri meets my eyes, but then turns his gaze down the road. His ears pink at the edges. I should let him go, but I see an unexpected opening. I want to climb Point of Heaven, and Henri likes to make me smile.

So I will flirt to convert my fate of cooking lessons and missed hikes.

"Henri." My voice drops into a low purr. "Don't you think I should go to Point of Heaven? I mean, it'll be your last day in town. Do you really want to spend it listening to Blank chatter and watching Monsen impersonate a stone?"

Henri's face contorts through a dozen expressions in less than seven seconds. "No," he says so quiet that God would have to ask him to speak up. "I'd rather spend the day with you." His eyes meet mine for a brief second, and I feel like I'm in the centrifuge at the county fair.

But then he collects himself. He smiles and leans against the gate. "But my mom would kill me, and the Elders are your Priesthood leaders. They all say no, so you're stuck making beans." He pushes off and walks away, laughing at me as I rattle the bars.

"Oh, you rat!" I shout at his retreating back. "You rat! I want to go!"

He waves over his shoulder.

Ydria won't hear my pleas, either. All through dinner, I make my case. She kisses my head and repeats no at each pause.

My tantrum mounts as I gear up for evening work. "I don't need a mother, Ydria. If I want to climb Point of Heaven, I'll climb Point of Heaven."

She checks my bandage, and then looks me dead on. "You don't even know which mountain leads to Point of Heaven. And you've proven, more than once, that you, of all my missionaries, needs her mother." I'm kissed again and pushed out the door.

I put my desire to stalk and tantrum aside to help Olsen acclimate, especially after a rooting hog takes us by surprise and she full-on cries in fear. We avoid all the scary stuff from that point, opting for a good tour of town that includes the ice cream shop and very few animal encounters. The never-working fountain is a highlight, and the marker for the path down to our area. Olsen enjoys the pause in the park while I beat a pair of old men at dominoes. We pick up a few contacts who live in our area and claim they've never been baptized.

A loud whistle disrupts our touring as I'm contemplating taking Olsen down into the real dregs of our area. Tavo races towards us from where his car is parked in front of the government building. He grins when he reaches us. "Tuesday. Six a.m. Meet at the crossroads. That's how you get to Point of Heaven."

"Why, Tavo, you're my new best friend."

Tavo laughs and claps me on the back. "You're better company than the Elders. The whole thing was stupid. It's not that bad. Liliana went last year. My mom goes up sometimes." He shoves a bright pink waterproof bandage in my hands. "I got that from the doctor at the Red Cross. He said wrap it tight and then wear long sleeves. When you get home, check for any mud. Come see him if things go wrong. So the arm problem is nothing, but don't be late—I can't help you if you're a minute late or slow us down."

"We won't do either. Thank you," Olsen answers from beside me. When I turn to her, there's a glimpse of the old Olsen. Her eyes gleam and we squeal in unison.

The days pass like we're waiting for Christmas, but finally the morning dawns. We arrive fifteen minutes early at the crossroads.

Blank walks right by. We accept silence as consent and join the entourage to climb Point of Heaven.

It's not an easy journey. Two hours of continual upward movement and several free climbs over cliffs. The final arduous steps drag us over a rim to a broad plateau above the fog line. My thighs and hips burn, but my breath catches over the vista. The rainforest snaps and breathes below us with a hissing fog that slithers in and out of the green canopy. At this height, we can see the thousands of birds that orchestrate our days. Their colors paint the gray morning sky with brilliant blues, reds and purples. Beyond everything, the ocean kisses land, and then it's gray-green as far as I can see on every side. We're adrift on a small pile of rock and fauna.

"Gorgeous," Olsen says. She's tough and wiry despite her anxieties, never paused a moment on the four hard hours up the mountain. Now she stretches and pops her neck.

"Is this how God sees the earth?" Olsen asks me with a happy sigh after her exercises.

I grin at her, one of our first moments of real connection. "I hope so. Would make dealing with our crappy human stuff easier, wouldn't it? Impossible to be unhappy up here."

"Complete, utter, divine splendor," I say on a sigh. Olsen moves past me to drop her backpack. She plops next to it and stretches before digging into the bread, cheese and bananas we packed for lunch.

"My mom sent *bandera* for us. There's plenty to share." Henri stands behind me. Warm energy runs through my shoulder nearest his. Something about happiness makes me too aware of him and how he makes me feel. "Come sit with us to eat."

The men gather close to the edge. Tavo removes brown clay pots wrapped in rubber bands. Savory beans spice the air with cilantro and garlic to contrast with the sweet wildflowers blanketing the plateau. There's a juxtaposition of my old and new lives at play. The arid landscapes of my youth combine with the pungent flavors of my current world.

But thoughts of home are too far away to be real. This grassy flat belongs to its own time and I'm my own person. Memories meld into the mountain. Worries slip over the side to be caught up by fog fingers. Only camaraderie and peace survived the hike.

The Elders break out dominoes. Henri tosses his mom's card deck in my lap. Blank raises his eyebrows at me, but then the dominoes move aside for rounds of blackjack and poker with flower buds and grass leaves as betting chips. Blank ignores my attempt to gamble over the photo in his album, which is wise since I beat him every hand. Yet even my concern over mission gossip winds into the wind as the hours stretch.

Olsen spends her time removed from the crowd, surrounded by her scriptures and a small journal with a cracked spine. Loose papers spill from the pages and get swept into her bag with everything else. I've not figured her out yet. The anxiety comes and goes without obvious stimuli. When she sees the cards, she stands above us with her hands clutched around the edge of her shirt and issues a reminder of the evils of gambling and graven images.

Blank takes note with a cranky mutter. "Loosen up, Olsen. No money changed hands."

"Oh, let her be," I say. "She's got a right to do this mission the way she needs to do it. Doesn't hurt us to be a bit stricter in our obedience. We need blessings, right?" The cards stow away again in a rubber band.

Blank grumbles again under his breath. He lies back and pulls his baseball cap over his face. Olsen returns to her pile of books much happier than before. The magic of the mountain undoes any permanent upset.

I rest near Henri and Tavo. Tavo takes advantage of his data plan, nothing new there. Henri reads Three Musketeers out loud until the sun slips past its center.

"Time to go," Tavo announces.

Blank complains and tugs his cap further down. "Really, man? We just got here."

"Harder on the way down. No shortcuts." Henri and Tavo have warned us of this reality over and over again.

Tavo carried a large rope up and now he unwinds it. He stands at the edge of the plateau with the rope wrapped around his waist. I didn't spare a thought to the reality of this descent with every deep step up the mountain. Glancing over the edge, I realize that everyone spoke truth.

Straight up. Straight down.

The fog has risen to obscure the path we took. Henri and Tavo argue about whether the fog is too wet and might have drenched the rocks. They switch descent plans and cross over to another lip. Blank and I follow, obedient and silent.

Blank whistles, low and long, as he looks down into the gray nothingness. He kicks a few stones off and they slip into the fog without a sound. "Is there really a ledge down there?"

"It's there." Henri grins as he ties the other end of the rope around his waist. "Don't worry. I'll find it."

He disappears over the edge, free-climbing past the rim of fog. Shadows contort into phantoms, and, as he disappears, my heart races. Time expands to encompass a single, endless worry. The rope slips right and left and then slips quickly over the side. Vertigo and fear threaten to send me tumbling with the length of rope.

The rope catches, and Tavo stumbles forward three steps with a harsh oomph. The taut rope goes still. Too still, and too silent. My racing heart begins to pound.

Then Henri shouts back up; he's found footing. We all exhale and then laugh at ourselves.

One by one, the men and Olsen slip over the side with their hands on the rope. There's initial trepidation but everyone goes without resistance. The rope tugs twice and Henri shouts up as each person finds him on the hidden ledge.

My palms sweat. In all our hikes, my dad never took us anywhere like this.

I won this ride up the mountain on sheer gumption, but I can't hide the truth under these circumstances. My unsteady feet will be my doom. A tumble down this mountain is the fitting end to the goat story.

Tavo gestures to me, his stance wide and a soft smile on his face. "Henri's at the bottom. He won't let you fall. Relax and jump over the edge."

Never. I'll never do this. There's no way I can hold that rope and stay on my feet. I fell twice on the way down to Paue Crossing this morning.

Tavo presses his hands onto my shoulders. "Hermana. Relax. Trust me and trust Henri. You think we'd let anything happen to you?"

Trust. Not my strong suit. But Blank is below me, and he's got to be having a good laugh at my reticence. "I'm embarrassing myself by staying up here, aren't I?"

Tavo flops his head back and forth, then nods. "Elder Blank is counting every minute."

"Alright. Let's do this. And no offense, but, if something happens, I don't want to be Catholic at my funeral."

"None taken. I don't want to be Mormon at mine." He shows me how to place my hands and then walks me backward until I'm forced to make the jump. My feet hit the rock wall and slip as I slide, but then hands wrap my waist and I'm safe. Shaking from head to toe, but safe.

"I've got you." Henri lowers me to the ground, his palms superheating my sides.

He places me close behind him and tugs the line. At Henri's shout, Tavo performs an act of bravery that makes me want to vomit. He runs head-first down the mountain, past us, and leaps over the edge to take the lower post for the next leg. Blank and Monsen anchor Henri until the line goes taut and Tavo shouts.

This terrifying cycle carries us down the mountain. I glean courage from each exchange of smile and brief touch.

Water drops on us after five downs. Henri covers his eyes to peer into the black cloud that has slipped around the mountain. He shakes his head and confers with Tavo. Then he re-ties the rope around his waist but begins a horizontal free climb as he searches for something along the cliff. Tavo side-steps along with him as the rope moves.

A rope jerk and shout announce that Henri found his goal. Tavo reaches out for me first. "There are caves below us where we can wait out the rain. It's not the usual path, though, so stay close to the face. Lewis first. Her arm earns her the driest spot. The rest of us get a little wet."

With a nod, I'm expected to navigate, in a reverse crawl, over the side, which is probably the ugliest thing I've ever done and the bravest. Water has begun to gather in the rock and I slip as I wiggle down the ledge.

Henri's hands wrap securely around my waist well before I land on the small ledge. He directs me into a small cave to his left, nestled against the mountain with a strong rock overhang. I'll be safe there. The inside is almost completely dry. The rain falls in puddles now. Each drop pops like an overfilled balloon, sending up a brilliant burst of sparkling liquid. More mud than water flows over the rim after each splat. The Elders and Olsen pass in front of my cave, one by one, on their way to other pockets. The cave feels darker and creepier with each passing figure. I've lost my love of being alone. Instead, I feel spiders ascending the rocks and wonder if a cave-in will capture me.

A figure pauses at the entry to wait out a rush of muddy water. When the deluge changes back to steady drips, Henri enters the cave with me. I'm uncomfortable—this is not right—and worried and yet—not. I want to talk to Henri. I'm tired of passing niceties and novels. I want to talk like we did at the cathedral. I'm a little lonely, in general, I guess. Without Schulz, fun is set on low. Olsen is a silent entree with a side dish of nail-biting and worry.

Henri isn't talking much, either, though. He crosses to the back and sinks to the ground beside me. I wiggle away, as if there's anywhere to go. We sit shoulder to shoulder, huddled with knees pulled to our chests. Our arms and legs brush against each other. Each move bumps him somehow, so my attempts to insert space only add friction and awareness. We're both growing more embarrassed by my wiggling. I need to relax. I've had guy friends, at least a few. I've sat next to them in caves when we camped in Zion. So, I'm being ridiculous. I can sit next to a guy without drama. I let my shoulder lean into his and my knee brushes his. Henri relaxes. His mouth softens and the taut muscle against my shoulder goes soft.

Water obscures the entrance with an opaque sheet to form a noisy privacy curtain. My cheek rests on my knee to look at him. His shirt clings to lean muscle. Water droplets rest on bronze skin and shimmer at the edge of dark eyelashes. He's really too beautiful.

Henri pulls me out of missionary space and plops me into girl space. Today is worse than all the others. I'm dressed in jeans and a t-shirt and my badge sits on the dresser at the house. I'm Lannie again, but not the old, insecure Lannie. I feel brave and new in this cave, sitting next to Henri, and that can't be mission-appropriate.

Something in my posture or face must speak for me. Henri points to the wall to answer a question I didn't ask. "Technically, Olsen is only eight feet away."

"Not much to be done, right? Last space left. That's what you get being anchor for this leg."

"I had my choice between three Americans I don't care about, and one I do." He knocks my shoulder with his. "Did you think only my mom prayed to meet you?"

My heart cracks down the middle and the missionary half falls away. Sometimes, someone fits snugly into your soul. Ydria and Henri are my soul people. I've missed them my whole life without ever knowing they existed.

Henri looks at me expectantly. It's too easy to lock eyes with his, too simple to smile back at him. "Guess I hadn't thought about it."

Our cave darkens as the storm intensifies and the mud falls in a cascade over the cliff. Occasional glimmers of light flit around the cave like fairies. I want this magical moment to exist outside of time and responsibility. I want to be the woman Henri wants to be alone in a cave with on his last day in *Los Limones*, and I don't want to feel guilty tomorrow.

And I imagine that's exactly how my dad felt about meeting Mikala. Henri fades until all I can see is Mikala's spiked blue and black hair and my very-married father in a tight production studio. The truth is all too obvious. Moments in magic caves – and music studios - ruin lives. I sigh heavily and lean my back against the cave wall, closing my eyes against every promise and risk inherent to two people in close proximity.

Henri lets me withdraw until light filters back into the cave and the fairies stop their work. Everything feels safer once the magic slips away with the clouds.

I peek up at Henri once he moves a few inches away. "So, what's your favorite book?"

Henri brightens again. He stops chewing his lower lip and the crease between his eyes softens. "I don't know. I haven't read them all yet."

Conversation takes flight. Words hover and soar like birds. One sentence removed our awkwardness and we need to speak the mundane things that matter too much. Books. Music. *Telenovelas*. American cinema. Stories from childhood and stories of Ydria. We have to lean our heads together to talk once the rain starts again, but there's no more space for silence. Emotions shift with the sunlight, at times serious and then with levity. We've been granted one hour to fill with a lifetime. When the water slows, we settle into silence, smiles and sighs.

When the water hovers at the cave entrance in heavy drips but rarely falls, Tavo pokes his head into the cave. "I think we give it fifteen minutes? Let it dry a little?"

Olsen stands behind Tavo. Lannie melds back into Hermana Lewis. Henri and I part without a word.

The whole group stands at the edge of the cliff, readying for a return to the harrowing descent. Tavo has coiled the rope and looped it back over his head. About fifteen feet below us, a path winds down the mountain. Brown water creates races down the mountainside.

The earth cooks quickly under tropical sun. The thick mud changes from malleable clay to hardened pottery. Tavo and Henri kick at the cliffside. We're ready to move again when earth falls off in chunks instead of clinging to their heels.

The fifteen-foot free climb covers us all in clay-like mud and ups the fun factor. Blank throws a lump of wet mud on my head. My retaliation involves shaking a broad leaf above his head and laughing as the resultant waterfall plasters his hair to his head. Monsen, Henri and Tavo toss leaves and mud at each other, too. Olsen stays above the fray until she slips on a rivulet and slides on her rear end all the way to the next turn.

Laughing, Blank runs after Olsen to repeat the slide. We all follow suit, six dumb kids playing in the mud. Some slide on their feet and others on their ends, but all of us hit the next bend muddier and sillier than toddlers on a riverbank.

"Lewis has dreds," Henri teases.

He's right. My hair came loose from its ponytail and falls in ten thick sections. I shake the remainder from its hold and do my best zombie walk. Then we're all chasing each other again as we play at zombie apocalypse.

Blank stops the game when the sun drives long sheets through the haze. The orange globe lies deep on the horizon like a buoy bouncing in the sea. Blank covers his eyes to stare at it. We all left our phones at home to avoid a gray-area confession if something got damaged. No one has any idea how much of that mountain lies within our work area or what punishments might await if none of it does.

"Gotta hurry, guys. This day is getting away from us. We've got appointments."

Sadly, so do we. Our run abandons fun for desperation. Duty calls.

Tavo's phone rings as we get to Paue Crossing. He hands it to Henri who flinches several times while the phone presses to his ear. He hangs up and looks at us.

"Mama says to bring you to our house. There's not enough water at yours for the mess. And if we even think about dipping in the river, she'll call the president."

Tavo laughs and whistles over three *motoconchos*. "Wasn't my idea to bring the women," he grins with a wink, his phone clasped between his teeth. "Pick you up at six tomorrow morning, brother."

Henri clasps his hand and pulls him in for a one-armed hug. They're university students again, and I'm a missionary in big trouble with her *mamita*. This great day has a downside.

I whistle for a *motoconcho*. "Best to get this punishment over fast, right?"

I get one more happy-grin before Henri climbs onto the back of a moped and speeds away. My heart has a brand-new rhythm called forth by that smile. The rhythm puts the events in the cave on repeat accompanied by little waves of happiness.

Ydria jumps from the porch to shout at us as soon as she sees the *conchos*. She physically hauls me from the back of the moped to field dress me proper. "Of all the stupid, irresponsible ideas! It's a miracle your arm is still attached. Look at you! How much of that mud is under the bandage? Ridiculous, stupid—"

"Mama! Don't yell at her." Henri maneuvers between us to clasp his hands over Ydria's small shoulders.

Ydria shakes him off. She points at him. "You're lucky everyone is back in one piece. I'll be fired for sure if she ends up back in the hospital. We're supposed to keep you safe."

Worry crosses Henri's brow. He glances at me, and I shake my head to deny her words. But I don't know if her job could be at risk over rules I choose to break.

Ydria goads us along like oxen towards the back courtyard where she's hung large sheets to obscure the neighbors' view. Three large barrels of water hold down the curtains.

"Get those pants off," she orders.

As soon as we're free of our thick jeans, Ydria grabs a cleaning bucket and tosses five gallons of water over each of our heads. More buckets follow, one right after the other, suffocating and freeing us as clods of mud fall from our hair and bodies.

The dirt and water clog my throat and blind me. "Torture is illegal in most countries," I gag in between deluges.

"Not here." Ydria pauses to allow us a breath, but then restarts the barrage until the water runs clean. Then she scrubs our skin and nails with a giant, coarse brush. Then shampoo, oil, and water work through strand after strand until our hair hangs in silken sheets.

Olsen is dismissed first. Ydria points her to a pile of clothes. Our black tags lay atop each respective pile. Olsen disappears behind one of the curtains to change.

Ydria hauls over a stool. She doesn't speak until my arm is unwrapped. The pink skin beneath the soggy bandage lacks any tinge of mud. Relief flows out of her in an exaggerated sigh. Her hands shake, and she dabs at her eyes with the back of her hand.

My hand covers hers. "Ydria. I'm sorry. I didn't think—"

"No. You didn't. You didn't think at all." A fresh, brown wrap begins its circle around my forearm. Ydria exhales on the third round. "You're never not the Lord's servant, Hermana. Every word, every thought, every moment belongs to Him. Nothing should happen without His counsel. How would He feel about a day caked in mud running about with boys? Do you think He smiles on you?"

My mind turns to Henri and the cave, to each whispered, *I've got you*, and the feel of his hands on my waist. Worse, I feel the weight of my desire to slip into a world beyond my tag and to serve no one but myself.

Ydria secures the bandage with butterfly clips. "You're in charge now. What was cute yesterday is unacceptable today. Time to put away childish things, dear. Past time."

Tears sting my eyes. They're wiped away on my shoulder as Ydria slips away to give me privacy for dressing.

The black tag hangs heavy on my heart when I pin it in place. Each letter traces under my fingertips. Hermana Lewis. The Church of

Jesus Christ of Latter-day Saints. That's who I am, who I agreed to be. Who I must be.

Ydria waits in the kitchen with sandwiches wrapped in dishtowels. Her eyes burn into me, and she only knows a small piece of all my sins. She'd raze me to the ground if she knew the entire story. She presses the food into Olsen's hands, and then nods toward the door. "Get gone. You've an hour to serve the Lord. Make it a good offering."

Olsen hangs back to offer an apology for her part in my mess. I walk through the door, my arms wrapped around my middle. Everything good is gone. I'm empty, completely empty.

Henri leans against the railing on his porch, fresh and clean. I duck my head and hold my breath. A few steps and I'll be past him and in the street. No need to think of him at all.

But he speaks before I get down the steps. "Did she give you her worst? You look like she gave her worst."

"Nothing I didn't deserve." It's my turn not to meet his eyes, to look at my shoes and down the road like he used to do when we first met.

"You're leaving this week? For sure? You're going to the Capital?"

"That's the rumor." Maybe it's the badge or my sins or the effort of the hike or some tropical illness carried in the mud, but everything aches, and the darkness feels darker. I need sleep, to be covered in blackness. If only Olsen would hurry. Maybe I could convince her to let us go straight home.

"So tell my mom where you are. I'll come see you at church."

The idea throws me outside my walls. The reality of it. The risk. Brave, new Lannie punches at the demons in my darkness. She wants in control of this conversation, but the badge pleads for a miracle transfer to *Barahona*. Brave, new Lannie seizes control of my tongue before my brain offers a counter-attack. And I smile. Heaven help me, I smile at Henri. "Ydria will always know where I am. How else could she lecture me?"

Electricity buzzes and crackles around us as Henri grins back. "Good. That's good. Then we don't have to say goodbye."

Fool that I am, I extend a hand to shake on this non-committal bit of stupidity. Our palms fuse together with intense energy that draws him a step closer and calls his other hand to shelter mine in both of his. My knuckles nestle so close to his heart that the beat caresses my knuckles. The warmth from our hands spreads to my smile and warms his eyes.

"Be safe, Hermana." My title is quiet on his lips, as though he didn't want to say it at all.

"You, too." Regret shades every word, but I can't cry. I can't feel any of this at all.

Olsen emerges from the house behind me. Henri's hand slides away. I shiver at the loss and the sudden drop back into the pool of my guilt.

# Chapter 13

Over the next ten days, work is the only *panacea* for the turmoil in my head and heart. Every time Henri crosses my mind, I push us harder. Discussions, street contacts, reactivation lessons, and pure exhaustion, can keep the happy-terrified thoughts at bay. Obviously, I can't ever see Henri again. The solution to my mess is simple: transfer out and don't tell Ydria where I've gone. In three days, my sins disappear along with my luggage. In the meantime, I keep my head down and follow every rule. Obedience will bring redemption.

The earth groans at my heresy, a strange jolt followed by unseen construction vehicles digging at concrete. I lose my concentration while guilt fades out reality. No, probably not even anything real. Olsen barely looks up. I shrug to clear out vain imaginations. Must focus, think.

The yellow agenda is crammed with appointments and contacts and new finds. I'm the busiest bee in all of Deseret. "So, I think we should go to Hetty's. No guarantee she lets us in, but I can show you where the Elders live again and maybe we'll run into those two women we met at the market—they said they lived by the liquor store, right?"

The earth shifts again with a terrible thud.

Olsen's head flies up this time. The buildings shiver as a barely-audible vibration expands to a giant wavelength. Dirt rises to meet us and then our feet float above. We stumble over shifting ground, tripping at the unexpected earth in unexpected spaces while we struggle to cross the street.

Luck or providence placed us at the crossroad as the earthquake hit. Ydria waves to us from her doorstep, her knuckles white where she clutches the doorframe. Her mouth moves, but cracking concrete obscures any sound until the earth sighs the briefest of breaths and we can find footing enough to run to her.

We race to the back courtyard to huddle as one in the doorway around a quivering Liliana whose fevered, twelve-year-old body seems twice as small as it did. She leans into my skirted legs. My arms wrap us all like the hen gathering chicks in Christ's parables.

Earth's sigh turns into a quiver that becomes a quake and then God picks up the earth to shake off the inhabitants like crumbs on a tablecloth. Screams erupt around us. We bury our faces in my skirt and cough through wave after wave of pulverized stone.

On and on, the earth howls. Giant palm trees tumble behind us adding bangs to the creaks and whines of earth. The crashes crescendo to a cacophony of destruction with no rhythm or melody. Liliana jumps with every boom until the destruction sounds so continually that she can't distinguish one crash from the next.

A giant trunk pounds against the house as it rolls down the street. Screams write themselves on each face during the thud-thud-thud of the battering ram. Olsen's eyes are distant. Her mouth has frozen into a living representation of Van Gogh's Screamer. My head bows to pray for miracles so huge they're undeniably impossible: for this house to stand when others fall and for survival when others die.

Eventually, the trembling stops, but the crashes and bangs don't. Structures tumble. Trees fall. And then the hum turns to a rumble all over again. Over and over, the terror builds and subsides. The cycle repeats so many times we lose count. No one dares to move except to tug up our shirts to stop dust from invading our lungs. Another house sways and collapses. Tiles from the roof roll off and crash at our feet, yet Ydria's house holds strong through it all.

Our legs and bladders ache after the last earthly sigh gives way to extended silence. I strain to hear the voice of Christ to speak calm to my soul as it did in the Book of Mormon. Only silence greets me. Silence and Ydria's gentle hand against my cheek.

"I think it's over. But let's pray first." Olsen's quivering hand grips mine; Liliana shelters in the circle of our arms.

Words slip past my tongue, pleas for safety and safe travels and safe anything. I pray for everyone, one by one, by name. Every name I have in my head. Ydria sobs when I say Henri's name. An earthquake this large may have reached the Capital. News will extend far beyond the impact of the quake. Somewhere in Utah, my mother will bow her head as Ydria does now and pray for my safety. I add her to my prayers. Olsen's family, too. Everyone gets their moment before God.

When I open my eyes, Ydria smiles at me. Tears hover at the rims of her eyes, then slip back inside her lower lid. "God will take care of us. But we've got to make it to the church. Everyone gathers there when these things happen."

We can barely see and still cough when we drop the cloth from our mouths. The swirls of air slowly progress past us as the dust cloud rolls down the hill. The sun shifted at some point to stand in front of us, hidden behind a thick layer of dirty air. The touch of afternoon sunlight wakes everything. A cowering cat unfurls from beneath an overturned pot to hop onto toppled stone. He hisses at us and runs off. More animals break free, and then people, too. The sounds of life infuse bravery into our group. We, too, shake off the dust of inaction and prepare for a journey to safer ground.

Outside the house, long tree trunks lay like a tic-tac-toe board across the road. Boulders rolled down the mountain to park amidst the rubble. The road itself has cracked. Fences lie face down with their barbed wire grabbing at us like ghouls. Dead pigs and goats stare up at us from under tree limbs. Water rushes down the road, sprung from somewhere unseen, diverting around piles of rubble from collapsed houses. From beneath these piles of wood and concrete, muffled voices call for help.

Men and women rush by us towards each sound. Ydria's hand shackles my wrist when I move to join them. "Please, Hermana, stay with us. We have to stay together."

The murmurs beneath the rubble intensify again. Men strain against the fallen concrete. One by one, large blocks get tossed aside so the men can lift the bodies trapped beneath. A boy's limp frame is the third pulled from the wreckage. The boy who shines shoes in the main square, the best businessman in *Los Limones* as I've called him. The men place his lifeless body on a wide slab of concrete. Beside him, another man lays an elderly woman. Her empty eyes reflect fear. I knew her, too. She sold chickens at the market.

Olsen's chin quivers as the men pull more people from beneath what used to be a house. My gut is a stone. This can't be happening. Not to us. A few hours ago, I worried where to eat lunch and thought my flirtation with Henri the worst thing that could ever happen. This morning was dull, unremarkable. Not a day for death. Nothing said death would consume *Los Limones* today.

The boys' parents emerge from beneath a beam and rush to their little one's side. The mom collapses and pulls her son's limp hand to her mouth. The father stands, stoic, to look at other things and try not to believe in what's plainly at his feet. My heart wants to join them, to weep with those that weep and mourn with those that mourn. Liliana wraps her arms around my waist and Ydria begs again.

For once, I listen to Ydria. She, Liliana. and Olsen, are my primary responsibilities. We push on in the not-simple task of getting to the church.

At the town square, water shoots in a single line from the broken fountain, and the marble fish have all lost their heads. The cathedral has a giant crack from bell tower to foundation. Our church could be in ruins. Still, we pick our way across the debris field to the painful crescendo of all-encompassing grief. The wails wind around every corner, as ubiquitous as salsa and merengue used to be.

The sun has almost crossed the entire sky when the white chapel comes into view. While the white stucco is untouched, the glass has blown out of several windows. Inside, every piece of furniture lays on its side. The metal chairs remain intact. Perfectly intact. When the apocalypse comes, Mormons will set out metal folding chairs to wait on the Lord. They're as indestructible as cockroaches.

President Andres waits in front of the chapel. "I was here when it hit, a mercy of the Lord. I've been able to receive everyone. The Elders have come and gone. Hermanas, you're to take up the effort to call the President. The cell towers must have fallen."

The power hasn't come in a very long time, so long that even my backup battery is out of juice. My phone shows twelve percent battery remaining. Olsen's phone's battery life is down to 50%. The reality is that we will all soon be cut off, cell towers or no.

Ydria winds arms around our waists. She kisses us for what must be the hundredth time. "Get a message to your mamas. Let them know you're alive. The President can wait."

Then Ydria and Andres dig out some pens and paper. They begin to make lists of emergency supplies: rice, beans, water, mattresses, gas, candles, and matches. The list grows as more members arrive.

And I feel useless. Everyone has something to do except Olsen and me.

Not that Olsen is up for much besides staring into space. Occasionally, she rubs the tops of her shoes together and hums a hymn. That's about it.

"Hey? Are you okay?" Her elbow quivers when I touch it. No, she's not okay. I guide her into a classroom with little damage. I take out her journal and scriptures to lay them next to her, but all she does is stare and rub the worry spot on her shoes. "I'll be outside, okay?" I say.

Out in the courtyard, the women have begun to organize into scavenge crews. The Relief Society president shouts orders to the groups. "We can cook here. The kitchen still works and there's plenty of gas. But we need supplies. We'll share everything, ladies. So bring everything you have." The United Order is the *de facto* emergency plan of the church.

"What about our house? What can we get from there?" I shout back, eager to contribute something—anything—to the cause at hand.

Ydria shakes her head with the pen pressed to her lips. "Nothing. It belongs to the mission. The *hermanas* will need it all."

The women and Andres erupt in argument. We have water barrels and Ydria buys rice in bulk and the house is secure—the members make so many other logical arguments. Ydria's jaw sets. She'll protect us, no matter the cost.

I link an arm through hers and slide my head on her shoulder. "Ydria. I want to help. We're a part of this, right?" Scriptures flow from my mouth without bidding. "Bring ye all the tithes to the storehouse, that there be meat in my house... and prove me now herewith... if I will not pour a blessing out over your heads."

For the first time since the hike, Ydria looks at me with respect. Without hesitation, she hands her keys to Andres. "Anything we have is yours."

Andres' older face breaks into a dozen smile lines.

An hour later, the supplies begin to arrive. Bags of rice and beans pile in the kitchen. Mattresses find homes in the chapel. Pots, pans, water jugs, bleach bottles, and other items fill every corner. Laughter clatters along with the random offerings. The courtyard overflows with children, whose games cannot be interrupted for anything as trivial as an earthquake.

We've been lucky so far. Every active family is intact.

Night has fallen when I sit and twirl my phone. I'm down to 5% battery after attempting three calls to the President. If I'm going to text my parents, I need to do so now.

Blackness consumes the rubble and hides the quake, so everything feels almost normal. The liquor store has generator power. The *bachata* has resumed its place in the daily soundtrack. Everything feels okay right now.

Texting Mom is easy.

*Hey, I'm all right. Everyone's at the church. It's crazy, sad and happy.* DON'T WORRY!!

I hesitate a moment before adding one more sentence: *I'll text dad.*

There's a chance he doesn't know. He never watches news. Other people's tragedies distract him from his own greatness. He'll be a jerk somehow if Mom calls, though. Or she'll have to talk to Mikala.

The battery slips to 4% while I write and erase. He's my dad, for heaven's sake. I only need to write two sentences.

Mom's reply sucks away another percent. *Oh, baby. I've been worried. Watched the TV all day. Thanks for this. Did your dad respond? Love you. Love everybody there. Prayers.*

Mom is awesome. That Dad didn't see it makes me dislike him more.

But I must do this. He's my dad. Christ loves him and commanded me to do so, too. Staring at the lit screen takes me to 2%. The keyboard icon mocks me. Whatever I write is fine. It's not like he really cares. I tap it and start a message. *Hey, dad. I've survived an earthquake. Hope the pregnancy is going awesome. Lannie.*

Then I power down the phone. I don't want his reply. Not yet.

Blank and Monsen return when the last light slips away. Monsen sits near the church, where dim candles provide some light. Blank drops beside me. For a long time, he says nothing. We both stare at flickering spots of candlelight popping up amidst the rubble.

When the blackness rests on everything, he slouches down to lie on his backpack. His hand wraps into my skirt. My skin crawls away from his hand. I force stillness as he starts to talk in a broken voice, far away and distant, like a recording of an old radio show. There's a rule for everything, and I'm sure even comfort isn't allowed among opposite sexes, but he needs nurturing and I need to have done more than sit on a hill all day. So I let his hand crumple and release my skirt dozens of times as I rub his arm.

"I'd never touched a dead body before. All the death I've seen here, and I've never touched a body before today. But I swear there was someone I knew under each piece of concrete. Dozens of them. Dozens of dead bodies."

He starts to list names, people he's known and taught. He's been here longer than I have and knows more people—more dead people. Each name, each person, each memory drags him further into the quiet. He starts to shake. "Would you sing something, Lewis?"

My fingers move through Blank's straight, brown hair while I sing, *Be Still My Soul.* Blank's shoulders quiver as I sing the lyric—*sorrow forgot, love's purest joys restored.* My hand moves from his hair to still his shoulders while I raise the volume to cover his muffled sniffles.

Blank falls asleep curled on my backpack with a hand still wrapped in my skirt. Sleep won't come for me, even if I could move. Instead, I watch over my city. Every so often, Ydria or another woman crosses near me while all the men sleep.

Eventually, Ydria sits next to me. She slides her hand into mine. "On nights like these, I realize how long it takes for the rooster to crow. Did you hear from your mama?"

I nod. She tucks a strand of hair behind my ear. Her own silver hair has fallen loose. Moonlight glistens on the strands and the dust sprinkled over her shoulders and face. She's my version of what an angel should be. Tough. Hardworking. Selfless. Always right.

But her heart must be breaking. Both of her own children are beyond her reach.

"Did anyone bring word of Hetty?" I ask.

For a moment, her mouth is a thin line as a dozen doses of sadness get dry-swallowed. She shakes her head. "But don't you worry. Hetty's a fighter. She'll surface."

I squeeze her hand. "I heard some women say that the radio in the liquor store said the epicenter was near San Isidro. The Capital didn't seem to take as much damage as we did. So he's okay. Henri's okay. We'd know if he wasn't."

My voice catches, though I try to hide it. The too-long hours of watch and wait produced dozens of fear-filled fantasies. In one, Henri slips over the edge with his cocky grin, but the rope never pulls tight. He's lost in that fog, fallen somewhere we'll never find him…

Ydria guides my head to her shoulder. "The answers will come, Hermana, but not tonight. Tonight, we wait on the roosters."

Maybe I sleep and maybe I don't before a thin line of light sets off the roosters' alarms. Their cock-a-doodles bring hope even as the sun illuminates the rubble that hid the bodies in Blank's stories.

# Chapter 14

The next morning, Andres spreads out a map to start the hunt for the missing members. Andres points to me as he hands out slips of paper with streets and member names. "The *hermanas* will stay here and—"

"Excuse me?" Frustration boils out of my chest on a harsh and ragged breath. Honestly, everyone but me needs a day off. Blank looks at me side-eyed, tight-lipped, and restless. He needs to sleep without nightmares, not search. I lost count how many times I hushed and sang him back to sleep last night. Monsen's eyes are blood-shot and he's not spoken a word to anyone in two days. Olsen? Well, Olsen is the resident nutcase. She tends a pot of oatmeal, humming *Teach Me to Walk in the Light*. Ydria worries over her. One hand touches Olsen at all times while the other busies itself with breakfast.

Not a one of these people should be going anywhere. But me? I need to work. Yesterday's inactivity killed me. "I'm not tending a group of perfectly capable women. I want to go—"

Andres gives me the look. The Priesthood holder look. The be-quiet-woman look that I don't appreciate at all.

Blank bumps my shoulder to further quiet me. "Sorry, Lewis. But Olsen looks like she's two bad ideas away from creepy. Maybe we can rescue you later and send you on splits."

My next sigh is ignored as much as the first. Andres continues all the plans that don't involve me. I will seriously lose my mind if I have to sit at this church another day.

A half-hour of pouting later, the Elders' *mamita* interrupts Andres with a wave and then gestures towards the road. "What's he doing here?"

The Priest stands at the gate. Cement dust chalks the hem of his robe. His bushy, gray eyebrows hang with sadness. Andres beckons him forward.

"I thought maybe we could be of service to each other," he says with an extended hand, which Andres eagerly clasps. "We could save time, avoid duplicating efforts."

"Everyone is everything in *Los Limones*," I mumble.

"Sadly true. More so today than ever." The Priest withdraws a white handkerchief to blot the sweat beading above his eyebrows. "I'd like to take the *hermanas* along the river if you don't mind. They trust her." He nods at me.

"I'll go." I seize my moment before Andres can object.

"Not alone," Blank interjects. "She can't go alone."

"He's a Priest, for heaven's sake." They're going to say no. They'll say no and I'll be stuck here all day while the men do the real work of salvation.

"I'll go with her." An out of place voice speaks behind me accompanied by a baby's babble. When I turn, Celia greets me with a tired grin. Little Issa reaches for me. Ydria makes a strangled cry and runs towards Hetty and the baby where they stand behind Celia.

"You're not a member," grumbles Blank.

"Close as I can get, right, Lewis?" Celia argues with Blank, who recently denied her baptism. I really don't want to be in the middle of this argument when there are so many people who need help. I hush Celia with a warning glance to Blank.

Graciela continues to take discussions, too, and the membership is firmly on her side. Murmurings pass through the women behind me. Husband thief. Prostitute. Celia and I pretend not to hear the worst, but her color heightens. Celia sells fruit at market now rather than her body. She deserves a chance and a little forgiveness, not gossip.

"I'll come. I want to come," Olsen rasps, gasping around what the wraith left of her brain.

"So, it's settled. We're going." I throw my backpack over my shoulder. Olsen does the same, though she clutches her journal and hums eerily instead of speaking. Celia passes Issa to Ydria, and then joins our small procession.

The Priest leads us down the hill toward the river settlement. Olsen's journal serves as our record. She's less crazy when she writes in it. Most are too traumatized to really note the oddity at all. They tell us their story and report their dead or missing.

Depending on whose hands gets clasped first, that person leads the spiritual portion of the visit. For all my complaints about the Priest, he backs off quickly when it's my hand clutched or my shoulder that absorbs the tears. I give him the same respect when a hand clutches a rosary.

We visit every house along the river and then start up the mountain. Celia has done her part in helping us find the scattered. She knows everyone. Sometimes, she disappears when we approach a house of a former client, but she finds us again as soon as we leave the house.

Toward the close of the day, she steers us towards the *sancista's* collapsed tin cottage. Wails rise from behind the cottage along with a strange, green smoke.

"They tell me she lost her man," Celia says in a whisper.

The Priest hesitates a moment with eyes on the green smoke. Then he picks up his robes to cross the mud from where the river sloshed its borders during the quake. When we turn the corner, we're all confronted by our prejudices. The *sancista* has erected an altar. Bowls sit within chalk-drawn symbols. The saints and Virgin Mary stare over candles that flicker as the fire hisses and coughs. The *sancista* jangles a bell and sings under her breath between wails.

Olsen's foot plants in the dirt outside the circle. Her fingernails turn white where they press into her journal. Celia directs Olsen away from the fire. "I'll bet she hasn't eaten. Could you help me with the cooking, Hermana?"

Olsen and Celia retreat. I focus in on the *sancista*. Her shoulders shake as she tosses powders and bones into a pot. Her wails emerge from such a broken space, a whistle through a crack. The Priest moves behind her to place a hand on her shoulder. I pull her wizened hand to my heart. The woman who greeted every death *in Los Limones* with love deserves the same from me.

The *sancista's* tears drop on my arm. I rub her hands while I quote Paul's second epistle to the Corinthians. "Blessed be the God of all comfort; who comforteth us in all our tribulation."

Then the Priest prays the rosary above us all. My mouth works as does the *sancista's*. After all we've done together, maybe it's true: everyone is everything in *Los Limones*.

Celia fetches rice and a simple soup. We share the meal over the fire that changes from green to brown to red as the *sancista's* mood changes. By meal's end, she cackles along with the Priest as they recall old shared rituals and people long gone.

Near the meal's end, the *sancista* scoots closer. "I see you've accepted *Anaisa's* kiss, my darling. Is the young man as handsome as he is worthy?"

I haven't thought about her warning in ages. Nabihah's death got lost in the mission fathoms. "I can't accept anyone's kiss. I'm a missionary. There's no young man."

"Why would you lie to an old, grieving woman? When *Anaisa* sends you love, child, you'd be smart to accept it. My Paolo was a gift from *Anaisa*. Fifty years... we spent fifty years together..." Her lip trembles and she starts to wail again.

We read her a few more things for comfort, but the light fades. Curfew approaches. We need to get back before the world plunges into darkness again.

The Priest rests a hand on her knee with a smile of true affection. "Well, old woman, we'd best take our leave. Let me know if you change your mind about a formal burial."

Her leathery lips press together. "I'll stick to the old ways for Paolo."

The Priest's face softens into a smile. "I'll have the nuns come by in a few days to check on you. No joining Paolo. Your people need you."

"I can't leave them alone with the likes of you." Deep smile lines form around the *sancista's* eyes.

The *sancista* clings to me as I offer her one last kiss. "We'll come and see you again soon. Please remember to eat." She nods, and I extract my hand.

"Remember, girl. It's not wise to anger *Anaisa*. Remember the offering." I kiss her again and then stride off more confidently than I feel.

"What was that about?" The Priest asks as he falls in step with me.

"I don't know. Lots of stuff I don't believe in."

The Priest chuckles. There's more than a small amount of humor in his voice. "Why do we put up with that old witch?"

"Because we love her." It's that simple.

The Priest and I walk in silence as we cross the borders of the village. The people call my name as I walk by. They wave and smile at us, several children run up for a final hug.

When I peel off the final pair of small arms, the Priest looks at me for way too long. "I don't say this often. I've only said it of Andres among Mormons, but you've been touched by the hand of God, Hermana. I hope you remember that where much is given, much is required. Satan stands eager to fell any tree the Lord has planted."

"I'm popular among all the gods and the devils, it seems," I say with good humor. I've had my fill of spiritual warnings today. I'm grateful for his return to silence as we ascend to the ward building.

Blank and Ydria stand at the gate, their faces lined with concern. The light fades fast this time of year.

The Priest grins at them. "We've returned, as promised. A very successful day. I think you'll be pleased."

"Hermana. I hope we can work together again. Perhaps in the outer villages?" The Priest extends a hand. I'm supposed to kiss his ring, I think, but I shake it instead. A look of pure amusement accompanies his small head shake.

Blank interjects. "The *hermanas* don't go that far out of town, but we're happy to go with you. Want us to stop by tomorrow?"

"Perhaps wise to keep the women close. These are dangerous days full of wolves." Then the Priest heads down the hill to the gate without responding to Blank's offer.

"Gah, that man is impossible. Can't fathom a moment of real connection to the Spirit."

I grimace at his dismissal, thinking of the *sancista* and the warm spirit by the fire.

Blank rambles on, "But let's get you home before the sun sets. Both the missionary houses survived the quake and were deemed safe. Ydria's house only needed a little cleaning. So we're all good to get a decent night's rest." Blank yawns and rubs his hand over his face.

Ydria wipes her hands on her jeans and then snaps for Liliana. "Walk us to the crossroads. We'll be safe from there."

Blank yawns again, and then he grabs his bag. "Fine. To the crossroads we go. Come on, Monsen. The faster we put the ladies away, the sooner we're in our cots. I'm hammered."

Andres intersects us on our way up the hill. He's back from a trip down the highway to assess damages. "I'm glad I caught you. The bridge is out, and the water is too high for a quick repair. For now, nothing moves in or out. The market at the crossroads had some food and better phone reception. We bought what we could carry back up. But I've got good news. I reached my Molli in the Capital. She's seen Henri. He's safe."

Ydria exhales audibly, probably her first real one since the quake hit. She hugs Andres while squeezing my hand. "We've a lot to thank God for tonight."

"Definitely. Be safe in town. The police will be in charge until the road opens."

Everyone lapses into silence for the long walk home. There's so much debris in the streets that even small outings take hours. Human resilience emerges from every inhabited corner. Two bulldozers pile debris in the town square. Tin sellers scavenge collapsed roofs. Children laugh and play amidst the rubble.

Life goes on, no matter what disaster brings.

At the crossroads, Blank shoves his hands in his pockets. "You got a solar charger at the house? Backup battery? Anything? You have to be able to reach us."

"We have seven carrier pigeons out back, I think. Will that help?"

"Shut up, Lewis. I'm trying to lead here. What if something happens? Another quake? How will we know to come dig your stupid head out of the rubble?" There's real fear in his eyes.

"I think I'll notice the rubble." Ydria sets her mouth in a tough line.

"But a charger, Lewis. You can't rely on the electricity. Take my phone tonight. It's got one call left. I've got a backup charger at home for Monsen's phone."

Blank yawns and rubs his face again. He's got no fight left.

"Fine. I'll take your phone. Get some rest, okay? You look like death."

"Just trying to fit in around here." Blank grins. He's handsome once you move aside the misogyny. Maybe yesterday's bonding did have some good outcome.

Monsen grabs my shoulders for a moment. It's weird. Totally uncomfortable. He nods once and the exchange ends. The Elders head towards their house.

Ydria needs to be dismissed next. She's got bags under the bags under her eyes. "You head on home. Worse we'll find at our house is an opportunistic rat. You're exhausted and need a real bed. Liliana, too. She's still got her fever."

Ydria hesitates, but I swoop in to reassure. "Seriously, Ydria. It's straight up the hill. Nothing to worry about."

"Your bandages need changed—"

"I can change a bandage, Ydria. We're fine. Go home."

Exhaustion overwhelms reason. She takes Liliana's hand and heads down the hill. We climb up. The sun follows Ydria's course, dropping further and further. We're immersed in darkness as we pass a large, concrete block building.

Shadows move at the corners. From a pitch-black doorway, a hiss slithers to us. "Aye *rubias*. Come here."

Olsen jolts. My hand locks her elbow. The earthquake made for looming, unexpected shadows that make everything feel weird, but this is nothing new. Cat calls follow us up the hill every day.

"I said come here, girls." The voice growls. Shadows shift again and a distinct clatter sounds as metal strikes metal. My heart bolts to a gallop.

"Just keep moving. We're almost there," I whisper to Olsen. She clasps her journal and hums *Give, Said the Little Stream*. The phone is in my pocket. I tap it but keep a steady pace. A few more steps will carry us past the building.

More noise emerges from shadow. Murmurs and scrapes. Footsteps fall in line behind us. Two men step forward from the shadows and block our path. Four more surround us. All are fully armed with automatic weapons, knives and bullet clips draped over their shoulders.

The most heavily armed man steps forward. He has a black beret and loads of curly hair. "Hello, *hermanas*. What keeps you out past curfew?"

Olsen whimpers beside me. I squeeze her hand and hope she prays real thoughts and not her semi-crazy babbles of the last forty-eight hours.

A quick 'please, God' echoes around my heart. My mind races through a thousand options, many of which are based on Hollywood action movies. Lacking the requisite muscles, I settle on safety in numbers. I'll take them back to Ydria's.

I smile and bat my eyes, playing at the dumb blonde. "There's a curfew? We hadn't heard. Care to escort us to our friend's house?"

"Happy to help you out. But there's a fee for service. And a fine, for breaking curfew." The man steps closer. His metal-covered canines glisten in moonlight, a terrifying cliché straight out of Hollywood.

"We're short on cash at present." I hope I've employed the swaggering action hero's bravado in my reply.

There's a general tittering among the men. The circle closes in. "Money isn't the only form of payment."

"We're servants of God. You can't touch us." Please, let this be true.

My words provoke laughter, not fear. "God doesn't watch over *Los Limones*," a man sneers too close to my ear.

Olsen sobs.

"Please, please don't do this. We're American citizens." I stop talking and pray. Make them go. We're afraid and they're powerful. Let that be enough.

"Do what? We want to show you a good time. Come inside. Lots of fun inside." The leader kicks open a door. Something sharp nudges me forward. We can't go in that door. Everything ends inside that door.

I drop into defensive stance to stop the forward crawl to the door. Fists ready at my sides.

Then a loud whistle pierces the air followed by my name.

There's a murmur among the crowd as the whistle repeats. The leader mutters a phrase I don't know, and the men break formation. Their guns stow away. But I stay ready to fight.

"Ho, there! Lewis!" The voice is closer, as is the form. I don't turn.

"Is that Tavo? I think that's Tavo." Olsen's voice shivers with relief.

I take my eyes off the men. Tavo races towards me. "Hey, Lewis. My parents are expecting you. Come on." He grins at the small crowd. "Sorry they're out after curfew. My dad'll get them home. Thanks for doing your duty." Tavo claps hands with each one to exchange yellow bills. The men grin, easily appeased, as happy with twenty-*peso* bills as our flesh.

Strong arms drop over our shoulders, something Tavo's never done. There's pressure and speed in his movement up the path. "Move fast. He'll remember soon that my parents are still in the Capital. I don't want you anywhere he can find you when that happens. Without that bridge, they know you've got no money and no protection."

The chilling words hurry my feet. While we walk, Olsen bites her nails off in long strands, an activity she's previously reserved for moments of quiet study and sleep.

Tavo turns us up a small, paved road with an electric gate. He pushes and tugs until the gate gives way. As soon as we're inside, he wraps a giant chain around the gate and snaps a padlock closed over top.

"Wait, Tavo. We can't be here alone—"

"Relax. Ydria should already be upstairs. I was waiting at her house. This is the safest place for you guys tonight. Tomorrow, we'll make a legit plan."

He leads us up a long set of stairs to the giant, modern home that looms over *Los Limones*. "We'll stay here, in the guest quarters. My mom protects the upstairs like it holds the bones of St. Peter. I don't even go up there when she's not home."

He flips on a light to illuminate pool tables, a sixty-inch flat screen TV, and a full kitchen. An ice-cold Coca-Cola finds its way to my hand. Everything hums and buzzes on generator power. The whole thing feels like I've stepped through a portal back to the States. No earthquake. No poverty. No bucket showers. No cockroaches. Everything exactly the way it was before I stepped on that plane.

I take a long swig of Coca-Cola and relax into fantasy. "Guess we know why Henri keeps you around, eh?"

"Sure. Yeah. Henri's real shallow like that. Doesn't explain you, though. Best you've got are wicker chairs and a pet gecko."

"Back off, man. Nobody mocks Max. I planned to catch him a nice, fat moth tonight to help him past the trauma. If he's alive."

I sink into a leather couch with reclining end-seats. Was this really what life was like? Clean and cool with no aches anywhere? "So why am I just learning about this piece of heaven? You're pretty selfish leaving us to rot in the streets when you've a sweet pad."

Tavo plops next to me on the couch. "I used to have the Elders over all the time. Ydria found out, though, and pitched a fit. Guess you're not allowed fun."

Olsen makes a small noise of approval where she sits at the bar. She's got wide-eyed doe look, caught in a moral quandary of safety versus obedience. I vote for safety. My obedience manifests in not asking for a movie. He has several I haven't seen and there are seven speakers placed around this room. The acoustics would be amazing.

The door opposite us opens. Liliana pokes her head in. A red Popsicle colors her mouth with each lick. "They're here, Mama."

Ydria pushes past her daughter. Olsen gets immediate attention. "Are you alright? I had the worst feeling when I got to the house, the worst. Were you in trouble?"

Truths and lies all collide together. I'm not sure where kindness lies. Tavo jumps in. "Yeah. Bad stuff out there, Ydria. Good thing your mama-radar never fails."

"Not my radar. The Spirit. While they're here, they should teach you about it."

"Catholics have the Holy Spirit, too, Yds."

Ydria dismisses him with a soft hiss. She demands the story, every detail, and twice. Then she clucks and paces while Tavo insists she calm down. "The only solution is to keep them off the street until the bridge is back."

"That could be months. Remember the last hurricane? Two months. We waited two months for the Capital to fix the road."

"I can't stay inside for two months." It's part-whine and part-reality. I'd rather face goons with guns than live prisoner in my own home. "I'm here to serve God. I can't do that locked inside a house."

"She's right, Yds. Servants gotta serve."

Ydria pushes Tavo's feet off the couch. "So what do you propose? That they get raped and killed on the streets of *Los Limones*?"

At that, Olsen makes a small, quiet squeak like a disheartened mouse about to let the cat have the kill shot. Ydria rushes over to hold her and stroke her hair. The two disappear into a bedroom and close the door.

"She's a bit fragile, isn't she?"

"I guess. She comes to life during discussions, then sinks back into... whatever that is. Being stuck in our house is probably the best thing that could happen to her. But it'll kill me."

"We kinda figured that. Henri bet you were already on the streets this morning. Looks like he wasn't wrong."

"Is he back, too?" I ask the question around the bottle to hide my emotions.

"Nah. He and Molli are on scholarship, so they had to report to uni this morning. I'll bet they close the place this semester, but until then, he's stuck. I'm under orders not to let you out of my sight until it's safe again. Henri practically shoved me onto the helicopter this afternoon, didn't care what I wanted." My heart warms at the image.

Liliana wiggles in to snuggle me on the chair. My arm slips around her small shoulders. She offers me a lick of her too-sugary treat and I take a bite instead. Liliana wrestles me when I demand more bites, both of us laughing as if the world didn't fall apart yesterday.

Tavo watches the whole exchange. "What's your story, Lewis? The real one? I've been trying to figure you out since we met. You've got all these parts: tough girl, nun, American princess, awkward geek. Are you worth all the trouble?" Tavo half-grins, his harsh words both a tease and a challenge.

Slow, purposeful truth winds its way free from self-importance. "Me personally? Probably not. I've got a badge on my chest that carries value. But we're all on a cheap exchange. One dress equal to another."

Maybe it's the earthquake or simply two bad nights' rest on cots at the church, but my limbs and brain hang like over-ripe melons at the ravine. At any moment, I'll drop to the bottom.

Tavo clicks his tongue in dismissal. "Nah. Nothing cheap about you, Lewis. Maybe you want comfy chairs and a nice bed—I'd be a liar if I said I preferred cots and dirt floors to my house—but you don't look down on us for being Dominicans. You're more than a badge. To us."

Liliana's black-lashed eyes hold all Seven Wonders of the World. "We love you." She tucks her head into the crook of my neck.

Ydria opens the door across the room. "Olsen is asleep. You should be, too. Tomorrow is soon enough to figure out the problems of the world."

A thick mattress drops me back into days of luxury and dreams of home. English words run through my brain in disorganized passages, and every dream ends in my mother's arms.

# Chapter 15

"Hey, Lewis, share that hammer." Blank reaches across the space atop a roof downtown. It's been a week since the earthquake. *Los Limones* is still in pieces. We're a few people with hammer, nails, stucco, and determination fighting back against Mother Earth.

Tavo or the Elders must be with us every minute outside the house. During the days, we burn through service hours in our yellow Mormon Helping Hands jackets. At night, the Elders hang with us until ten. Then Tavo and the male ward members stand guard all night against the men with guns that pace in front of our house, supposedly on a march about town. Our door gets extra special attention. Andres confronted the men about it and almost took a punch. So, for now, we are housebound twelve hours a day and never alone. But I'm here, with my hammer, doing good for at least a few hours each day.

The hammer changes hands. Bangs resume as Blank pounds a patch into place. I smooth stucco over a patch I hammered into place minutes ago. Available workers have tapered off as families begin the mourning rituals. *Los Limones* lost 123 of its thousand souls in the quake. The mass funeral will fall on the tenth day when the families can resume public appearances. Until then, we're down to ten of us, four of whom are missionaries.

Tavo swings behind me on a rope that lets him jump between buildings. He presses a water bottle to the burned skin on my neck. "You look like a papaya."

"Squishy and stinky like one, too." Three drops of water bead on my fingers after a quick swig. I let them fall onto the heated skin. The drops cool my neck, and I ignore the longing for more. Water has become a precious commodity. The days have turned hot and dry and the earth sucked the rivers dry, so buckets from the river require longer and longer walks.

Ydria rations smaller amounts each day. She put out one 32-ounce glass of treated water for each of us this morning.

We've given up all but the most crucial hygiene. The Dominicans bathe on their trips to the river. Our rules preclude public baths. Deodorant and perfumes cover the smell; nothing relieves the crawl of skin beneath dirt.

"You're pretty rank. Dad says the Red Cross water truck will be here tomorrow. If you don't get enough, then I'll make Ydria bring you up to the house."

It's nice but not possible. Tavo's mom has returned. An icy glare to cool my skin is the only service she'd do us. Tavo's dad is slightly more useful. He carries messages to the President on his frequent trips to the Capital. We get back the usual responses. Be safe. Be obedient. Get to work. With so little guidance, we guess at what's best. Be safe means trust the members' curfews and rules. Be obedient means read the Book of Mormon until my eyes bulge out. Get to work gives approval for me to be on a rooftop.

Blank scoots over to work by me once Tavo slides away. He's got missionary zeal written all over his desperate face. "We've need to get some real work done. Maybe we should team up and do some discussions. We're the last district to still be strictly on service hours."

The stucco fills my hands again. Goop oozes through my fingers. "Not like we can baptize anyone." Immersion requires water, that thing we don't have.

Olsen speaks from where she drags boards up with a rope. "Probably not, but spiritual comfort is as important as physical comfort. I would love to give a discussion or visit those in mourning." She broached this topic in the morning.

The stucco slides over boards and hardens immediately. Another hole patched. Real work getting done. The river people sleep exposed, their babies at the mercy of the elements. Tavo thinks we can rebuild ten huts before dark. Ten families served. But I've already lost the argument. Olsen and Blank chatter about which investigators to visit and how best to use our limited time. Monsen suggests we trade off areas every afternoon. Estimates of finding and discussion numbers jump into the fray. Baptism expectations follow closely behind.

Another plop of stucco obscures their ramblings. I'll miss my stucco. I'm good at stucco.

The afternoon morphs back into the regular day-to-day of mission service. Too many have re-entrenched into old beliefs. Daily visits to the cathedral increase contact with the Priest and comfort rituals of Catholicism. The *sancista* is busy, too, walking from home to home peddling candles and promises of prosperity. We trail behind, mopping up what crumbs don't gather on Catholic and mythological plates.

Blank grumbles about the frustrating afternoon as we trudge back up from the river. "See, this is what happens when we neglect the work. It's too easy here for people to shift their beliefs. Before the quake, we had two full lists. Now, we've only got the reformed town prostitute eager for baptism. And she can't get baptized without clearance from the mission president, thanks to that abortion. So, we've got no one we can baptize once the water turns back on."

"Maybe. Maybe not. I think we should talk to President about Celia. She's kinda impressive, Blank," Monsen says, distracted by a growing growl somewhere down the road.

The repetitive vibration reminds us of the earthquake. The guys glance at their feet, stable on the ground. I rub my arms. Olsen's teeth chatter despite the heat. We're all relieved when a helicopter with a large Red Cross appears. It flies over us and lands in the middle of town. Two pilots hop off and start to fill a large plastic tank on a truck.

Water. Blessed water.

As the pilot connects the hose, spray covers the people gathered around the truck. They spin and rejoice in the wave of cool salvation. Then they hold up buckets to catch water, hoping for ongoing relief from this community-wide thirst.

The plastic tank reaches the two-thirds mark, and the pilot disconnects the tube. Hundreds of people wait with buckets outstretched, but the pilot climbs aboard the craft and the truck moves away. Shouts overwhelm the noise of the truck, barely. The truck picks up speed as the helicopter prepares to take flight.

"No. That can't be it. That's not—that amount won't fill a single tank."

"It will. It'll fill the only tank that matters." Monsen looks up at Tavo's big house with its large water tank. A giant dust cloud obscures most of our view as the truck turns up the path. Sounds of protest break through the loud whir of the helicopter.

The helicopter reels and pitches five feet off the ground. Ten men have grabbed the hose to pry open the tank. The police shoot guns into the air and pull the men off one by one until the helicopter rises out of view.

Like a colony of fire ants, dozens more rush the truck on its slow progress up the hill. People swarm over the top and around the sides. Five men rock the tank from its moorings.

Olsen grabs my hand as the police rush at the crowd with guns level and at the ready. There are faces we know, faces we love, in the crosshairs of those guns.

The tank rocks back and forth and back and forth, and then it topples. The water spills over the people. Some catch it in buckets and run off back to their homes, but most of the water pours onto the ground. The thirsty, dusty, broken ground sucks up every drop.

Something grabs my heart and twists out a sob. The water is gone. The Red Cross passed us by. The bridge is out and we've no money, no power, and no water.

"We've only got twenty pounds of rice and about half that of beans to feed almost fifty people every day. There's no water. And look at the sky! Blue forever. Where will we get water? Where will we get food when the rice is gone?" I'm shrieking. Panicking. Insanely rocking and grasping at my own skin. This woman can't be me. I'm never hysterical.

Blank crosses his arms and stares at me. I'm sure he rolls his eyes, but I can't see much through the veil of tears. I'm shocked I can cry. I haven't peed since morning.

Monsen speaks, his eyes full of pity. Monsen has been a surprise. He's more like me than I thought. We like service. We dig in to service. So, I'm not surprised that he understands my shattered heart. "Take her home, Olsen. We could all use a break."

Olsen leads me up the mountain to our house. My knees draw up to my chest on my bed and I rock and imagine my own burial at the cathedral. Max turns his head left and right as I stroke one finger along his scaly spine. The tears dry up, though the rocking sobs continue until Ydria comes, summoned by the Elders, to tell me lies about safety and fairness and a God who won't forget us.

All of life's injustices roll into this one. Divorce. Earthquakes. Poverty. Then there's my dad's baby, the small thing that makes sobs erupt again. The injustice of a baby. In the divorce, my dad gave up custody to save himself three hundred dollars a month child support. Joe and I were bargaining chips. Mom wanted full custody. Dad wanted money. Joe and I were reduced to bylines in a contract. The people of *Los Limones* fare no better. They're dispensable. Like Joe and I to dad. The world is full of injustice.

It's dark when I venture outside my room to scavenge food. Ydria left me an almost-rotten banana, watery hot chocolate without cream and hard bolo bread. Inedible, except my rumbling stomach welcomes any food.

The light from Tavo's cell phone casts baleful shadows that contort his face into an overturned barrel of water. Ydria's cards sit on the ledge, a shame offering.

My heart carries the pain of the wronged. He's better than this, better than entitlement and injustice. I settle my hands on my hips and stare at him hard. "They're all thirsty. Everyone needed that water."

One arm rests on the large bars as he leans towards me. Apology etches deep lines in his face. "There's only so much water in those helicopters. We have the biggest storage tank."

"Oh, planning to share? Like you've shared the electricity? The money?"

Tavo looks at the ground. His mouth tightens. "That's not how things work here."

That's not an apology. He has no apology to give. Sometimes people suck, even nice ones like Tavo. That's all the explanation you ever get.

"I don't understand this. Not at all."

Tavo looks at me. He shrugs and there's a cruel certainty in his eyes. "You really think America is any better?"

"I don't know." But I pick up the cards and start to shuffle.

Tavo settles into the chair outside the patio bars. He straddles it to face me. The cards deal out for two-handed Pinochle. You can only play so much poker before you realize luck never lasts long. Life is a lot like Poker that way.

So, I shuffle and deal our way back into friendship. Amazing how anything you don't focus on fades in importance. The water is gone. Tavo is here. The day's stress turns to ash next to friendship's embers.

It's late when we pack everything away. "Who replaces you tonight?"

"You'll see. I wasn't sure I could convince you to stay out late enough. Good thing you can't resist a card game."

A low whistle emerges from somewhere in darkness. Three footsteps sound before candlelight catches on silver-brown curls, and firecrackers explode in my gut.

As if Henri isn't gift enough, God has granted me a miracle. My black violin case hangs at Henri's side. I stamp my feet like an eager kid on Christmas morning while I fumble at the lock. The gate swings open and I run to take the case from him and hold it in my hands, hefty and wonderful as ever.

"How... How did you...?" The case cracks open. The smooth brown wood and black strings. It's back. It's here. I never imagined, never even dared to hope.

Henri crouches with me, as goofy-grinning as I am. "I thought one hundred twenty-three people deserve a special farewell. The Priest agreed. He wants you to play at the mass."

"Then my dad made a call to the President to convince him. Pays to be rich sometimes." Tavo shrugs but his glance at me carries several layers of meaning.

If I weren't a missionary, I'd punch him in the gut for that one. But I am a servant of the Lord, and my hands are too busy stroking my beloved's maple belly. The guys clap hands in stupid ritual above me. The silly men know they've done well tonight.

# Chapter 16

I play all the time. Nonstop. I perform *Ave Maria* at the mass funeral. That's only the beginning, though. Ydria digs out a music book from some forgotten corner of the local school. As the weeks go by, our house becomes a gathering spot for locals to hear my rehearsals. I play everything I know, from religious music to the classics I've studied since I was four years old.

As days turn into weeks, my nightly rehearsals become a bit of a stress reliever for the whole town. The Elders set up some chairs across the street where five or ten people gather to hear me practice. They usually dissipate at dark, but, tonight, a small boy atop a donkey listens for forty-five minutes after everyone else leaves. He leans over the donkey's neck with eyes closed and taps the music out on the bridle. For a moment, I give him beauty and his weepy eyes give me hope.

Then I pack up my violin to join Olsen for evening scripture study. She's doing better, maybe. If we stay within the safety of the gospel, Olsen seems balanced. And Ydria presses anxiety meds on her at night. Once she pops one, she's out for twelve hours.

That's more a curse than a blessing for me. I'm bored and restless once she passes out. Unfortunately, entertainment waits for me on the porch every night.

The university closed due to a fundamental crack somewhere that caused a wall in the engineering building to fall down during a mild aftershock on the day classes resumed. The broken building means that Henri and Tavo are permanent fixtures in *Los Limones* for at least a month.

Every night, Henri comes for the midnight shift that the ward members were plenty happy to hand over to him. When Henri's voice weaves through the house to dismiss the first shift, my feet hit the floor.

The chair clangs against the bars. Henri sits facing the street, one of our funny customs to stay in line with the rules. We make minimal eye contact, and engage only in small talk about books, current events, gossip and food.

Most nights, our empty stomachs force a focus on food.

The last bag of rice lies crumpled and empty in a corner at the church. There's officially nothing left. The women will scavenge *cassava* and fruit from here out. Every three days, a few men make the long walk to a lake to bring back buckets of water. Sometimes, water flows through the river and the women and children join the march. But not often.

We write letters to the President explaining our situation, but they all sit on Elder Blanks' desk in the Elders' apartment. With the power off, we've no access to email or money. Tavo charges my cell phone every few days. The fickle service renders phones useless, though. Blank broke his phone in frustration after a call to the President dropped for the third time.

We're stuck up here. Even if the President is trying to reach us, he'd have to hike in and Henri told me that hike requires free-climbing over difficult terrain. There's no way he could bring in food or water or anything but his own body. Everything waits on the bridge.

Ydria tells me not to worry. God will provide. She has dozens of disaster stories: hurricanes, floods, fires. All of them ended with the Lord providing for the missionaries. Maybe the Lord will provide for us, but there are hundreds of people in this town without our blessed title. And little will be nothing in another few days.

Henri's thin t-shirt confirms my darkest thoughts. Thin muscle and sinew wrap harsh bones. He works too hard and eats too little. Most of his food goes to Issa and Liliana.

Each bone in his shoulder spurs my guilt until I can't stay silent. "I hate that they feed us first. We're a burden. On you. On the ward. There are children and Andres' mother to consider. The old and young won't last forever, Henri. You won't last forever."

"We're used to being hungry. We serve God by serving you."

Henri retreats deep into his brain. Muscles in his cheeks work a slow pattern. He's not like anyone else I knew here. Dominicans bathe in color every minute, full of noise and music and energy and nature's brilliance, but Henri is quiet and subdued like the tranquil blue sky. He carries too many burdens for someone our age, and I doubt anyone hears the thoughts bringing clouds to his sky. He has to talk to someone, even if that means we violate our small talk rule.

"What's bothering you tonight?"

The chair adjusts. Henri adds an inch of distance between us. "I called my dad today. I didn't know what else to do. We need food. Maybe he can help."

"Oh." A small, unimportant statement in response to a very important change. My worries add energy to the air. We don't need more bad news or bad people in this town.

"I'm to hike down to the crossroads to meet my dad. Tavo thinks he can drive me part of the way. That'll save a day's hike. I should be back in two days with real food, not rotten *cassavas* and sunbaked melons. Or at least money. Money would be okay, too."

"Oh. Okay." Stomach acid churns at the idea of Henri not being on my porch tomorrow.

We lapse into silence, both hungry and tired and me feeling stupidly girlish and weak. Not talking at all stops me from saying the things that make tears form in my eyes.

I should be in bed. I should always have been in bed. The sugarcane husk seat of the chair crackles when I stand.

Henri turns towards me in surprise, and then stands when he sees I've gone. I've never left so early. "Where are you going? This is the last night we've got, Lewis."

There are books of poetry written in his watery green eyes. I walk forward to read each word until I can curl into the space he covers outside the bars. This is why I can't open the gate and why he doesn't ask. The bars offer too little protection as is. I grasp them, grateful and not for my imprisonment. Henri's rough fingertips roll over my knuckles in slow and purposeful motion as he traces each fall and rise.

Body and Spirit go to battle at the simple touch. Yet, as always, the badge wins. Almost at the same time, our hands come off the bars and tuck inside our armpits. Tomorrow, he'll be gone. Someone else will stand outside the gate. Then, one day, the bridge will be back. There will be money and food and no reason Henri has to stand guard every night except that I want him there but wanting him makes me the worst sort of hypocrite.

"Good night, Henri. And good luck with your dad." He doesn't challenge my retreat this time. The mission rules have been drilled into both our heads since childhood. The reasons I'm here and who I serve hang heavy between us like meat on a slab at the market – necessary and foul. We need to stop killing each other a little every night.

Three days later, a dark cloud appears on the horizon that matches the one Ydria and I carry in our hearts at Henri's extended absence. The cloud is small at first, barely a bit of conversation starter for the young family we find near Paue crossing after an exhausting day building tin huts that left scorch marks on our hands and legs. Once again, I've thrown myself into the work to try and force my heart into the lockbox other missionaries carry so effortlessly.

The family agrees to read the Book of Mormon as the thunder rolls in. The single dark cloud blocks the sun and promises rain. Each clap summons watchers with water buckets piled on their heads and tucked under arms.

"You need to go, *hermanas*. This could be our only water for weeks." The mother pushes us out the door. Her children grab every bucket, pail and pot in the house.

Pain splits my side as we run up the hill to fetch our pails of water, a funny little reverse of Jack and Jill. My arm aches a bit, too. For the most part, it's healed. Or I hope it has. Without doctor intervention for weeks, I'm stuck with whatever scar or muscle damage is beneath the bandage Ydria still changes twice a week.

Our shampoo bottles sit beside the house door. Ydria shouts from where she and Tavo wrestle with the water bucket. "Go. Wash your hair. Find a gutter and scrub away those bugs." Lice and critters that flourish in poor hygiene have left bug bites all over our skin.

The air thickens as the cloud drops. Large drops plop on our backs and shoulders. Then the water falls in glorious sheets over our upturned faces. A true tropical downpour douses the town. For the first time since my arrival, no one runs from the rain. They set their buckets and dance to the rhythm of salvation. Mouths stay open to the sky to drink mana directly from heaven. We run to the gutters we recently installed on businesses around the park.

The water rushes off the beauty shop roof in a harsh, roaring flow. Laughs bubble up along with soap while our fine hair comes clean. We don't stop at our hair. Mango shampoo strips grime from our arms and legs. The townsfolk point and laugh, but nothing matters except feeling clean again. Then we dance, letting the water sop us to the bone. I whip my hair around in joyful wonder at this unexpected miracle.

Olsen comes out of the water a renewed woman. She chatters as she did at the MTC. Opinions emerge from behind the veil of anxiety and she offers them freely on our walk home. "I think we should focus on Celia. Sometimes I feel like Graciela only pretends at wanting baptism to make sure that Celia gets delayed. We need to focus on where the Spirit is strongest—"

A horn honks behind us. We've grown accustomed to walking in the streets, so we jump aside before either of us remembers we were on what remains of the sidewalk. Our own stupidity and the levity of the day sets us to laughing.

A loud whistle accompanies a second honk. This time, we look around. Henri emerges from a plum Plymouth. The people and street noise fade into a glittery black-and-white backdrop. He doesn't hide his excitement. I force every muscle in my own face to freeze.

He jogs to greet us while the low-riding car bounces around debris. "They've got the road rebuilt down to the bypass. We waited so that we could bring more supplies. It wasn't easy getting the car across the dry riverbed and it'll be impossible again with all this rain, but we have food. Plenty of food," he says with a smile broader than the riverbed.

Daylight places stones on my tongue. Olsen's bright and aware eyes scan over us and seem to read more than the nothing happening in this friendly exchange.

"Is that your father?" Friendly. I'm being friendly. Maybe a little weird, given the puzzled glances from Henri and Olsen at my bright tone and too-proper sentence construction.

"Yes. Would you care for an introduction?" He uses the formal you with an extra grin and wink at me when Olsen looks towards the car, but I look away. He can't do that. Not here, not on the street. He can't be anything to me on the street.

"Hey, all!" Celia shouts from across the street in her usual red bra and torn denim shorts. The discussion on modesty—all three discussions on modesty—have not taken root. Olsen bolts forward to greet Celia. She's made up her mind about Celia.

Henri waves, then turns back to me. "So, Olsen's a no on the introduction."

My laugh stays hidden behind the cheeks clasped between my teeth. The street has sprouted, and every tendril bears a dozen eyes. "I voted maybe, so…"

"You don't get to choose. Get it over with. You know how this goes. Smile a lot and let him talk. My muscles are stuck. I'll probably need weeks to get back to my usual serious scowl."

"Too bad. I like your smile." The confession slips out between anxieties. I'd shifted from worrying about the street to being terrified of the jerk dad. The resultant dead space undid two days' hard repentance. Both my lips clamp between my teeth. I can't be trusted.

"Then I'll try to smile more. Now come meet my dad so I can complain about him later."

The plum Plymouth burps and shudders to a stop beside us. The man who slides out looks more like Liliana than his twins. He's darker and stockier with bushy eyebrows. Henri's similarity to his father ends at the small dimple between the eyebrows. Luis' harsh lines come from scowling; Henri's from thinking.

"I'm Hermana Lewis. Nice to meet you."

"*Americana.*" He ignores my extended hand and my official title. To Henri, he says, "Go tell your mother I've arrived. Take the food so she starts dinner."

Henri throws a fifty-pound bag of rice over his shoulder and tucks a small bag of beans under an arm. "There's more for you. I'll bring it up later. And two bags for the church."

A yellow pinwheel spins in my low stomach when Henri stops and looks back at me before running towards his house. I lock down my reactions. No flinching is the standard untrustworthy parent protocol. I do know this drill. The less info your dad has, the less he can hurt you. I've not given my dad any real information in the seven years since he left, not even when I lived with him. He's on a strict need-to-know basis, and I've never found anything he needs to know. Luis has earned even less.

Luis regards me with equal distrust. "You're *muy poca cosa* for so much loyalty," Luis says. *Muy poca cosa.* A small thing. Nothing. A person of no consequence.

"Their loyalty is to God, not me."

Luis' chest rumbles on a deep laugh that adds no light to his expression. Hetty emerges in his smile. Mean and empty, dipped from the same genetic pot of inborn arrogance. The family toggles on this single characteristic: humble like Ydria or cruel like Luis.

"Spoiled American girls are my son's weakness. I like it as much as your daddy would like you slumming with black boys, right, Princess?"

As if my father or Luis gets any say in my choices. I'm not a spoiled American princess, and I'm not shopping for a husband of the island or continent variety. But all that falls under banned information. "I'm a missionary, Luis. I'd have thought Ydria educated you on our dos and don'ts."

Luis crosses his arms. We each offer and accept mutual disdain. "You're not his first *Americana.* Not his first anything."

Anger simmers on low near my base brain. The idea that Henri bubbled over with news that can't be news makes me want to be my nasty self. "That's not my business. Can I help you with something, Luis? Perhaps directions to the church to drop off that food?"

Luis ignores my kind offer. He slides back in the car and speaks through the open window. "You Americans change up every few months, right? When do you leave?"

"I'm sure I'm leaving soon. I was supposed to leave before the earthquake."

"Good. He goes to school. He has a future. He's a smart boy."

Pretense falls away. Henri needs school, and I'm no one worthy of the sacrifice. I'm a bad missionary and a waste of a woman. I won't cost Henri his potential. "I know. School means everything to him."

"Then think on this, *Americana*: religion doesn't pay for his life. I do."

The white flag waves above me. Full retreat. "Good to meet you, Luis. God bless for the food you brought."

Olsen gives me a puzzled look when I join her. I'm lost in a very surreal moment, barely verbal and worried over everything I've allowed to be true. I don't make sense to myself. Here in the light, with my secrets common knowledge, nothing fits. Misfit Lannie doesn't inspire romantic drama. I've had zero dates. Not one. Then something about long nights and waterfalls locked me in a fantasy. My reality has slipped away, and I've lost the mission dream where Misfit Lannie learns to be something useful. Olsen is still there, in our reality, but I can't connect to her. She's become a radio station out of reach. A sound that comes sometimes but then fades.

Maybe nothing is real. Oh, it would be nice if I had a reality where I'm on a lovely mission in Tulsa. Or a visitor's center at a temple. I spend all day clean and safe and fed. When I pinch my hurt arm, the fantasy world refuses to fade. I'm still standing on a rubble-filled street filled with threats while a short, angry man glares at me from a plum Plymouth.

# Chapter 17

As with any dream, once I notice the disreality, everything goes weird—an orange clown pops out of cupboards and you forget to wear pants. *Los Limones* is no different. My town transforms after Luis arrives. He seems to be everywhere—at Ydria's house, at the church, at our house to pay the new security guard he hired for us. Everywhere.

Ydria barely speaks except to yell. She forgot to change the dressing on my arm, so I pulled the bandage off for good. I kept messing with it anyway. I've developed a dozen nervous tics, including biting off my nails *à la* Olsen.

I haven't slept well since Henri left. The quilt haunts my nights. My dad pulls out the stitches as fast as I can insert them. Sometimes, Henri helps him. The quilt has grown to cover the earth. Miniature people replace the tacks, scissors and needles that scattered the top as I worked. When Lazy grabs a corner and shakes with all her might, the people fling into the air and scatter. I scream and search the floor and quilt top. The quilt comes apart as I look for them. Squares float above me like oversized snowflakes caught on a breath of wind. I catch them, but the people are gone. I'm alone—abandoned—atop a mound of fabric and unspooled yarn.

Last night, the dream got stuck in a loop. Ydria was on the quilt top. She dropped four times. Over and over and over. Her scream still echoes in my ears. In the light, my brain stays stuck. She's all I can think about. I mention her by accident in morning prayer. Then every work-related decision I make somehow crosses us by her house. I imagine unseen, dark fingers curled around the door. Black and ugly, so ugly I'm sick inside, but the sounds in the house are the ordinary din of a family. I try to move on, and then find I've circled right back to Ydria.

I can't stand all day staring at a door. Not today. Celia needs me.

We'll meet the Elders and Celia at Hetty's house. The President will come once the bridge opens, which should be next week. If everything stays on schedule, she'll be cleared by the end of the month. We knock the door on the precipice of a very big mission win.

The Elders and Olsen go full zealot and scare Celia to death with talk of perfect obedience and risk of hellfire. When I can't take the scary preacher act any longer, I retreat with Issa to the kitchen. I adore this baby. She walks and stomp-dances in time with the *merengue* music. Her adorable laugh lifts my sour mood and drives away images of Ydria.

A bump sounds at the wall behind me as I cuddle Issa to sleep.

Hetty leans against the doorframe. Her smile warms a little when she looks at Issa, though shades of Luis darken the edges. "Do you think she looks like her mom or her dad?"

Issa snores into the crook of my neck, her drool both disgusting and wonderful. "I don't know her dad."

"Sure you do. You've been cozy as anything with him for weeks. He and Celia have been off and on since we were all fourteen. Once she's baptized…Well, it's a world of possibilities."

The gut-punch finds that sweet spot that explodes pain and steals breath, but I learned to take a hit and recover well before I met Hetty. My smile is genuine. "They're a cute couple. I'd feel better if I knew she had a champion once Olsen and I are gone."

Hetty's eyes narrow. "You don't care?"

For once, Hetty isn't the only heartless one in the war of words. "I'm a missionary. Baptism is my game. Members answer to God for what they do afterward."

Celia squeals from the other room. She's thrown her arms around Elder Monsen whose face turns red.

"Back away from the Elders, Celia." My usual humor doesn't brighten the phrase. Despite my strength with Hetty, the world shakes like my quilt in my dreams.

Celia is unphased by the darkness in my tone. She merengues through the house. "Two weeks! They think I can be baptized in two weeks."

My lips press against Issa's fluffy black hair. In her perfect baby smell, I find my center. A baptized, not-prostitute mom and plenty to eat. Maybe even a good dad. That's a dream come true for this little one. That's what really matters here.

*Bachata* music pounds through the window slats. A familiar horn honks. Luis. Everywhere. He's everywhere. We grab our bags to leave.

But it's not Luis that honks. Outside the house, Henri rests against the stupid plum Plymouth on the other side of the street. I'm not excited to see him. Hetty's words froze anything that might have warmed to him.

Olsen grabs at my arm. "Do you think Henri'd give us a ride down to the river? I want to see the Moregas family before nightfall. Maybe Celia would come so we're not technically alone with a member of the opposite sex."

Henri reaches inside the car to honk the horn again and wave us over. My grandmother scolds me for looking. Any man that honks for you should get ignored by you. Good advice from a great woman. No rides. Not from Henri and not in that car. Not ever.

Celia shimmies towards the vehicle, aglow with her good news. She throws herself at Henri who laughs and hugs her. A very snuggly kind of hug.

"Want a ride?" Henri calls to me with the smile I once thought rare.

I stay rooted to my spot on the stoop. "I'd rather be bitten by a snake, thanks."

Henri's face settles back into the over-thinking grimace. He pushes off the car to jog over to me. "Where'd that come from?"

Hetty's accusations throw spears at the part of me that's way too aware of Henri. "Ask Hetty. I've got to go."

Olsen falls into step before I pass the liquor store. "We'll visit the Moregas tomorrow. I need to stop by Ydria's. Something's... wrong." The gnawing need has returned.

Olsen's sharp intake of breath is her only response. I pick up the pace. Inside me lives the strange, growling beast from Revelations. Its thousand eyes see everything, but the images bring confusion. My head swims a dark sea filled with something unseen that snaps and splashes.

And it speaks with either the devil's or God's voice, as large and powerful as anything I've ever experienced. *Go*, it whispers. *Go now.*

I bolt forward, dragging Olsen along at a near-run. We pass the fountain, wave at the old men playing chess and dominoes in the park. I refuse invitations for ice cream, for visits, for a moment of rest. No, I have to go. I have to stand in front of a green door for who knows what reason. The beast growls and yells louder and louder and I pick up my pace with each command. It doesn't quiet until I'm standing in front of Ydria's house with no idea what to do.

A hard thud tells me the house isn't empty. *Go*, the Spirit seems to scream.

Olsen follows me inside with ongoing protest about intruding. We cross the living area and head toward the courtyard. A strangled little sob grabs my attention. Liliana hovers behind a tree in the courtyard with both arms crossed over her face.

Olsen runs to her. She holds Liliana close. When Liliana lifts her eyes to meet mine, she points to the bedroom and whispers, "Mama."

The voice and gnawing need push me in the direction she points. Over my shoulder, I issue orders I hope will be obeyed. "Get Liliana away from here. Take her to our house."

They move toward the dirt path between the clustered houses. Both the fragile things need not to see whatever the beast intends because now it's angry. A burst of heat that rushes up my neck and inflames my temper.

The closed bedroom door seems to pulsate. It flies open when my palm touches it, as though the beast has given me his strength.

Luis stands over Ydria, hovered in a corner. Her hands bleed as they cover her head.

A shriek of rage unlike anything I've ever made, erupts from deep inside.

I rush at Luis and push him aside with the same force that bounced the doors off its hinges. He hits the wall with an oompf. My arms wrap around Ydria, and I lift my face to Luis. His fists form as his eyes flash.

The beast roars out my own mouth. "Do it. Hit me, too. Make me bleed, too."

"Hermana, no," Ydria whispers around a bloody lip.

"Hit me!" I scream.

But Luis turns and leaves without a word to me. His dismissal hurts worse than a hit. My screams could wake all the dead I've sung into the ground.

"Shh," Ydria whispers. "It's over now. It's okay." She wraps me in a safe cocoon while rage and tears and everything else subsides.

When I'm me again, I pull back to look at her. My beloved Ydria is deformed from swelling and blood. Bright red bruises surround broken skin. She flicks away bubbling blood from the crack in her lip with her tongue. "Ydria... your face... He should be in jail."

Ydria's face softens as much as it can. Her beautiful hands come up to cradle my face. I kiss both her palms and then the cuts on her hands. She must have fought back, of course she fought back.

The unbroken part of her mouth lifts into a grin. "You are a very foolish girl," Ydria whispers. "This isn't your fight. It's mine. You need to let me finish this."

"Let me help. There's nothing I wouldn't do for you, Ydria. Nothing."

"I know. You love us. We love you." Her eyes fade into a wistful resolve that forces her gaze to the wall. "I made a promise to God that night we met. I promised him I would walk away from this life if He sent you here. No more beatings, no more sleeping with a man I hate, no more of any of it. I knew if He heard my silly prayer to have the music I love so much... If He sent you to me... I knew that would mean He loved me enough to help me through what may kill me. Has almost killed me. But then you came, and Henri looked at you and... we all..." Ydria swallows and winces around an unseen pain. "We dreamed the wrong dream. And now I must keep my promise to God. Even if it kills me and breaks Henri's heart."

Ydria pushes up, hunched over and cradling an arm. She grabs two sheets of paper from the bed, official papers with the province seal. "Would it do any good to ask you to stay inside this room while I handle this?"

"None at all. If he kills you, he kills me, too."

Ydria drops her hand to my head for a moment. "My beautiful, foolish girl." Then she turns and walks as fast as her broken body allows.

Luis tips back a beer in the kitchen. Beer bottles are strewn about the floor of Ydria's usually-pristine kitchen. He doesn't look at us, not even a nod. The beast inside me growls again.

"You forgot to sign these papers," Ydria says, strong and resolute.

Luis looks at her. He's all smiles now, like I'll forget why Ydria bleeds. "I said we'll talk about it tomorrow, Yds. Why don't you go to the house and rest?"

"This is my mother's house. You're the one who's leaving. Forever." She places the papers on the counter. They shake and wiggle like a bag of snakes, the only sign of her fear.

Luis doesn't look, but I do. A bill of divorcement. And a birth declaration for Liliana that only bears Ydria's name as parent.

Luis tips the bottle three or four times. For all I complain about my dad, I've never known violence. I don't know how to interpret the silence or the growing darkness in his eyes. The bottle threatens me, the way he wields it in two fingers, as though he's mastered both the beverage and the weapon.

Finally, he speaks. "Where are you going to get the money to file those documents? *Americana* paying for that?"

My mouth opens to tell him I'd pay any price to be rid of him. Ydria beats me to the words, though. "I have it. I've saved for it since the day you brought Liliana into this house. And now I want to be free."

My calling to *Los Limones* finds its purpose. I'm here to be Ydria's strength and her salvation, a living symbol of Christ. This is why the President had his dream. This is why I'm here.

I lift the pen toward Luis. "You're going to sign it. And I'm going to witness. Or you can beat us to death and answer to the authorities as to why an American princess lies dead among your beer bottles. If you think my parents would stop before you spent every day of the rest of your life in jail, then you don't know American royalty beyond the catchphrase."

Ydria moves the papers closer to him. "I said it earlier. Either kill me or sign it. But we're done. Forever."

Luis' eyes show that he's still contemplating the first choice. But he shrugs. He signs the birth declaration.

"What do I need with another girl?" he mumbles.

"And the other one," I say the moment he lifts the pen. I won't leave Ydria in this mess of a marriage. Not for one more minute. Like her, I'd rather die.

The Plymouth burps outside. Henri. Luis catches my eye with a strange smile, like he's won the game, the same smile Hetty gives when she thinks she's outsmarted me. "Maybe religion will get you another son, Ydria. The one you've had leaves with me tomorrow."

Ydria pushes the other paper. "He's a man now. He'll have to make his own choices. This... This is my choice."

Luis' smile deepens and grows crueler. I don't really know what we're bargaining over. I'm treading water in cultural depths no MTC ever prepares you to navigate.

Luis signs the paper at the sound of footfalls on the porch. He shoves it at Ydria. "I'll go tell him the good news. Have him packed and ready to go by sunrise." Luis turns and walks out the door. We hear the footfalls retreat from the porch. Ydria wails like someone's died, then gulps around the sound. It stays, though, rumbling in her chest. Silenced, but not silent.

I don't know what's been gained or lost—did we win? Or did we fail? I hold Ydria and let her sob on my chest.

Nothing makes sense. Everything is nonsense once you realize the dream is only a dream.

When the world fails me, music always makes sense. So, I rub Ydria's back and hum. When there's a break in her wailing, I whisper, "The Priest had a copy of the *Verdi Requiem*. I was going to surprise you with it tomorrow."

Ydria pulls in a tortured breath. "Maybe you could play for me tomorrow."

"No, tonight." I'm worried Luis will return. "You have to come with me, Ydria."

I pick up a cloth from the sink to blot the blood from her face. In the distance, the plum Plymouth roars back to life and squeals away.

The front door bangs off its frame and rattles the fragile wood slats on the front window. Henri stands in the doorway, his face an odd mixture of emotions. "Mama! What have you done? You must go. We have to fix this." He sees me and his expression changes again. "Why is Lewis here? How long has she been here?"

Rage erupts again. The beast squawks out an angry shout of rebellion. The rag flies at Henri and makes contact, splatting against his face, covered in his mother's blood.

"What will you buy with your thirty pieces of silver? How much of your mother are you willing to sell to keep yourself comfortable?"

Then I rush at him, all rage and no thought. Another man who betrayed me, only I'm no child this time. I've faced the devil more than once, and I've plenty of fight left. This isn't the beast. This rage is mine, all mine. I've hated my father for years. Now I add Henri to the list.

Henri holds my shoulders to keep me at bay. His eyes stay on Ydria. He's perfectly still, except his fingers dig into my shoulders. Then he pushes me aside to run from the house, leaving me to press hands into my thighs and heave giant, gasping breaths that want to be sobs.

Ydria links her arm through mine, a rag pressed to her eye. "Maybe I'd like to hear that requiem. If I lean on you, I think I can make it up the hill."

Yes, we need to try. We trudge up the half-mile to our house, one painful step at a time.

Tavo is closing his gate as we pass. Ydria tugs us towards the shadows. "No, Ydria. I need to talk to him."

Tavo grins and jogs towards us at my whistle. Ydria hides her face in shadow, but the reality registers on Tavo's face. "Guess that's why I got a panicked call from Henri a few minutes ago. I'm supposed to meet him at the bar where Hetty works. I figured Luis was involved."

My lip chews inside my teeth. So many things cascade through memory. They seem to circle around the water truck like the angry villagers. I don't understand how everyone can know about Luis and be so accepting. I don't understand how Tavo can have so much and be content that his best friend has so little. The culture feels foreign to me, more foreign than it did on my first day outside the mission training center.

Ydria raises her face to Tavo. "You have to convince him not to take Henri out of school. He can't make him quit. He'll try to make him quit."

Tavo rubs Ydria's arms. "Don't worry a minute, Yds. Luis likes me, right? Two beers and I'll have Luis convinced. Henri's not going anywhere."

Two tears squeeze out of Ydria's swollen eye to run into the crack in her cheek. Tavo kisses her forehead.

I chase after him as he walks away. "Tavo, wait."

He turns to me. I don't even know what I'm asking, maybe it's laughable. "Remember the truck? The water truck?"

"Yeah. I remember you spitting fire at me for two hours over it."

"So, make it better. Right here. Now. Make this be okay. Don't be the rich guy that can't get through the eye of the needle. You're too good for that."

Tavo kisses both my cheeks, which earns a sharp hiss from Ydria that comes out more like a two-year-old's slobbery raspberry. Tavo and I laugh, a little.

"I got this, Lewis. Have I let you down yet?" Then he jogs off.

My shoulder hitches up under Ydria's arm. She wilts against me. "I don't understand any of this, Ydria. Not a bit of it."

"Good. I pray you never do. Now get me somewhere I can sit down."

# Chapter 18

Later that night, the first and second hiss at our door go unheeded. I'm too familiar with footfalls and change of guard not to recognize Henri. But if you ignore something, it's supposed to go away, so I ignore him and wait in the dark.

Olsen stirs, wide-eyed and worried. middle-of-the-night visitors aren't common to her, at least, not the corporeal kind. Her chatty sleep indicates she's got an active dream social life.

"It's nothing to worry about," I whisper. "Go back to sleep."

She nods, then rolls to her back. Neither of us can find sleep. I didn't even bother to undress. I've laid on my bed, clothed, after hours of confessions.

There have been lectures—too many lectures—from Olsen as I sobbed my heart into the pillow and told her all the things she missed in her month-long blackout. Olsen is terrified Luis will come for us all. She's terrified of all the truths of her life, I think.

The third hiss startles us both. Henri speaks my name through the slats in our bedroom window. My real name. I don't know when he learned it. Lannie, he whispers again. Intimacy breaks against the wall of rage. He has no right to my name.

"Go away," I say from my cot. "It's late and creepy that you're staring in our window in the dead of night."

"I'll go away when you talk to me. And hurry or we'll wake Olsen and my mom."

"Too late," Olsen says.

Henri's dead silence is comical, as though we can erase a month's worth of sins through pretense. Olsen inclines her head toward the door, granting permission for a final audience. The whites of her eyes in the candlelight remind me we will be watched and judged for every word.

My *chancletas* slap against concrete along a hallway that was once too long and now too short. The door post before I enter the moonlit porch invites me to pause for prayer. Only God knows what's coming and how I should react.

Then the door slides away. Henri stands there, same as before, with his usual insecure grin and hands in his pockets, as though he vanquished his evil twin a few hours earlier. Now he's my Henri again. The rage I want fades into the love I feel. Neither emotion feels right, though—too much like putting on dirty clothes after a hot shower.

I ignore my usual chair and instead lean against the door, the most space I can insert between us without retreating into the house. Henri leans against the fence. The crease between his eyes deepens. He looks ready to speak several times but chooses silence.

"You're unbelievable," I say first. The black badge cuts into my arm as my arms cross hard over my chest.

"Stop. Lannie. Stop. I don't get you today. My stupid head won't make sense of anything that's happened. And you've got my mom here? Because... Because she's not safe with me? Is that where you've gone in that brain of yours?"

Me. He thinks this is on me? My arms wrap tighter. Truly bizarro world. I rescue his mom and he shows up without an apology and expects me to explain myself.

Henri pushes up against the gate, trying to erase more distance. "I talked to Hetty. She told me what she said. But think, won't you? If I were Issa's father, wouldn't I claim her? How can you think my mom and I would leave a child to die if it was our own? We took in Liliana! But I'm a Dominican, right, so I've got to have a bundle of ignored babies? I thought you weren't like that, Lannie."

My arms shift lower to wrap my belly. The window slats cut into my back as I rock back and forth. That piece of today does make me feel foolish, but it doesn't forgive the rest.

He continues without response. "No. I wouldn't. That's the answer. It was Hetty's stupid way of finding out if you cared about me. She watches too many *telenovelas* and has serious communication issues, in case you haven't noticed. And then you call me Judas, like I'm okay with my mom getting hurt? We've been trying so hard to get my dad out of town by playing perfect, trying to keep Mama safe. Hetty asked Mama to come to her place while I was gone, but she said Mama insisted she had errands. Hetty and I didn't realize she was going to ask for a divorce. I wouldn't have let her alone for a minute if she'd told us her plans. How could you believe that I would let him hurt her? As a kid, I had no choice, but now—she's my mom, Lannie. The most important person ever to me. You know me. I thought you knew me."

Henri rubs the back of his neck, sighs and rocks back on his heels. "My dad—and Tavo, even—say this is part of the American Princess act. You come. You flirt. Then it's time to leave, and you can't have anything real with a Dominican, but you can't admit you'd rather be with someone like Blank than a black man, so you come up with reasons we're not good enough."

At this, I interject. "Wait. Let's be clear about something. I'd rather play Russian roulette with a firing squad than be with Blank." His truths stripped me bare. Humor is all I have left.

"Don't make me laugh, Lannie. I don't want to laugh. I want you to tell me the truth to my face. I can't follow your good example and slink off on assumption."

"Hey! Don't diss my methods. My assumptions were fueling a clean getaway until you blew up my self-righteousness with reality bombs."

This apology is all mine to give. He's been honest with everyone while I've hidden us in corners and pretended at being two different people at once. I deserve every accusation and more. The things he says—my own behavior condemns me, even if they weren't what I meant at all. I take the two steps forward, though I keep my hands at my sides. "This isn't me making a racist getaway. My daddy issues did the *merengue* all over a situation I didn't understand."

"You can't judge everybody based on what he did."

"I know. I was wrong. And I'm sorry."

"Lannie—"

"But you've got to stop that. That's not my name." My fingers brush against my black badge, and then I tap it twice. Henri grimaces and looks away.

"Could you take that off tonight? I have to say things and I can't with that badge—"

"No, I can't. There are lines, firm ones. You can't say things at all."

"Lannie, please," he begs on a half-breath,

"That's not my name." My voice swells. "I'm Hermana Lewis and I belong to Christ. It's on my badge. I won't fail Him. There's no one I love like Him."

It's the first moment I know the truth of what I've said. Even as Henri's eyes squint and he looks away to hide pain written all over every feature, I know my choice: as much as I want Henri, I want my mission more.

And my mission is to help others come to Christ. A flashlight seems to turn on at my heart center. "But I want to help you. Do you have to go with your dad?"

"Tavo talked him out of pulling the money for school, but I'm tired of being his puppet, too. I want out of all of this, but if I don't finish school, what hope do any of us have if I can't finish school? Mama needs money for Liliana's tuition. Hetty has the baby now. I have to finish school and get us all out."

"Maybe the church can help. We can talk to Andres tomorrow. He'll have some ideas."

"Andres isn't always nice to me. I'm supposed to serve a mission and marry Molli. The mission thing isn't possible because Mama and Liliana need the money my dad sends me, and Molli is okay, but she's not what I want." Henri looks at me too intensely.

The firecracker fuses ignite, but I douse them with holy water. "We'll try to keep arranged marriage off the table. The mission, though? Missions are never a bad idea."

Henri's eyes fade. He shakes his head and looks back down the road toward his mother's house. "You really don't know anything about being poor, do you?"

No, I don't, but I've learned for myself why missionaries should be in bed all night. "Turns out, I don't know a thing about a thing. I'll see you at church tomorrow."

"Good night, Hermana Lewis." His voice sounds resigned.

I don't turn to look at him. My silly girl brain constructs a half dozen ends to this conversation that have nothing to do with church and missions while my heart shatters. I glide past Olsen and barely hear her praise for my heroic—and possibly stupid—sacrifice.

The Lord is as good as His word. Once my duty to Ydria was complete, my transfer was certain. The bridge opened on Tuesday, a miracle just in time for transfers. My name was the first announced. I'm Capitol-bound, as promised six weeks ago. I've been in *Los Limones* for five transfers, almost half my mission. My heart hurts as much as it did the last time I hugged my mom.

Over the past five days, I've asked—no, begged—to know the fallout from Luis. Tavo tells me everything is fine. Ydria is silent except for pithy, meaningless phrases intended to make me focus on missionary work. Henri avoids eye contact and conversation. I feel shut out.

I am shut out. Another *hermana* in a string of *hermanas*. No different from the rest, no better than the next. Maybe even a little worse. I doubt it will take long for the memory of Hermana Lewis to fade into a really great story about a runaway goat.

I wipe off the tear that falls from my nose. My tiny town glitters beneath the chapel porch while the farewell party for Blank and I rages inside.

I voted for a quiet slip out of town, but Ydria refused. "You need to say goodbye."

But I don't want to say goodbye. I want to stay in *Los Limones* forever.

The door behind me opens and closes. I don't turn around. The smell of soap and musk announces that Henri has decided not to avoid me tonight.

Cold metal touches my chest, and then very warm fingers touch the skin at the back of my neck. His fingers against the side of my neck carry a dozen storm clouds. His voice rolls soft and low like thunder on the horizon.

"Could you hold onto this for me? Until we see each other again?"

Again. Will there be an again? No, there probably won't be. This is life, not a romance novel. There aren't love letters and longing looks and feelings that never fade. Reality says he moves on. He forgets me. I'm forgettable.

But even my inner cynic can't deny the gesture. My fingers twirl the two tiny silver hearts linked together on the pendant. "I can hold onto it forever."

My fist closes over the pendant. This is what I have. This little bit of love that hangs about my neck. It's all I get in exchange for making the choice my father didn't make. I'm walking away. I'm saying no. I lock my knees and force my posture to stay straight and strong.

Henri presses his forehead to my hair. "Goodbye, Hermana Lewis. Don't forget us." His fingers disappear, pulling back the storm and leaving winter's chill.

My arms wrap my middle to try and find warmth in the lonely heat of a tropical spring. Two tears squeeze out the corners of my eyes. Even though it hurts so deep my toes ache and my guts seize up and every cell screams for the storms to come back and quench the frozen thirst that's killing me, there's an odd pride. My father's long-winded speeches about love's immortal power have a counterpoint that includes a different kind of happy ending. Henri will have a future; one built on his own abilities, not my citizenship. He'll marry a Dominican woman and two lives will be made better. This, Dad. This is what sacrifice does. It exchanges pain for salvation. And though I stand on a patio and cry, I know there will be joy.

Celia knocks on the door post unknown moments later. The tears have mostly dried, though a few cling to my eyelashes. It's easy to compose myself and turn to greet her.

Issa babbles in her arms, dressed in red silk and white lace. The dress drowns the skinny little girl. "Oh, you beautiful thing. Get over here. I need one more snuggle."

Issa clings to me. She presses messy baby kisses to my neck. She's so much stronger. I can barely see the starved creature inside the puffy baby. Celia has weaned her to fruit, rice gruel and goat's milk, a sustainable food supply.

Celia watches us cuddle and play. "She loves you like you're her mama."

"Ah, we're friends. She's an old soul that remembers me from the pre-existence." Issa squeezes my cheeks together and kisses me on the mouth. Frenches me, practically. Celia and I can't stop laughing, which makes Issa's advances more ardent.

"Probably not the passionate kiss you expected tonight, was it?"

Baby slobber clings to the sides of my mouth. I rake at it with a nail, but the sticky residue remains. "Baby kisses are the best kisses. Only ones I ever need."

Issa wiggles until I put her down. Then she toddles off to stare at flowers. She's too perfect, too precious.

Celia slips her hand in mine, her eyes also on Issa who puzzles over a white moth. "Take her to the States. Make her your baby with Henri so she stays alive."

"She'll be okay. I've told them to keep taking you rice. But please be calm with them. Go to church. And no sex. They need to see you trying."

"It's not about food. It's about what's right. She'll end up like me if she stays here. But you and Henri can educate her. She'll have a good life."

"Celia, Henri and I are friends—"

Celia sucks in a half-kilo of pre-tears snot. The sound counteracts a laugh to make a goopy guffaw. "Why do you even try to lie? You suck at it almost as bad as Henri. He tells me the same lie. I've known him since I was six and I've never seen him such a hot mess over a girl. First, he couldn't talk around you. Then he couldn't shut up. Now he's silent and handing out jewelry. That's love. He loves you. And you almost crawl out of your skin to hand him your heart whenever he looks this way. You're not dumb enough to let that go. You'll get married and then you can take Issa. Give her the life I can't."

No, I can't hear this. I'm too young and a missionary, and true love is a concept invented to sell Disney merchandise. "Babies need their mamas, Celia. You'll find a way to care for her. She'll get her education and she'll be loved by the person she loves most."

Tears flood Celia's eyes. "Why do you have to go? I can't do this without you. Can you come back? For the baptism?"

"I'll try. Sometimes the president grants permission. Ask him when he comes." Our hands squeeze together tightly.

"I'll beg. You need to be there. This wouldn't have happened without you."

"Please be good, Celia. God saved Issa—"

"I know. And he sent you. But you better come back and check on me. I'm a mess. If you don't come—"

Tears take turns sliding off our noses as we sniffle through our final goodbyes. Issa pats our legs while Celia and I cling together and cry until the Bishop calls me in for cake.

The ward members sing *God Be with you 'til We Meet Again*. They're a small portion of the crowd. The farewell party churns up people from every corner. Families with whom I've mourned or for whom I built houses. The Priest sits regally in the back corner with the *sancista*. Ydria baked three cakes and all disappear in the breadth of a sigh.

As the dancing starts, I'm pulled into a sea of well-wishes for the better part of an hour. The crowd dwindles until only Ydria, Tavo, Henri, the Elders and a handful of ward members remain. I lean against the door to watch this last faithful wave prepare to see me away.

Henri dances with his mom, but our eyes stay on each other over her back. His are red-rimmed. Celia's words repeat and then are dismissed.

Blank comes to stand by me. His eyes watch Henri watching me.

"You know, I had hopes for you. I knew you sucked at missionary work, but I thought your head was somewhere in the game. If people find out about all this, the missionaries might eat you alive like those mutts in *Hunger Games*."

He shoves his whole piece of cake in his mouth and walks away to talk to Andres. For a while, I thought Blank and I might come to some sort of understanding, but that one night under the stars after the earthquake got washed away in the rain, I guess.

An hour later, only Ydria, Henri, Olsen and I remain. Ydria stands in the kitchen, doing dishes in her white Keds. I wrap my arms around her middle. Her arms cross mine. Her head collapses to my shoulder as her own shoulders shake. But it's Henri's periodic sniffles that break my heart.

# Part 3: Macoris

*O thou afflicted with tempest, and not comforted. Behold, I will lay thy stones with fair colours, and lay thy foundations with sapphires.*
—Isaiah 54:11

# Chapter 19

My hair could burst into flame at any minute and no one would notice. Passersby float by me and each other, barely coexisting in the impersonal city, while I wait on a breeze to cool me after the long drive to this gleaming pink church.

Luggage piles high in the cultural hall amidst loosely organized chaos. Elders and sisters mill about, discussing assignments and catching up on gossip. Each sound is amplified by the wood floors and vaulted ceilings. My ears can't adjust to all the noise. I haven't had to process this much aural stimulation in months.

An Elder I've never met shakes my hand. "Hey, welcome to the Capital. You'll meet your companion inside. Everyone sits together based on area. Just tell me where you're going, and I'll point the way."

"Calista Ward? I think. I only heard it once. I'm Hermana Lewis. From *Los Limones*." My throat is thick, parched. I glance about for any sign of water while the elder rustles some papers, but there's nothing. I return to awkwardly staring and waiting.

Finally, the elder points to where the female missionaries sit in the back rows. "That's Hermana Barrera with the black leather bag and sunglasses. You're in for a great month."

Hermana Barrera, my new companion, reclines in her chair with sunglasses perched on her head and her arm slung over the back of the chairs. "*Hola, campesina*," she greets me without standing, referring to the fact that I've only ever served outside the Capital—in the *campo*, the rural areas.

I'm not sure what to say after I shake her hand. Barrera is serious business, per Schulz and Elder Blank. Her name is always at the top of any leadership board. She studied management at the university and applies what she learned to the art of mission service. She's also a hard-core *capitaleña*—she'll never serve more than twenty miles from city center. Some Dominicans get that privilege. Usually, it's because they have extended family in the *campo*, but rumor informs me that Barrera is a straightforward snob. In her first mission area, she was so condescending to the less-affluent members that the stake president requested she transfer back to the city. Her current baptism numbers make up for any inconvenience her prejudice may cause the Mission President.

Barrera rambles off lists and numbers and names and none of it sticks in my head until she says, "We'll have to cancel our appointments tonight. President wants to talk to you."

"With me, why?"

Hermana Barrera wrinkles her nose at me. "You think he goes over his agenda with me? President says stay and we stay. That's all I need to know." She turns away to talk to another Dominican sister on her right about possible splits next week and whether we can share a baptism date with her investigator. I sit on her left, speechless and sick. The lights and heat hurt my head, and I'm queasy from the drive. I wish I'd accepted Ydria's offer to pack me a lunch.

An odd buzz starts at the front of the chapel where two elders pass out flyers. As the papers move through, there's silence followed by a ripple of laughter, and then heads turn toward our area of the chapel.

Barrera notes the change in the room. "What's got them all talking?"

The sister to her left leans forward and squints. Then she shrugs and sits back. "Guess they finally made a decent Care and Feeding manual. I never find them even a bit funny."

To me, Barrera explains, "Office Elders have too much time on their hands. They've created a mission comic, a complete waste of time and resources. I wish the President would shut it down, but he says the boys need to play sometimes."

The fliers have reached the first row of sisters. Laughter turns to groans. An American sister shouts over the din. "The Care and Feeding of Sisters? This is a new low, Elder Pace!"

Elder Pace, long-term Assistant to the President, gives a thumbs-up. He stands next to Elder Blank, his new companion. Mission leadership makes no sense sometimes. Maybe this is a case of the President wanting Blank close to keep an eye on him.

Groans turn to chaos as sisters begin to read the pamphlet. The office sisters grab ten or fifteen folded pamphlets to shove under their seats, but the Elders boo the reduced circulation. The sisters give in and resume passing the sheets.

Barrera leans forward to peer over the shoulder of one of the sisters who got a copy. Then she pulls her whole chair forward for a better look. "What's that?"

Barrera grabs the pamphlet to shove it at me. "What's this?" she practically screams.

That embarrassing photo from Blank's mission yearbook appears on the front page, copied in full color. That skin-tight shirt and pin-up pose. The stupid blown kiss. I want to run away, to hide in the bathroom like a middle school girl afraid to walk by the cool kids' table.

"I…" I can't come up with an explanation on the fly. My mom and Ydria would tell me not to engage the rhetoric. They'd tell me to have grace and compassion and permanent red spots on my knees from hours of prayer—that's how women of God manage a blow to the ego. I've never felt less able to take their good advice. The most I can manage is to sit still while others gossip and laugh.

A door opens and the whole room falls silent, saving me from Barrera's interrogation. The President walks to the front with his wife on his arm. He pauses before the pulpit, his eyes on one of the comics. Then he whispers at Elder Pace who nods once. The office Elders shove the comics aside. Everyone else in the room follows their lead as the President moves to the pulpit to begin the transfer meeting.

I survive the first and second hour of migraine coupled with a dose of humiliation. Not that I hear anything. I do a pretty good impression of a living chair. Back straight. Eyes forward. Every muscle tenses. At each break, eyes and whispers follow me. The hours tick by in slow, successive, torturing twists of self-loathing.

As soon as the meeting ends, Barrera points me towards the Bishop's office where the President stands with crossed arms. That lamb to the slaughter doesn't feel so proverbial as I walk toward the office. The President holds the door open until I pass in front of him. Then he pushes the door closed—a reverent slam, if such a thing is possible.

He perches on the desk and then temples his fingers so tightly that the pads turn white. His eyes close while the red in his neck slowly fades back to his usual perfect tan.

"This can't have been an easy day for you," he says, his eyes still closed.

Tears prick my eyes. "I hate that stupid photo. It was just a joke."

The President waits until I fall silent. "Did you know the missionary dress code when you selected that outfit?"

"It's not... I didn't choose it. My clothes were ruined, and our investigator gave me..." I gulp around my shame. If only I'd never accepted that sweater. Why do I do such stupid things? But, grace. Accept responsibility with grace. "Yes, I know the rules. I should've stayed in the ruined clothes rather than walked around town dressed like that."

"Those aren't the only rules you supposedly broke. Elder Blank tells me there was a young man." The President sighs when I whimper. "I had hoped the hospital was a turning point for you. I admit I'm disappointed." The word raps the gavel that declares my judgment.

My voice squeaks around a widening lump. "I'm sorry." I've shrunk smaller than a cockroach and silent as one, too.

The President stares at me. Then he sighs and rubs his eyes. "Where was your *mamita* in all this? It was her son, yes?"

My head shakes wildly to deny every word he says. God may thrust down the liar, but I'd rather roast in brimstone than let Ydria be fired. I swallow my pride and hope three half-truths don't make a lie. "Elder Blank is right. I wore that shirt and I flirted, and I broke rules, but it's all on me. Ydria wasn't aware of anything. She's the best *mamita* on the island and she loves the Lord and the missionaries. She wouldn't have let anything happen."

The President nods. His eyes soften a little. "The Elders definitely went too far with this joke. I've told them to collect every single pamphlet and see them destroyed. But what's done is done. I can't stop what people say. The best way to avoid gossip, Hermana, is not to do anything worth gossiping about. If you'd been following the rules, this wouldn't have happened."

I can tell he wants all of this to make me feel better but throwing a bunch of papers in the trash seems like very little punishment. Still, it won't help me to quibble with the terms. I nod and hope I look deeply penitent.

The President looks past me toward the painting of the Savior on the wall before he speaks again. "There's a quote I like from a movie. *A Man for All Seasons.* Do you know it?" He moves on without my response. "Thomas More is on trial and he says this to a man who betrays him, and it's really quite profound. *It profiteth not a man to gain the whole world, and lose his own soul, but for Wales?* I want you to think about that. Have you lost your own soul? For Wales?"

I have no idea what he's talking about. I wouldn't know the reference except Thomas More is on Henri's list of people he wants to meet in heaven and one night he went on for a half hour about this story. But what does it have to do with me? Are Ydria and Henri the worthless Wales? If Ydria and Henri are Wales, then I would give up my own soul. I'd give up everything I have and more to see them happy.

The President leans forward to force me to look in his eyes. "And that begs another question. Who is Hermana Lewis here to serve? I can't answer that question for you. Only you and the Savior will know for certain." He pushes up and walks to the door before adding the last, more to himself than to me. "The gossip will blow over. It always does."

The President is wrong. Gossip lasts an entire mission lifetime. I've passed along enough of it to know. But I let the door open and close with no resistance from me.

My fingers stumble on the clasp of the two-hearts necklace the moment the door closes. I never should have worn it. Blank might know, might think he knows, where I got it. When the chain comes free, I shove it in my bag. If the President had taken it—my breath turns shallow and nostrils flare. I can't lose my necklace. It's all I'll ever have.

In the courtyard, Hermana Barrera flits and flails in frustration. Her rant becomes audible as I step outside. "But I'm in the lead in the competition for discussions. Can't someone else rehabilitate his fallen starlet?"

She's hissed into silence by one of our other housemates. Barrera drops the sunglasses onto her nose and motions toward the car. "Let's go. We'll do everything by the book because the book brings results."

The fire of lashing tongues and burning sun beat on me. It's hot in the Capital. Hellishly hot. I float along the river Styx as other souls pass around and in front of me, trapped in purgatory with their outcast sister.

The river Styx is predictable in its excruciatingly slow turns. Sadness and loneliness inundate each day and soak my nights, too. Sleep brings nothing but nightmares. Mostly about my quilt. I've shrunk to become the needle, pulling through the fabric on endless repeat. Now, when the dog shakes the corner, I fly through darkness, the thread snapping behind me. Then I drop and drop until the hardwood floor in the living room slams into my metallic face. I wake shell-shocked, surprised by my own intact state.

During the day, Barrera drags me all over the city to meet dozens of *Capitaleñas* with their loud cars and filled pantries and lack of caring for the poverty in *Los Limones*. I hate them for every bite of food they press on me. Barrera insists that I wear upscale clothing and cake my face in makeup to impress them. The weight tears at me, riveting my feet into the ground.

Yet my silk-ensconced shoulder is at the wheel. I push along. Slowly.

I thought I'd done something fantastic and faithful when I left *Los Limones*, but I hadn't. I convinced myself that a small show of loyalty meant I'd overcome some great weakness. How pathetic. I miss Ydria. I long for Henri.

I am *tigra*—a tiger, a word for a fallen, rebellious missionary. Everything reminds me that I'm a sham like my father.

I wonder how long my father plowed along in false piety before he realized the gates of heaven would never open. I make it two, then three weeks. Each day, I drop a spiritual practice. Each night I pretend I'll repent. But heaven and I are both content to spin an endless cycle until my mission service time commitment reaches zero.

Or, that's what I've convinced myself until the will of the Lord suddenly inserts itself into my life once again.

In the middle of the third week, I'm summoned to the door as soon as I finish in the bath. Elder Pace sits in our living room, his feet on the table and his mouth full of brownies pressed on him by our *mamita*. Elder Blank hangs back, shrunken against the wall. He's not looked at me, not said a word. Not since that last night in *Los Limones*.

I stand by the table without greeting either of them.

Pace points his brownie at me and then speaks around a giant mouthful. "Pack your bags, *Tigra*," Elder Pace jokes in poor taste. "The *campo* is calling you back on special assignment. Your new district leader will be here tomorrow morning to pick you up for training."

"Who am I getting?" Hermana Barrera asks, her eyes alight with relief.

"Geez. Can't even say goodbye first, Hermana Barrera? That's harsh." Pace grins at her as he slices off another brownie.

"Where am I going?" I ask, my face still.

"*Macorís*. The resort area's been a mess since the quake. Lots of stateside money pouring in, but the town is still a mess. President wants missionaries he thinks will make good ambassadors to help.

You're training with the humanitarian missionaries tomorrow morning."

"She's our ambassador?" Hermana Barrera looks me up and down. "But never mind. Who am I getting?"

He grins at Barrera. Brown bits of cake are stuck in his other-wise perfect teeth. "President must have heard your whining. You get to kill Hermana Āngel."

"Yes!" Hermana Barrera begins to dance around the apartment. I snag a bite of brownie but then spit it out. Even food in the capital sucks.

I head to my room without another word. No one here will miss me much. I won't miss them, either.

As I pull my luggage out of the closet, I close my eyes to imagine the mountains. The cool air kisses my skin, but too soon the fantasy transforms into Henri. I sigh as I open my eyes to return to safer activities and thoughts. Barrera calls before I've finished packing. A day of proselytizing and knocking doors will carry me through my last hellish day with Barrera.

That night, long after sleep claims Barrera and my suitcase sits beside the door, dark thoughts bully me until I can't lie in bed any longer. I wonder if Ydria hates me. My replacement was probably that picture-perfect missionary who baptizes by the thousands and changes every life she touches. A lump in my throat cuts my breath as a sob threatens, but I can't be that weak. Not anymore.

I get out of bed and creep over to the window where the cold air drives off any threat of tears. Then I fill my mind with mental recitations of challenging violin exercises. The repetition eventually calms me enough to half-sleep against the window. I'm still there when the knock comes the next morning. With only a hint of sunlight, I shuffle to the door, inviting a new world and praying for a better today than yesterday.

As soon as I wrench the knob, the door swings forward and I'm wrapped in a tight, warm hug. I know this hug – the warmth and kindness, the slight smell of peaches and cheap perfume.

"It's like two pillows hugging, no?" Hernandez squeezes and shakes me.

I grab onto Hernandez as though she's the last lifeboat on the Titanic. I can't cry, I won't cry. But I sure want to.

Hernandez grabs my suitcase. "See ya later, homies," she shouts over her shoulder in English. No one calls back or comes to say goodbye. "Eh, not a friendly one in the bunch," she whispers. She goads me with my own suitcase. "So, move it *gordita*, they're feeding us lunch at Panda Express."

I break into a wide grin, the first in way too long. "Finest restaurant in Santo Domingo."

# Chapter 20

I don't stop clutching Hernandez's hand the entire length of the car ride. We slide into the back bench of a Ford Fiesta that zips along city roads with spectacular ease.

Hernandez slides forward in her seat to chat amiably with Elder Gordon. Like most humanitarian missionaries, our district leader is a man in his sixties—one of the twelve senior couples serving on the island. I'm in awe of how much English Hernandez has learned. She was the most bilingual of all the Dominican sisters, but now she's fluent enough to chatter about construction materials with Elder Gordon, who is helping the civic engineers with a bridge and well project in the island interior.

Elder Gordon drives us to a large warehouse outside the city. I know from social media that church humanitarian services take themselves seriously. They roll out big numbers—wheelchairs provided, vaccinations given, wells dug, and people served. But while I've read every boast in LDS Living, I've only seen a few yellow Mormon Helping Hands shirts during my time on the island, so it was easy to assume that the entire country had been forgotten after the earthquake. Here lies the evidence of my error.

Elder Gordon parks us beside two giant bulldozers. Golf carts zip by filled with people in jeans and business suits. Every so often, a forklift travels past carrying large crates marked with various commodities. There are piles of clothing as high as you can imagine and food crates that reach ten to fifteen feet in the air. I can't imagine how many people you could feed and clothe with all of this. I follow Elder Gordon in awe, not certain why I've been picked for this grand adventure.

Hernandez has spent her months since the earthquake in this building. She's proud of every moment of her mission and eager to educate me on every nuance.

"Right after the earthquake, the President and some government people did a survey of the island from helicopter. The ambassador from the United States came to a meeting. And then three general authorities came down along with the donations." Hernandez continues chattering as we walk past giant mounds of mattresses. "The resort regions need restored – that's a given. Tourism drives the entire country. Broken resorts make for lousy vacation photos on Facebook. I've been mostly subbed out to the Red Cross with one or the other senior sisters to do surveys and deliveries. But *Macoris* needs more than a few days' work. They want us on semi-permanent assignment to help the volunteer effort. I said I would, but only if you came with me."

"Me? Why would you want me?" I honestly can't come up with three good reasons why anyone would want me in any job besides crash test dummy.

"Because people talk to you, stupid. I told them all about Phillipe and Luis in *Los Guaranas*. Miracles that no one else could accomplish. And from what I hear, you did the same in *Los Limones*."

She whistles at a group of men in suits. They wave us over with big smiles, eager to greet me. Stupid Hernandez has filled their heads with all sorts of stories that the President didn't dare to deny. My stomach knots so tight that it could raise the Titanic. This is my chance—my big opportunity. But all I can sense is impending doom.

A Latino man with silver hair holds out a hand to shake ours – Elder Juarez per his nametag. "Aye, sisters, it's good to see you. We have a lot of work here to do and the president assures us that you girls are the right guys for the job." He smiles at his own sexist pun, which I must admit was impressive for someone whose thick accent betrays his rather recent acquisition of English as a second (or third) language.

Elder Juarez points at the bags and materials being organized for shipment. "These will go out to goodwill ambassadors as early as tomorrow. Necessities for them to distribute to their own practitioners." I contain a grin at the boxes marked for Catholic Relief Services. The old Priest of *Los Limones* disdainfully accepts the offering in my mind. I miss that old curmudgeon and the dusty hem of his otherwise-pristine robe.

I'm lost in memory until a man walks out from behind a nearby crate and startles me. I do a double-take when his wavy hair and bright smile give me goose pimples. He could be my dad's twin. The young girl in me whimpers as my actual dad's disloyalties counter the reality. In my mind, I see a specter of the choices my dad didn't make, a path carved through these crates. My mom would've loved being here, serving by his side. The ache I usually feels becomes a snake that tightens around my chest.

I wish I understood why my dad didn't choose this life. I wish I could make any sense of his new life and all these choices he claims make him happy at our expense. If only I hadn't wasted my one chance to hear his side of the story.

I shiver as the snake constricts again, doubling my agony. The day we almost talked feels so close, like I could change that day if I only tried. Dad had been drinking and wandered in while I was reading scriptures. I expected him to rail against the church, but the beer had made him mellow. He told me that he'd loved the passage I was reading in Alma, and that he sometimes missed the scriptures. He rambled for a while before he said, "I couldn't reconcile it all after a while, though, you know? I wanted to be more, to have more. I couldn't push myself aside and abandon my culture anymore for the sake of someone else."

That *someone else* were my mom, brother, and I, and the *more* was his barely-legal live-in girlfriend. At the time, I couldn't handle even a piece of that conversation. I let silence shove him out the door.

I regret that missed moment as I wonder at the specter down a corridor of corn meal and powdered potatoes. I have questions I wish I'd asked. *Did you feel as unworthy as I do when you tried to go to church after meeting Mikala? Did you stand proudly, holding your sins up for judgment? Did you hope you could hide your sins like I hope I can hide mine? And what would've happened if you'd made a different choice? Could you have made a different choice? Why didn't you love us enough to make a different choice?*

I don't have any answers, not for me or for him. I wonder if anyone else knows what it feels like to be so deeply disappointed in yourself that you're not sure who you are anymore or who you could trust to help you sort it all out.

A woman steps into our line of sight. She has peacock-blue, curled hair straight off the Magic School Bus. I read her name tag: Sister Juarez. Is she married to Elder Juarez? Why does that shock me so much? My tongue is tied through the whole introduction.

After greeting us, Sister Juarez gestures toward the bounty around us. "Isn't it marvelous? Don't you just feel the love of the Lord?"

Yes? Maybe? The warehouse has started a happy buzz in my core. I wish I'd been here for the past few months as Hernandez has been. Maybe then I'd be as mission confident as I'm pretending to be.

Hernandez and Sister Juarez jump immediately into planning. Hernandez has thought of so many different places that we could go and people that we should meet. Shop keepers, politicians, shoe-shine boys. The names and titles are dizzying.

But something inside me niggles and wiggles in protest. The *sancista's* face keeps appearing to me. Her kind eyes and grizzled hands reach for me.

"Has anyone spoken to the *sancistas*?" I interject. Then I grab my lip in my teeth. Both women stare at me in confusion as though I've suggested we borrow the Magic School Bus. Was that wrong? I've heard so many people speak out against the sancistas. Did I just confess to Satanism? Gah, I wish I could control my stupid mouth. I wait for a dose of guilt and shame and then feel confused when I feel peaceful instead.

I clear my throat to try again. "I know everyone is baptized Catholic, but that doesn't mean everyone trusts the Priests. In *Los Limones*, the *sancista* was a friend and in every home."

Sister Juarez has tipped her head to the side. Hernandez looks shocked to her bones. I'm pretty sure she's going to cross herself and toss a case-worth of salt over her shoulder.

The story of the *sancista* gets swallowed up by nerves, but I do manage to murmur, "I think anyone who loves the people could help us."

Sister Juarez tips her head to the other side as a soft but wide smile grows. She closes her eyes briefly, then nods. "Love is the reason for all we do. The Lord can use anyone to accomplish His purposes, that's what I've always said."

I love her. Completely. She's strong like my mom and happy like my grandmother.

Sister Juarez turns toward Hernandez. "As our cultural liaison, do you think we could find the *sancista* in *Macoris?*"

Hernandez shrugs her shoulders as she looks at me. "I guess so, but you'll have to help. I couldn't find a *sancista* at a fire circle."

"Let's talk to the men. I can't imagine they'll object, but it's good to get their input." Sister Juarez slides up to Elder Juarez to lay her head on his shoulder.

"They're married?" I ask Hernandez.

She tips her head toward mine to whisper. "Met in Columbia. Sister Juarez was the mission nurse; he was a widowed branch president. The Mission President made her swear not to tell anyone here or else we'd all get ideas of the naughty kind."

"An island husband," I say, miserably, the guilt exploding so hard that my face turns red and I want to vomit.

"A what? Oh! Gah, *las vampiras*. They were obsessed – blaming all the Americans for their lonely, single status. But I say, find love where you find it. The Juarezes are adorable together. Should they have to be apart because they were born in different countries?"

I wish her words alleviated my guilt. I smile anyway as we settle back into the discussion.

Sister Juarez interrupts the men at the first pause. "Excuse me, gentlemen. I think we asked these ladies for some advice, and they have a bit." The men turn toward her. They watch us expectantly.

And I shy away, unable to express my own ideas. Sister Juarez suggest the *sancista* and then I listen to the men make all the necessary plans to enact my idea.

I don't know when it happened to me, but I've become the person my mother raised me *not* to be. I've absorbed all the stereotypes that I never believed. I wait to be told. I wait to be instructed. I wait for someone else to figure things out. Every word in my mouth feels like a lie, even the ideas I know to be true.

After ten minutes of impersonating wallpaper, a door opens and the President walks in. The mood shifts as the men begin the mad hand-shaking. There are no silly signs like the Elders throw, but it's the same level of brotherhood. Elder Juarez shakes the President's hand twice, clapping him on the shoulder. Sister Juarez and Sister Stathos don't shake hands. It's odd that women shake hands so much less than men, though I can't really decide what that means, or if it means anything at all.

Elder Juarez beams at the three of us. "We've a good crew here, President. Well chosen. The sisters will be a great asset."

The President nods, a small concession to the idea that I can't be counted as drivel. As the men gather their books, the President levels his gaze on me. "This is a great opportunity. One not to be wasted." Then he turns and walks off with the regional leaders.

Oh, he does know how to get to me. My withering confidence deflates. I'll probably be as useless here as I ever was in the Capital. I cross my arms over my chest and squeeze.

Sister Juarez returns to us before she leaves. "Okay, you've got some downtime while we talk to the President. Then we'll get you both some lunch and off to *Macoris*." We both nod. The constriction in my chest has moved to my stomach. I'll never be able to eat. I slide into a crouch beside the boxes.

Hernandez turns to me as the older missionaries dissipate to their various assignments. "What is up with you? I've never seen you so quiet. It's weird."

I don't know what I could say that would make any sense, so I look up at the big stacks. "What are we supposed to do with all of this? Is there a plan?"

She squats to unzip her backpack and then hands me a bottle of water from inside. "I guess we'll do some good, make some friends. We're good at that, right?" She smiles at me from where she's crouched, and everything feels right for moment, as if I can undo all the wrongs of the past few months.

"Yeah, let's do some good," I say as I jostle her with my knee. She falls backward, fake-cursing as she tumbles onto her backside.

And I laugh. For the first time in way too long—I laugh.

# Chapter 21

*San Pedro de Macoris* feels like the three previous areas of my mission were placed in centrifuge. The resorts have flourished, creating a sprawling city. Chain restaurants abound, bringing a flavor of the States to the coastal city. But despite the visage of wealth, each neighborhood contains a *barrio* much like *Las Guaranas* with its house-based storefronts and food stands. The further out from city center, the more resemblance to *Los Limones*. In the periphery, I see people and places as destitute as anything I've encountered.

We live in my first real apartment near the city center. The block building survived the earthquake though the sidewalk suffered significant damage. But despite being in good condition, the building is mostly empty. The people have emigrated to healthier areas of the island, mostly to the west. The resorts suffer from lack of workers and from the damage done by the earthquake. Our first task has been to document the damage that limits workers' ability to earn a living and find food.

We've spent two weeks tracting out various neighborhoods with volunteers from the Red Cross. The task is daunting. The *barrios* are often uncounted in any census, so the population estimate is way off. The giant piles of goods in the warehouse have shrunk from abundant to merely sufficient. There's also a stranded contingent of American and European tourists living at the resorts. Their needs seem endless. They want double what the natives consider adequate.

We meet with the Juarezes every evening to try and configure a distribution plan, but we end up more confused. Last night, we didn't even try to put anything on paper. We only knelt in prayer and asked God to show us how to serve the people. I wish we'd had a collective lightning strike of inspiration, but we left unilluminated.

Today is our last day to figure out a plan. The trucks from the warehouse arrive tomorrow at dawn, transported in the dark to avoid black market pirates. I woke with a crick in my shoulder, a harbinger of great things, I'm sure.

I knock the bathroom door as I pass. "Ten minutes, Hernandez!"

"Aye, aye!" she shouts back, her usual lament. Her beauty routine has not lessened over the course of her mission.

The two sisters who share the apartment are already gathering beside the door. I join them in prayer. As I close my eyes, *Jesu, Joy of Man's Desiring* plays in full orchestra. I played violin II at a wedding with a string orchestra shortly before I left. The jerky syncopated rhythms overwhelm the version in my mind until I can't hear the words of the prayer.

I open my eyes, shaking off the sensation before bowing again. Again, the strains resume. The second violin drowns out the melody completely. I can't even hear myself say *Amen*.

When I open my eyes, the music doesn't fade.

The song repeats as I grab *pan de agua* and sip at hot chocolate. Then the music swells again as I go back into my bedroom for morning prayers. I can't form any words of my own. The music dominates my entire mind.

I give up on prayer, but, as I go to stand, I notice my violin beneath the bed. On a whim, I lean down and flip the latch, opening the lid to see the faded, unpolished wood. I pluck at a string to let the A sound clear.

*Yes*, a voice inside my soul says as the song goes quiet in my head.

I sit on my bed to stare at my skirt and worry at the hem, tugging on loose strands and smoothing wrinkles. I haven't trusted myself much over the past few months. Every idea has been followed by second-guesses and self-blame. With Hernandez, I've begun to feel the spirit again, though I've not acted on my own intuition.

But the violin... It's alive today and asking to come along.

I finger the bow, enjoying the buzz of familiarity and spirit as instrument and body unite. My brain offers up a dozen reasons the violin is a stupid accessory to the day. It's heavy. I'll look stupid. It'll be hard to manage on a *motoconcho*. I might break it.

But I also shouldn't ignore a prompting. I've been working hard, maybe it is time for the Lord to speak again. What would it hurt for me to try and listen? Without giving myself another chance to second guess, I pick up the case.

Hernandez waits at the door, sucking juice from a mango. She's on an all-fruit diet trying to reduce her weight because her skirts are getting tight. Unfortunately, she eats her weight in fruit every day, so I doubt there's been much progress.

"You bringing that thing?"

"I think maybe God wants me to."

She snorts. "You look like a hobbit. So where should we carry all your things today?"

"Very funny." I hesitate. The violin has me doubting everything. But God likely has a plan. Isn't that what I tell people every day? I bite my lip before taking a risk. "I want to pass by *Barrio Uno* one more time," I say, as nonchalantly as I can.

Hernandez rolls her eyes. "If the *sancista* hasn't shown herself already, we're not going to find her today. She's not going to talk to a blonde American woman and I do not look like somebody who uses a *sancista*." Henandez's arrogance has not helped this effort.

"I can't give up, though it's probably a fool's errand."

"Not probably," Hernandez says, but she blocks out the next hour in our schedule without further argument.

We pull our backpacks onto our right shoulders. We're wearing matching bright yellow floral prints today, twins in everything except skin color. I'm not sure how I got talked into the dress, but Hernandez claimed that it would be good luck. The pattern makes me look like a cemetery on Memorial Day. But we could use the luck.

I dodge cracks that run down the center of each street in rivulets. Cars honk as they dodge cracks and people. The people turn and curse at the honking cars. A *motoconcho* speeds by. The female passenger clips my violin case with her feet and I stumble forward several feet with a gasp. She makes a rude gesture and yells at me. Hernandez yells back. This is life on the streets of *Macoris*.

Hernandez helps me get my gear and balance righted. "Gah, can you believe that? She knocks you over and then complains about it?"

I shrug the shoulder not burdened by the backpack. There's a new hitch in my lower back to squawk at the ache in my shoulder. Fantastic.

We head straight back through the city out to the edges of town. Here lurk the underpaid cooks and the nighttime housekeepers, the shoeshine boys and the sex workers.

So far, no one has admitted to using the *sancista*. Hernandez thinks it's because the resorts tell them *sancistas* are bad for tourism. I think they don't trust Americans. We're probably both right.

"This is so frustrating," I say after another claim that no one practices the traditional religions. "Can we pray?"

"For rain?" Hernandez asks. I roll my eyes at her. She dutifully folds her arms as I ask the Lord to help us find anyone who will help.

When we open our eyes, a boy on a bicycle stares at us. "You should look over there, behind what you can see from the road," he says.

I point in the direction he indicates. "Between those houses?"

He pushes on the pedals to ride away as though he never spoke to us at all.

I look at Hernandez who shrugs both of her shoulders and then turns in the direction indicated. We squeeze between two huts. Behind the hut, a small shared courtyard connects four houses. And in the center of the houses, there's a fire and that fire is burning incense. A clue. Our very first clue.

Hernandez rubs her arms. "I don't like this place," she mutters.

I look around for signs of life, though, and can't see a single soul, alive or undead.

"Well, she's not here," Hernandez says unnecessarily.

I sit down and drop my backpack for a minute, eager to roll my shoulder until the pain subsides a little bit. This backpack weighs a ton. The violin case has turned my fingers numb.

"Another goose chase," I complain, eyes closed as I pretend the pain is lessening with the return of sensation. Hernandez plops down beside me.

We startle when voices invade our rest. A woman's voice reverberates off the tin huts, seemingly coming from every crevice.

"There was a boy on a bicycle who said I needed to check my fire. I don't know who he was. Second time he's been after me, too. I'm getting tired of being chased by some stranger on a bicycle full of words and no money." The voices grow stronger until an older woman with silken hair cut in a fashionable A-line emerges along with a man covered in tattoos and gauges. They stare at us, blinking as they try to process two women who have arrived without invitation.

The older woman eyes us carefully. "What could you possibly want?"

"Are you a healer?" I ask.

The woman stares hard at me. "No. If you want healing, go to the hospital, *gringa*."

The word for an obtrusive white person shuts me down. Despite the Latin blood in my veins, I'm too blonde with accented Spanish. Anything I say in my own defense will be fodder for anger, not help.

"Please." I stand up and extend a hand. "I worked with a *sancista* in *Los Limones*. We were able to help a lot of people. Our church—we're representatives of…"

"*Mormones*. I know your kind," she says curtly. "I don't worship your Jesus."

"You don't have to. We have a truck arriving with food and other resources. We want cultural leaders to help us distribute it all fairly."

At this, she sniggers. She's probably been made that kind of promise a dozen times in her life. "For the believers, eh? The faithful? The people here pray to a dozen gods hoping for relief and then they pay for magic instead." She tosses a handful of silver pebbles onto the fire. The burst of flame unveils the cynicism in her smile. "Because magic is all there is."

That smile. Devoid of light. Empty of spirit. Cruelty disguised as wisdom. I've seen this look a few too many times.

I square my shoulders despite a terrible twinge and then face her. The fire crackles behind me while a different type roars in my heart. "I don't think that's true. I know God is in this." Do I? Yes. Absolutely. I doubt myself but never my God. I grin, pushing aside all my insecurity as I trust the scriptures. "And I'll prove it."

Hernandez jumps in. "And you can be part of it. We need everyone to help. So show up. Or don't. But God isn't going to let us down."

Hernandez links an arm with mine. We stand in solidarity before we walk past the *sancista*. We don't make a sound until we're back on the street.

"Glad we spent three days looking for her," I grumble.

I shift my backpack and accidentally clip Hernandez with my violin. She chuckles. "And that came in really useful."

I purposefully jostle her again. "I thought Spanish-speakers weren't supposed to understand sarcasm."

"Gah, the things they teach you *gringos*."

We walk arm in arm down the long expanse of road. House-front shops remain boarded over, evidence of a defunct tourist industry. Weathered signs advertise for beaded necklaces, authentic Dominican pottery and cheap t-shirts. The *"I survived…"* shirts with laughable taglines such as *21 margaritas* or *the bachata challenge* seem lovably ironic amidst the destruction.

But usually there are people milling about. Today, I'm in a ghost town.

"Does everything seem unusually quiet today?" I ask Hernandez.

She pauses to knock mud off her wedge sandals. I envy her foot freedom. She has a divine collection of sandals while I'm stuck in sensible shoes. My penny loafers are declining in value every day. Soon, they won't even qualify as ha'penny loafers. And I try not to think about how much they stink.

Hernandez looks around. "Yeah, it's quiet. Probably a market day somewhere close."

I accept her answer; this is her culture, but the idea sits wrong. It's really quiet, not even children run the streets. The only sound is a dog scratching its fleas in a shadowed alcove.

The quiet makes me uncomfortable. When silence falls, all I can think about is the working cell phone in my pocket. I've never had one that functioned reliably before, so I feel hounded by this never-ending urge to text my mom. Weirder still, I want to call my dad.

I've tried to trust Hernandez with my story, but it's felt so good to be accepted again. I don't want her to sigh or lecture me. I don't want to lose her respect like I lost Hermana Olsen's. The same fears creep in when I think about my mom. But my dad can't shame me. He'll probably praise me.

My desire for his approval makes me spiritually squirm. My dad's approval shouldn't matter anymore. We don't even share a last name. We have nothing in common.

Except that we understand church shame.

The cell phone tugs at my skirt where it sits in my pocket. The weight pulls me down—down, down, down to where my dad resides. Maybe I should start "forgetting" my phone. Or keep it in my backpack. Or accidentally drop it in the river.

Hernandez has finished repairing her shoes. "Argh, the soles are broken. Let's stop by the *zapateria* to see if Manuel can mend them. He'll probably let us teach a discussion if it means *veinte pesos* at the end. That'll make the President happy when he arrives tomorrow."

"Gotta keep the President happy," I say with a grumpy edge.

"Why do you do that? Say his name with so much... *animo*." She adds the last graciously. We both know that I can't say *President* without italicized-for-emphasis sarcasm.

"We have a complicated past," I retort with the exact same edge.

Hernandez pauses to look at me, her hands on her hips. "You've got quite a collection of those. Sister Lannie Lewis, featured starlet of *A Complicated Past.*"

I can't tell if she's trying to be funny as she waltzes to the tune of none-of-your-business. What does she know of my life? Nothing. Hernandez has it as good as anyone can. Her family has money. Her parents are married in the temple and her brothers have all been, too. Her earthquake story involves meeting dignitaries from three different world powers. Worst thing she's faced this mission is the stupid broken shoe.

I storm past her, making the next turn towards the *zapateria* without looking back. She doesn't catch up to me until I'm standing in front of Manuel's closed shop.

She grabs my arm at the elbow. "No, I'm not taking it back. I think I mean it. No matter how rudely you walk away. You've been moping since I picked you up and I'm ready for it to stop." She tugs off her shoe and plopped it on the counter as if Manuel is sitting right there. "It's your dad. It's your grandma. It's a bad companion. It's the president. Every day, a new reason you're the victim."

"This really isn't any of your business," I hiss across the space and then try to point to the closed sign.

"It is. It's my business when all you do is complain. We can't hear the Lord over the voices of your ghosts," She mumbles as she digs out a 20-note. "There's more to life and the gospel than figuring out who is to blame every time a sin gets committed."

"The shop is closed!" I shout at her.

"*Pftt,*" she says. She kicks open a small door beneath the counter. She slides the shoe and the 20-note inside. Then she slams it shut before she turns to face me.

"How are you going to get home with only one shoe?" I ask, ignoring her question.

She places two fingers in her mouth and whistles. I hear a *motoconcho* roar to life. It annoys me so much how easily she moves through this culture, even if it is the one of her birth.

The *motoconcho* arrives. Hernandez cross-mounts and then points with her lips to indicate I should climb aboard side-saddle behind her. Curse the mission rules. I really want to abandon her in indignation, but instead, I perch on the back of a one-seater bike with my ankles crossed politely. I contain my sniffle. A sniffle is one dramatic step too far.

Hernandez waves and calls out to the few people that we pass as though we weren't in the middle of a fight. I mope—okay, I admit to this one—until we get back to our yellow townhouse.

"You don't really know what I've been through," I say in self-justification after Hernandez pays the driver.

"Then tell me," she says. Then she holds up a hand to stop me. "But only if you're going to forgive everyone involved after we talk."

"What? You can't demand I forgive people."

"Can't I? I'm a representative of Jesus Christ, baby. I'm only speaking His truth."

"Not sure you can claim He's the master of your attitude today. And we're not supposed to speak for Christ," I mumble as I push past her. I drop my useless violin in the corner. Then I head off to flop down on my bed.

The phone beeps as it digs in my hip. Tears slip over my cheeks as the temptation to call my mom becomes painful.

Hernandez's flip-flops flap against the concrete. She sits on my bed, but I flop away from her like an injured seal on a beach.

I bury my face in my pillow as I lose the battle with tears and self-control. "It's not like I haven't tried. You don't simply take feelings like this and send them away like paper boats. I've prayed, and I even moved in with him…" My dad. Why does everything circle back to my dad?

Sobs overtake me. Hernandez places a hand on my back. I lift my head to stare at her. "Well?" I say. "What haven't I done? What's the big solution?"

She smiles at me around a slice of papaya between her teeth. Then she shrugs. "I don't know. They gave me a badge at the MTC. Told me it would make me wise."

A smile begins to tug at my lips, so I throw my hand over my eyes before I start laughing with her. Blocking out the light forces in a bit of honesty. "You're useless. And I'm useless if I can't figure out how to serve Christ."

I feel Hernandez shift away from me. "I think you serve Christ fine. It's letting Christ serve you that's tripping you up."

"What do you know about needing Christ to fix things?" I grumble.

Hernandez peels my hand from my eyes. "You'd probably be surprised. You think you're the only imperfect person on the planet? Christ died only for you?"

Her eyes are sincere and sad. I push up on my elbows, my brow pulling together in response to a question too impolite to ask.

Hernandez looks away, her smile wistful. "There was a boy," she says quietly. Then she looks back at me. Her wistful gaze turns to a steady, serene smile. "There was a boy. And then there was a need for the Atonement."

"I..." Oh, crap. I wasn't prepared for this. Stammering is the worst choice, but I can't find any other words. "I'm sorry."

Hernandez laughs softly. "Don't be. It brought me here. But no one can walk anyone else to Christ. You have to go on your own. I think you'd feel better if you did." She stands and stretches. "Want some papaya?"

I can tell from her grimace that she's hoping my answer is no. Enduring a little hunger is the least I can do for her. "Uhm, no. It's okay. You eat all of it."

I lay back down. Her shoes slap the concrete three or four times before she pauses. "Hey, I know a lot of missionaries like you. They don't do anything wrong, but they forget to do some things right. I thought I'd always hate what I did, but I'm glad I came to Christ. And watching so many of you... Maybe it's harder to come to Christ when you already think you're perfect, than when you know you're not."

Her flip-flops resume their slipping pattern until the noise disappears into the kitchen. I lay awake, silent and staring, but tear-less. There's a light in Hernandez that I've never known, a peace that I assumed was part of her personality. But maybe she's simply got the light of being *born again*. I want that light. I've wanted it since the day we met.

The phone beeps again. "Stupid thing," I murmur as I pull it from my waistband. Then I nearly drop it when I look at the numbers on the face.

My home area code.

My eyes zip up towards the ceiling. "Are you in this, Big Guy?" I ask, but immediately regret my familiarity. Diaz could pull off talking to Christ like they were besties. Maybe Hernandez could, too. But I worship God from at least twelve light years away, and I need someone on this planet to help me.

I key in my mom's cell phone number and then stare at it before I hit the green key. Then I pray that she doesn't answer... or that she hangs up on me for breaking the rules.

But God isn't one to get you out of trouble you made for yourself. The phone clicks. A soft inhale tells me my mom has picked up. "Lannie? Honey? Are you okay?"

There's a lump the size of The Dead Sea in my throat. All that I've gone through in silence chokes me. I clear my throat twice, willing myself to ease her worry. "Yeah. Mom. I'm here. I..." What? Why exactly have I called? "I wanted to hear your voice."

"It's here," Mom says, high-pitched. Then she clears her own throat. "I'm here, baby," she says, softly, as she would when I'd cry in my bed at night as a child. "I'm always here."

A tear slips down my face. "Hey, you know how you said that you met yourself on your mission? Did you like the person you met?" I ask, trying for levity and landing at gravity.

My mom pauses, a long thinking pause that ends up so pregnant it could deliver twins. Then she exhales, hard. "No. Not at first, at least. But I learned to."

"I hate that dad is having a baby with Mikala. I can't stop thinking about it. Obsessing about it." I say it plainly, acknowledging the thing that's been eating my soul to pieces and turning me into someone I don't want to be.

"Me, too," Mom confesses. Then we both let silence settle between us.

My tears shift to sniffles that beg for explanation. "What did we do wrong? Why didn't eternity work for us?" It's unfair to ask her this. I never have, and Joe would have my hide for dinner if he knew I'd said it. But I want out of this mess. I want to believe there is a way out of this mess.

"I don't know." Then I hear her sniffle. Guilt descends like a tsunami, but I can't let go of this conversation.

"It's all I can think about. Dad. Mikala. Our lost family. How much he hurt you. But it all feels so ugly… I feel ugly." An idea hits that I've never considered. Joe has been a shell since he came home from his mission. His energy sapped and emotions focused on bitterness. "Mom, is this what ruined Joe's mission? He came home so angry. Has he even spoken to Dad since he came home?"

There's another long pause. I've always thought of us as a super-honest family, but I've found the closet where all our agreed-upon secrets have been neatly hung out as moth food.

My mom doesn't exhale this time. She talks eventually, though. "I'm tired of what that man has done to us, you know that? I'm tired of how much he's taken." She sighs. "But I've been thinking about that scripture that says you should forgive *seventy times seventy times*? Do you know that one?"

I nod though she can't see me. I'm sniffling, too, so I wipe my hand ungracefully across my nose. "The one you always said made messes of abused women?"

"Yeah. I think we've interpreted it wrong, or at least that I have. I don't think Christ meant we should let people hurt us seventy times seven times—I think he meant that we might have to forgive seventy times seven times before forgiveness would actually stick."

I chew over her words, wondering if such a thing is even possible. "Have you gotten there with Dad? Forgiveness?"

"No," she says quickly, "but I'm willing to try." She clears her throat. "He called to ask if he could come when you get back. I've been going to tell you, but it won't go down right in a letter. I think it's your choice, but he wants you to meet your sister—it's a girl. I don't know if he's mentioned that."

A girl. Like Issa. Innocent and perfect without any piece in this. I squeeze my eyes shut until I can see Issa's giant brown-black eyes and pouty smile.

*Seventy times seven…* only 490 times until it sticks.

"I'll think about it," I force out. There's one act done. Only 289 more acts of forgiveness to go before this doesn't feel like being drowned slowly in a waterfall.

My mom chuckles. "It's a start. Honey, did you have permission for this call? I don't want you to…Well, as your dad would say, I never met a rule I wasn't excited to follow."

Blech, that man. I hate what he did to Mom. Forgiveness is not going to be easy with a father like mine. I shake my head against the self-recrimination in her voice. "Mom, that wasn't right or fair when he said it. You don't have to break every rule to be an independent, strong woman. And you are. You always have been."

"Ignore me. I'm working on my own *seventy times seven*. But I want to support you. How can I best support you?"

I smile into the phone. There's my mom. My rock. "By being amazing. And making me keep the rules. But Mom, I love you. And this hasn't been easy, so if I have some stories to tell…"

Mom chuckles. "Nothing turns us into liars like our missions. I get it—I went, remember. I'll be ready to hear everything you didn't say in letters when you're ready to tell it."

We both weep into the phone, the need to disconnect terrifying and yet necessary.

"I'll talk to you in a few months," I finally say.

"I'll be here. Always."

I hit the red phone icon. Then I hit the nine dots that cue up the number pad. I dial up my dad's number before I think better of the idea.

"Please don't let him answer," I say to the heavens again. I guess I've been a good girl this time, because the phone rings and rings. At his canned response, I smile up to heaven again. "Never give us more than we can handle—wise move," I whisper to the sky.

"Hey Dad. I wanted to say… I want things to be better. So, yeah, come. That's all I want to say. I'll see you in six months." The last is ridiculously cheerful. But it's done. And it's true. I want things to be better.

My next stop is my knees. I pray until I cry. Then I cry until I feel like praying again. Hernandez knocks when our rest break is over, but I wave her off, praying until I find peace. I can do one act of forgiveness at a time, but I know it'll be easier if I have Christ on my side.

I stand up at Hernandez's second, less patient knock. Our shoes flap against concrete and then we both groan as our bags hit our shoulders. We pray again at the door.

Again, the song worms into my head as soon as we start the prayer. With a sigh, I pick up the violin case.

"No, you're not serious," Hernandez says.

"Take that complaint to Jesus. He's the culprit." I grin at Hernandez. She grins back.

"Let's go tell the Juarezes that we still don't have a plan," Hernandez says as she holds open the door.

"These are the moments I am grateful to be demoted. Junior companion for the win, baby!" I pump my fist in the air.

Hernandez drops an arm around my shoulder. "Braver already," she jokes. "I'm not looking forward to tonight. All my inner squiggles are squawking."

To be honest, so are mine. An inner set of heavenly bells sound in joy and alarm.

# Chapter 22

"How late do markets stay open? Especially for people with no money?" I ask Hernandez as we mount our bikes for the ride up to the church. The uncommon silence has continued. Even the local *colmado* across the street has closed.

"I think market is even more exciting when you have nothing to spend than when you do. Everyone will be back tomorrow," she says, but sounds less certain. The sun has begun to set. Families should be gathering at fires, passing around the plate of chicken and rice that will sustain them through the night. But the houses are dark and quiet. We travel near-empty streets for turn after turn.

When the noise arrives, I'm in awe of it. Gritty and human but with a wolf's growl. Hungry. Angry. Each rotation of my wheel brings more noise. A crash of glass. Then a clang of metal. Hernandez pushes her bike hard, beads of sweat pouring from her head and wetting the underarms and front of her dress.

We turn the last corner toward the church and find the missing crowds from today. People press up against the gate. They scream into the private lot.

Hernandez abandons her bike a dozen yards before the crowd. I hop off, too, but take the time to chain up our primary transportation.

When I reach Hernandez, she's found Elder Juarez. He's trying to talk rationally to a screaming man waving wire cutters.

"They know the delivery is coming," Hernandez hisses at me. "They want their share first. They want it now."

The crowd lunges forward to press us hard against the fence. The wire cutters are poised. "We don't have anything yet!" Elder Juarez shouts. "I promise you..."

*Everyone makes promises*, I argue back in my head. A scuffle starts behind us. I hear the sharp crack as bone meets bone. How long before violence turns deadly? I remember the water truck in *Los Limones* and beg God for a solution.

Another jostle forward presses my violin to my back. I stumble into a wall at waist height.

A wall that climbs above the crowd.

Oh, wow, this seems stupid, but don't I always lament I've never had a Moroni or Samuel moment? The wall presses into my stomach again as I'm pushed further forward. My decision is made by necessity. If God has given me a wall, then I'm going to stand on it.

I jump up and start the climb, hopeful that I'll be granted balance I've never had. The wall rises slowly until I'm a good two feet above the crowd. From here, the scene is more terrifying. The crowd is large and angry. Someone will be armed.

And all I've got is a violin—albeit a violin that's worked an impressive array of miracles. I raise my own version of *The Title of Liberty* to my chin. The strands of *Come Ye Disconsolate* pour out, louder and more intense than I've ever played. I don't know what I expect. I stand on the wall and play, begging for Christ to change this scene.

One after the other, the songs I memorized in *Los Limones* play while mission memories slip by in a poorly-edited movie. I relive each debate with Phillipe, marvel at Ydria's tears in a courtyard, and hold Issa in my arms again. Then I watch as the iron stick shears skin from my arm, and as I insert myself between Luis and Ydria. Fearless and fierce in defense of gospel, love, family, and justice.

I thought I met me when I fell from grace, but that wasn't the whole of me. The woman limping along a trail as blood drips down her arm—the one who helped to save a baby before passing out—that woman exists every bit as much as the one who lost control of her heart and struggles with forgiveness.

Warmth replaces the melancholy that's chilled me for so long. I open my eyes, thrilled to find a growing number of people listening and watching me. Hernandez has jumped up on the wall, too. She makes her way to me with slow sideways steps.

When Hernandez arrives next to me, I end the impromptu concert.

"Please calm down," Hernandez shouts. "We want to help all of you. We *can* help all of you, but not if there's a riot."

I wait for the shouting to erupt with my violin poised under my chin, but there's an aura of peace that's fallen over the crowd. They're falling into lines to either side. In the middle of the crowd, the *sancista* winds her way from group to group, saying words that calm the most irate. I won't say she's changed—I see her taking coins in exchange for comfort—but she pauses as she comes to the base of the wall to look up at me. I catch her eyes and then nod with certainty. We *will* help these people. She has my word.

She bats her eyes at me and then shakes her head with a hard shrug. Not ready to feel or believe, but that's okay. She pantomimes me playing the violin as she guides the man with the wire cutters away from the gate.

I pull my bow down as instructed. The crowd's attention turns back to me. Parents direct their children to sit along the back wall while adults roll over trash bins to start fires. Peace and order have been restored, but no one will give up their spot in line.

Even as the crowd settles, their eyes stay fixed on me. I know what song needs to come next—the song I've prepared across a lifetime.

*Traüme* sings itself to the Creator across an open sky. The notes shimmer with the stars. My heart trembles with the vibrato, and each phrase carries a story. The crescendos spill love, while the decrescendos resonate with pain. I want the strains to be picked up by the birds and carried to *Los Limones* where they can sing my goodbye to Ydria in the language we both speak best. Tears spill out the sides of my eyes on the last held note.

The wind whistles through the mango trees and the palms above me clap. I'd probably still fail juries, but it's perfect enough for the island.

Perfect enough for my heart.

The crowd has been stunned into silence. Then a single shout ignites an explosion of applause. The finale we've all needed. As the sun slips into its final resting place, the crowd settles into conversation and laughter.

We stay with the people all night. Maybe it's not safe, but I'm not here to be safe. Christ called me to be a daring advocate. I can't claim to follow Him if I doubt why He loves me.

Somewhere in the dead of night, the President's car arrives. Behind him, the tractor-trailer groans its way up the street. The crowd rises up. Our careful *detente* cracks with clattering bangs as trash cans get shoved aside. The men at the front rattle the gate in warning when the two vehicles cross into the courtyard.

I speak to the President and his car of dignitaries before they fully disembark. "Please. We need to feed them first. I know the Americans want things, but...*please.*" I run out of breath four times trying to get the words out.

Sister Juarez steps into our circle. She squeezes my hand. "Feed them first. God will make sure there's enough for the resort."

*Somehow,* I add silently. A brief prayer rises in my heart. *Please.*

The President looks at Hernandez and the Juarezes, who all nod in agreement. "I'll make sure you have time."

The VIPs have joined him outside the car. The President turns toward them, full of smiles. They lead the resort owners to the inside of the church, away from our distribution.

"Okay, let's do the Lord's work," Elder Juarez proclaims. He and Sister Juarez pull yellow vests over their church clothes. Our small contingent of faithful members and fellow missionaries do the same. We're a motley army—perhaps the only kind God ever assembles.

Elder Juarez crosses his arms over his chest. We all bow as he prays for a miracle. I wet my lips and worry about the soon-to-open gate. We're outnumbered by the hundreds.

As we finish the prayer, the gate rattles. I glance up to see the crowd has parted for the *sancista*. She emerges with a collection of men. Large ones, mostly tattooed. The bishop opens the side gate to permit this contingent. He shakes all the hands and offers them a yellow vest that they quickly reject. But they all shuffle over to help unload. A few minutes later, a priest and handful of nuns push their way inside, again refusing the yellow vests. We have help, the right blend of help regardless of uniform.

Elder Juarez rips open a box of rice to signal the start. When the bag emerges, the crowd cheers. Then Sister Juarez tears open beans, greeted with a similar shout.

Sister Juarez and the *sancista* look to me with expectation. I slip through the side door to find my place on the wall. My fingers will be cracked and bleeding, but if it keeps the beastly side of crowd management at bay, then it'll be worthwhile. Two lines form as I strike up a chord.

I play primary songs as the sun slowly lights the eastern sky, happy tunes with worker energy. The missionaries and members sing along as they pour rice and beans into the containers. The sun rises harsh and hot, leaving us all drenched in sweat and sapped of energy yet we continue our pace until the sun finds its zenith.

When the last person has been fed, I pack up my violin.

Happy customers have stayed to express gratitude. The President and resort owners emerged at some point and now pass among the crowd to remind everyone to report to work as soon as possible. Hernandez has spread the same message. The resorts draw the tourists and the tourists bring the money that buys the food. This is the modern Caribbean economy, whether anyone likes it or not.

Sister Stathos approaches me with a cautious smile as I stow the violin. She reeks of bug spray, a reminder of her fears from our first meeting.

"I think you've proven you can suffer for Christ's sake," she says. She hands me a first aid kit to doctor my bleeding fingers.

"I can't resist blood and mud," I joke back. She laughs. Then she hugs me.

As she lets go, her fingers brush the skin on the back of my arm. She gasps and pulls her fingers away. The scar. I never really think about it. I've not thought how others might react.

Sister Stathos wraps her fingers around my wrist in earnestness. "Oh you poor thing. I hope they'll be able to do something about it in the States."

I cradle my arm protectively, appalled at the suggestion. My finger strokes the knotted tissue. I think I'll keep this scar, but I guess that's hard to explain in passing. For most people, it's the sign of poor medical care, not a relationship with Christ.

Hernandez whistles. They've started to load the truck for its trip to the resort. I stow my violin against a wall before I jog off to toss half-filled bags of rice into the bed.

When we've sent out the last load, Hernandez and I collapse against a wall. Everything hurts. We didn't sleep at all last night and the day has been exhausting.

The President sits down beside us. He hands us a cold bottle of water. "You didn't waste this opportunity. Neither of you. Well done."

We nod as we drink, unaware until the water hit our gullets of how parched we'd become. The water makes me think of food, too, but he doesn't offer that.

"I'll be sad to separate you. But I think it's time you moved on, Hermana Hernandez. You've been here a long time."

The man can't resist a gut-punch. Hernandez takes it in stride. "Ah, President. Give me a day to enjoy, okay? You're always pushing me where I don't want to go."

The President leans toward her. "It's for your own good, you know." He stands as his wife appears, looking nervous and eager to leave. "Transfer day is Tuesday."

"No rest for the weary," I say, hoping it comes off as teasing.

The President nods at me. We'll never really understand each other, but at least I'm back in his good graces.

Hernandez drops her head to my shoulder when he's out of sight. "Let's sleep straight through until Tuesday," she says around a giant yawn.

"Or we could work," I say, reflexively.

"Or we could work," she agrees with a grin. "Give me Jesus, right, Hermana?"

"Give me Jesus," I repeat quietly.

The days pass too quickly. The call comes on Monday. "Hermana Hernandez is going up north. Be ready at six tomorrow morning. We're bringing Lewis a greenie. First transfer after her trainer. You gotta break her into the real world."

"I'm going senior?" I ask in disbelief.

"Seems so," the Elder on the other end says. "Shine up your manners."

At six on Tuesday morning, Hernandez and I stand with arms around each other while the Elders unload a young brunette from the truck. They dump her luggage in our district leader's truck and then stand aside while Hernandez and I say our final goodbyes.

We hug, pulling each other closer with each sniffle. "Like two pillows hugging, eh?" Hernandez says through a sob. I can't answer.

The Elders honk and we let go. Our perfect partnership is over.

I look to my greenie, who seems fascinated by the differences between our shoes. I stare down, too, lamenting the state of worn leather opposite her perfect loafers.

"I'll stop by the *zapateria*. Manuel can fix them. Probably."

She looks up at me, a grin spreading. "No. Don't. My mom says you can tell the good missionaries by their shoes. I figure I must have one of the best by the state of yours."

I look back down at my feet. "I guess these shoes do have a few stories to tell," I say with a soft smile. I put my arm through hers to guide her through the streets to where our bikes rest against the house. Her body grows tighter and tighter.

"I don't know how to do this," she whispers after I lift my bike. "In a skirt? With a backpack full of books?"

My desire to laugh is swallowed up in memory. It's all so normal to me now, but I've never forgotten those uncertain first days. I drop my bike and move to her side. "Don't worry. We'll get you on that bike. And then I'll show you how to flush the toilet."

She smiles at me and then follows my movements as I hitch up my skirt. We'll be okay, this greenie and me. Maybe I'll tell her my stories.

Or maybe I'll leave her to create her own.

# Chapter 23

There are so many stories that get swallowed up in the last six months of my mission – the usual ones, the ones that I'll tell when the High Council asks me to speak. I can give great lectures on faith, obedience, and compassion. But I don't know that those lectures are the real lessons of my mission.

On the night before I transfer home, I fall asleep on my knees, as Callister used to do. I dream my quilt again. This time, someone else sits with me. I see His hands, scarred at the center, and calloused from work. He secures the fabric at the corners. He pulls each stitch tight.

The one hundred and forty-four squares have transformed into memories. There are squares for my grandparents. They sit on a bench in their garden and laugh at old jokes. A square for Family Home Evening with Ben Lewis the clown. Another for Joe and me, crying over a yellow apartment contract. A giant portrait of my mom covers the middle. There's an area dedicated to music school and a square for failing juries. There's one for cockroaches, and another for the blue plaque that will live with Ydria forever, I hope. There are squares of Henri and Tavo atop a mountain, Ydria in the kitchen, and Celia and Issa dancing. And a very large patch of me atop a wall in *Macorís*.

So many memories. Some beautiful, and others that break me a little. My tears form new thread, and the Master dutifully ties another corner into place before handing me a new square. In the dream, I take off my badge and pin it to the fabric. The badge merges into the fabric, soon to be another memory stitched into a life.

The dream gives way to aching knees that complain through my whole dead day. I've joined up with Hernandez again. We wait at a crossroads out of town for Diaz, still Hernandez's BFF though I haven't seen her since our first house. Diaz flies into town on a rickety old bus. She spent her whole mission in the wild interior of the island. The first we see of her is a My Little Pony umbrella that obscures all but her frilly anklets with pink bows and well-worn Mary Janes.

"You reek of the *campo*," Hernandez says as she plugs her knows.

Diaz cackles. "God uses pigs to guard his best miracles."

I laugh as I move to hug her. "Diaz, may God grant that you never change."

"Why would I ever change?" she says, puzzled, as her tiny arms try to wrap around Hernandez and I in a single hug.

Hernandez and Diaz drag me shopping to all the best areas in the Capital. We've saved money throughout our missions to put ourselves back together. Manicures. Haircuts. New clothes. Mostly, we talk about going home, but mission stories wind in – Diaz has seen her share of miracles, too. She wasn't joking about the pigs as much as I thought she was. My miracles were quiet, personal. But Diaz has seen the hand of God. I expect to feel jealous of her but I don't. I wouldn't give up my own miracles for all the wonders of the immortal realm.

Once we're prettied up, we go to the office sisters' house for a party for the dearly departing. My heartache blooms when Diaz starts *merengue* music and Hernandez hands me cake. Their beloved faces crash against old memories and, as much as I want to celebrate going home, my heart knows that the loss that happens tomorrow will forever eclipse the joy of going home. This place, these experiences— for good or bad—are frozen in time when I step on that plane.

A window ledge gives me shelter and comfort to listen to the trees whisper. Beneath the window, a group of women dance under a single strand of stolen electricity. The romance and beauty of their movements wrap me in a moment of pure connection to the island. I'll miss everything I ever hated about this place. I'll even miss chickens on the bus. American buses need more chickens.

The island taught me to love so deep it hurts, and to trust God so hard it seems stupid. Because crazy, stupid love for God and man is the point of the gospel, and, when you do it right, miracles happen. I've seen so many. Too many, maybe. Enough that my faith has roots that reach clear to my toes and branches that extend into every area of my brain.

My violin sits beside me in its damaged case. The latch broke ages ago. There's a dent in the plastic that bent a stay on the violin, held in place by black electrical tape. This violin served as many people as I did.

My violin's future is as unknown as my own. For the millionth time since my travel plans came, I wish for an instruction manual that will never come. I may know Christ, but Lannie Lewis remains a mystery. Music therapy is a possibility. The truth is, there are simply too many possibilities. They rob me of sleep most nights.

Olsen comes in to sit by me. She arrived later than most, having spent her last day working. "Can you believe it's over?" Her serenity seems in place, but the beds of her nails are as angry and red as they were in *Los Limones*.

"It already feels like it happened to someone else."

"I was glad to hear that you moved past *Los Limones*. I always knew you had a great missionary in you. You just got a little lost."

The *tigra* of *Los Limones*. That's how some will remember me. I made my peace with it long ago.

"Thanks. I'm glad we made it," I say simply, my eyes still on the horizon.

Olsen stands and leaves. Diaz replaces her. She has a pass-along card in her hand.

"Hoping for one last hurrah?" I ask her in Spanish.

"It's for you," she says with a sparkle. "Monsen wants you to have it."

I roll my eyes. I haven't seen Monsen since *Los Limones*. "I already got the repented *tigre* congrats from Olsen. I think I'd rather put *Los Limones* away."

She looks at the handwriting on the card. Her eyes sparkle. "Okay. Then I'll call the handsome boy when I get home. It's my lucky day."

My eyes fly to the card. Henri's name and email address has been written in slanted, male handwriting across the back. "I don't want that!" I say quickly. Maybe too quickly. "I can't want it... Can I?"

Diaz shrugs. "Monsen says he's sorry that he didn't stop Blank. He was…" Diaz's brows pull together. In English, she says, "…a big bully. But Monsen is… good guy." She grins at her successful phrase. "See, I speak English now, too," she says in Spanish.

Hernandez joins us at the sill. She wiggles herself into a nonexistent space in the middle. Dominicans supersede the laws of physics. This many rear ends shouldn't be able to squeeze into a single space, yet here we are. Friends until the end, crammed in a single three-foot space.

"Eh, what are you crazies talking about?" Hernandez asks, her head on my shoulder.

"Boys," Diaz says. "But Hermana Lewis has taken her vows. Now there are boys up for grabs. Tavo and…" she glances at the card before looking at me with mischief in her eyes. "…Henri. So, I'm going to call him. He's my type." She says the last in English and cackles.

Hernandez plucks the card from Diaz. She puts it in my hand. "*Anaisa* chose him for Lewis. Unless you've got some spare cigarettes, don't play with danger," she says with a wink at Diaz. We don't believe in *Anaisa* or her power over anyone, but there's something lovely in an old joke between parting friends.

She wiggles, and we all shift, teetering precariously over the city. As the *bachata* playing below stops bouncing its beat in the street below, Hernandez lays her head on my shoulder. "*En serio.* Don't just be defeated. I know it won't be easy and people might talk but don't say no because you think you should. When you're not here, when you don't have all the pressure, then you pray before you say no. Okay?" She physically closes my quaking fingers around the card.

"Okay," I say softly. Acceptance without obligation. The pass-along card with Henri's email flips between my fingers, and, in the hand dangling out the window, a small, silver necklace with two hearts dances in time with the couple below. Yes, everything is changing, and I have to decide what comes next, and what, if any, pieces of the past belong in the next story. It'll take a lot of prayer. Maybe more prayers than I've ever said in my whole life.

"How did it end so soon? I'm not ready. I want more time." Diaz begins to sob.

Hernandez sniffles, too. We sit in the window until every light we can see goes out.

The plane ride home rolls back time. Olsen sleeps the whole way to Salt Lake. I hold a young woman's hand and hear about her three miscarriages and failed IVF. We pray together somewhere over Tulsa.

When my seatmate slips into sleep, I pull out my mission journal for the final entry. There aren't many entries. Most of my mission will live only in my heart. I write down my testimony to try and capture the love I feel for God.

From the back of my journal, I pull out the letter I received from my dad a month after I called him. I slide my finger along the seam to finish every bit of my mission before I step off the plane. I begged the Lord to help me make things better with my dad. I need to try.

A photo of a newborn falls out first. My baby sister. As lizard-like as any newborn.

Then there are five pages of advertising for the great Benito Lantana. He has an album release pending. Yay. He's frustrated by how long Mikala wants for maternity leave. Not so yay.

They're planning to be in Utah for my return. All of them. But I knew this already.

In the last paragraph, my actual dad emerges for the first time in seven years, the one who taught me to reach for the stars and imagine Christ reaching back toward me.

*Baby, the thing my mission gave me that I'll never give back is the knowledge that something bigger than us is always at work. So maybe it's that energy, or maybe it's the baby, or maybe I just miss you, but I want to do whatever it takes to make things better for all of us. I know you blame me, and you won't understand what I did for a long time—or maybe ever—but I want to believe we can still be important to each other.*

And that's almost too much. Too much to think of feeling love for my dad again when forgiveness remains a daily struggle. But it's also hope in the idea that maybe love doesn't disappear, maybe it only changes form. Maybe there's always hope if there's once been love.

The plane whines and begins its descent. A familiar valley stretches below me. I search out all six temples and find State Street. Then I trace that street back to where my home sits.

Two bumps later, I've arrived in Salt Lake City. Olsen and I and a few elders wait out those precious final few moments: the last we'll spend as real missionaries. When I look over, Olsen has tears in her eyes, too. Her fingers fiddle with the corner of her badge.

My fingers fly to my own badge. I'll never be Hermana Lewis again. This thing that once felt burdensome is now a weight I dread to lose. I want to stay on the plane. I don't want to lose the mantle.

I follow the line of missionaries out the door and down the escalators to where dozens of people wait with handcrafted signs. One by one, the missionaries are re-enfolded into the chrysalis that formed them.

Mom squeals when she sees me. And Joe? Well, he pretends not to be playing games on his iPhone. My dad and Mikala stand aside. Close, but not really involved. A flame of anger flares like the first burst of flame on a stove when Dad waves at me, and I try to cap it and stop the source, but some pains don't heal in a day or a decade. And some never will.

Mikala waves, too. Her shirt rises towards her breasts. Celia swaps places with her. The baby becomes my Issa—with the same little zirconia in her ears—and I love her fiercely.

Maybe I love them both a little.

The Lord knots another tie in a corner of my heart. There are thousands more squares and ties to go in the quilt of my life, but, for now, he drapes the unfinished product over my shoulders.

And I hope that He says, well done.

*The End*

Dear Reader,

None of this would exist without you and a team of friends and professionals who believed in these words. The journey to bring you Hermana has enriched my life in so many ways. I've found a deeper, richer relationship with Christ and renewed my desire to help those who surround me. Sarah Arthur said, *"Story is one of the primary modes in which God speaks to us. It's one of the main vehicles for God's truth. The best, most ennobling stories have the power to shape our actions and play a vital role in moral and spiritual formation."* So, thank you for reading my story. I'd love to hear what you thought and how you're doing on your journey with Christ. Please consider leaving a review on your favorite platform or reaching out to me directly.

*With enduring love,*
Becca McCulloch

# About the Author

Becca McCulloch grew up in an idyllic town perfect for daydreaming and storytelling. Her gift for stories made long walks interesting on her LDS mission to the Dominican Republic. Back home, she earned a degree in nutrition, and worked as a dietitian among the diverse population of southern California. The miracles she saw as a friend and advocate for those on the cultural fringe serve as the basis of her creative writing. She currently works as a professor and lives with her husband, children and menagerie of pets in Logan, Utah.

Come find me on social media!

Email: **authorbeccamcculloch@gmail.com**
Amazon: amazon.com/author/beccamcculloch
Facebook: **https://www.facebook.com/WriterMcCulloch/**
Twitter: @WriterMcCulloch
Instagram: @WriterMcCulloch
Goodreads: **https://www.goodreads.com/GloBecca**

Made in the USA
San Bernardino, CA
19 January 2019